Maggie Ford ⟨...⟩ the East ⟨...⟩ the age of six she moved to Essex, where she has lived ever since. After the death of her first husband, when she was only twenty-six, she went to work as a legal secretary until she remarried in 1968. She has a son and two daughters, all married; her second husband died in 1984.

She has been writing short stories since the early 1970s.

Also by Maggie Ford:

The Soldier's Bride
A Mother's Love

Maggie FORD

Call Nurse Jenny

EBURY PRESS

1 3 5 7 9 10 8 6 4 2

First published as *For All the Bright Promise* in 1998 by
Judy Piatkus (Publishers) Ltd

This edition published in 2014 by Ebury Press, an imprint of Ebury Publishing
A Random House Group Company

The Random House Group Limited Reg. No. 954009

Addresses for companies within the Random House Group can be found at
www.randomhouse.co.uk

A CIP catalogue record for this book
is available from the British Library

The Random House Group Limited supports the Forest Stewardship Council®
(FSC®), the leading international forest-certification organisation.
Our books carrying the FSC label are printed on FSC®-certified paper.
FSC is the only forest-certification scheme supported by the leading
environmental organisations, including Greenpeace.
Our paper procurement policy can be found at:
www.randomhouse.co.uk/environment

Printed and bound by CPI Group (UK) Ltd, Croydon, CR0 4YY

ISBN 9780091956288

To buy books by your favourite authors and register for offers visit:
www.randomhouse.co.uk

Chapter 1

From her bedroom window Jenny Ross could look down into Victoria Park Road, where she lived. Her mother preferred the back bedroom, which was far quieter.

The houses at this end, coming off from the busy Cambridge Heath Road, one of the many arteries serving East London, were modest two-up two-down homes with tiny gardens at the back but none in the front. They weren't exactly poor or slummy – being in the better part of Hackney – but they couldn't match the fine houses further along, those that faced or backed on to Victoria Park itself.

Some were double-fronted, some three-storied. All had long if narrow back gardens. They had front gardens with low brick walls and shrubbery to shield them from the noise of poorer East End children who trooped to the park in hordes for a bit of fresh air with packets of sandwiches and bottles of lemonade, or to swim at the lido, costumes tucked under their arms, or to feed the ducks with stale bread or just to hang around the ornate drinking fountain and clink the dented metal cups on chains against its granite sides as loudly as they could. The sound could sometimes be heard clear across the park's lawns and flower beds and playing fields.

At her dressing table Jenny leaned nearer her window to see better the large houses once occupied by the middle class in a previous era: small business people, shop owners, bank clerks, all waited on by armies of domestic staff as their basements still bore witness. Now, in 1939, domestic staff were a thing of the past except for the occasional charlady who lived out and came and went at set times. Vacuum cleaners had taken over, and white vans that collected laundry once a week, returning everything clean and pressed the same day, and dry cleaners for finer clothes.

Lipstick poised, Jenny wasn't thinking much about these things. She was thinking more about one particular house, the first one in that row of houses which she could see well, almost opposite. It too was large, not as large as some of those further along, though fine enough, but in that house lived Matthew Ward with his mother and father and sister Louise.

Jenny had met him through becoming friends with his sister four years ago when she and her mother had first come to live in this area after her father had died. Mumsy, who had leaned on her husband all her life, had been inconsolable. After his death, unable to face living in their house in Approach Road on the other side of the park, it had been decided she and Jenny leave all their painful memories there and move. They hadn't moved far, but it was smaller, more manageable; it was comfortable and held no sad memories though Jenny suspected Mumsy still carried each and every one of them in her heart like little fetters. But had they not come here she'd never have met

Matthew. He had been sixteen then, and she fifteen.

She thought of Matthew now; how her heart raced every time she saw him. She thought of the looming threat of war, as most people were doing. Barrage balloons were already floating in the breeze on the end of their cables like fat floppy silvery fish, soldiers were digging trenches in the parks and anyone with a garden was sinking an Anderson shelter into it. And already children were being evacuated to the country to escape possible air raids. But mostly she thought of Matthew, whether he'd be sent away to fight – if there was a war.

For a moment, she took her eyes off his house, bathed in the golden light of an August evening, the sun still well above the horizon so as to make it still seem afternoon. It was no good watching the house forever. No sign of life from there. He must already have gone while she had been helping Mumsy to clear away the dinner things. Lingering dismay hung heavy inside her but she doggedly applied her lipstick in the dressing-table mirror all the same. Perhaps she could still make it in time.

Her bedside clock stated ten past seven and she was not yet ready. It was a good ten minutes' walk along Cambridge Heath Road to St John's hall. No good getting a bus, she might have to wait ten minutes for that. St John's Friday night dance started at seven thirty, but there was no guarantee that Matthew would even be there, though he'd said he would be.

She had met him closing up his father's electrical shop as she got off the bus from Leadenhall Street where she worked in an accountant's office. He had grinned at her as she passed, totally unaware how her heart had flipped at the sight of him.

'You look a bit hot and bothered, Jenny.'

She hated his shortening of her name. He was the only one among her friends who did. But she smiled. 'So would you be, working in the City. You're lucky. It's been a real baker there today.' She had hastily changed the subject to what had been uppermost in her mind, posing her question as casually as she could. 'Are you going to the hall tonight?'

Most of the young people she knew frequented the events St John's church put on. Matthew was a helper with the Boys' Brigade, she a Girl Guide lieutenant, and both of them, like most of their friends, would help out at bazaars and church fetes and Sunday school. And there was the Friday dance.

Matthew had lifted his broad shoulders in a gesture of doubt. 'I'll see how I feel come seven o'clock. Bit too hot for dancing. Might think of going to the lido for a swim. Did have a date for tonight. Mare Street Regent, but it was only casual. It's too hot to sit in the pictures.'

So that had been that. She had laughed lightly, nodded and moved off, feeling vaguely sad for the casual date waiting about outside the Regent cinema, golden hopes dying as frustration set in. That was how he was, quite unaware of the hearts he broke, hers included. But then, she'd never registered in his book. She was more certain than ever that he wouldn't be at the dance tonight, since his front door remained firmly closed when she glanced yet again towards his house. But just in case . . .

Hardly had the thought touched her than she saw the

door open. And there he was. Her heart that a second before had sunk into her very slippers now rose like a bird leaving a tree's topmost branch.

Mesmerised, she watched the tall, lithe figure stride with an easy grace along the road, crossing it diagonally to pass beneath her window. Gaining Cambridge Heath Road, he turned – and Jenny's heart leaped again for joy – in the direction of St John's.

The second he was out of sight, she jumped into action. Reaching blindly for the pillbox hat that went with her blue flowered summer dress, her unguided fingers caught the small froth of blue net and sent it tumbling to the lino from its already precarious perch on the edge of her dressing table.

'Damn! Bloody, bloody damn!' she burst out. Why was it that the mere sight of him sent her into paroxysms of clumsiness, she who at work was always known for being so calm and collected? One can always rely on Jenny Ross to cope in a crisis – she'd heard it said more than once and even derived a certain modest pride from it. Yet coming anywhere near or even seeing Matthew Ward was enough to make her no longer mistress of her own actions. And now, the mere thought of arriving late for the Friday dance perhaps to find him gone off elsewhere by the time she arrived, perhaps taking most of her friends with him, sent her into a panic she'd rather no one witnessed.

It seemed all the more precious to be near him these days what with the threat of war and young men talking of joining the Territorials, keen as mustard to have a go if the balloon did go up. Nothing their parents said of the

Great War seemed to be making any difference to some of them. And if Matthew joined up, it would be goodbye to her secret joy of being near him.

She had no illusions about herself. Even as she crammed the stylish little hat on her head, she tried not to acknowledge the ginger hair, which some called auburn but which to her could be nothing other than ginger, nor the milky complexion that went with it, typical of those of her colouring. She was well aware of Matthew's preference for dark-haired, petite types.

As far as she could see the hat did nothing for her. She smiled grimly at her reflection in the dressing-table mirror, the raging curls swept severely back from a high forehead into a comb at the nape of her neck; her mouth wide, her nose, in keeping with her firm narrow face, very straight. How she would have preferred to have a short retroussé nose like that of Jean Summerfield, Matthew's current girl, even though such a one would have looked incongruous on the face her critical green eyes now studied. A strong reliable face to match a strong reliable body.

Jenny gave a huge sigh. Well, make the best of a bad job. Mirror, mirror on the wall . . .

'I wish I was dark-haired and petite,' she'd remarked to Matthew's sister only a few weeks ago, her thoughts still centred on Jean Summerfield.

'Why?' Louise had said in her blunt, straightforward way. Louise was the type who offended quite a lot of people by her almost epic frankness, rather like her mother, never seeing it as offensive, though people knew where they were with her. Not one to falsely flatter, also

like her mother, one could always rely on the truth with
Louise Ward. The way she had said 'why' had given Jenny
a certain encouragement to open her heart to her.

'It's the sort Matthew usually falls for,' she'd admitted.

'And you'd like my brother to fall for you?'

That had been just a little too candid and Jenny
remembered cringing inwardly, wishing she'd bitten off
her tongue. 'Of course not. It's just that I hate being ginger
and tall. I hate my face and my frame. I'm so ungainly.'

'You're not ungainly,' Louise had said without
glancing up from the dusty old church hall bunting they'd
been sorting out ready for yet another church fete to raise
funds.

When she hadn't answered, Louise, still busy unravel-
ling strings of faded triangular pennants, had gone on: 'I
suppose you are tall. What, five foot eight? But you've got
a nice figure, and there's nothing wrong with your looks
as I can see.' Louise had stopped what she was doing to
search her mind for a comparison, 'A bit like Katharine
Hepburn . . .'

'For heaven's sake, Louise!' Jenny had broken in with
a self-critical laugh. If the girl had been a natural flatterer
she could have been forgiven, but this sweeping statement
set Jenny, crouching beside her, back on her heels. 'I can't
compare with a *film star*.' Hepburn of Hollywood with her
high cheekbones and dancing eyes was one thing, Jenny
Ross from across the road with her too-curly hair and her
wide shoulders was quite another. 'For heaven's sake,
Louise, don't be so silly.'

But Louise had looked up from sorting bunting to

regard her closely, comparison to screen idols forgotten. 'You haven't got a *thing* about my brother, have you?'

'No.' Jenny had also put aside Katharine Hepburn, her face warm before the younger girl's shrewd smile. Louise never smirked or grinned. She smiled, as she had then, in a lofty way, the way her mother did, making the recipient want to crawl under a stone.

'I think you have. I think you fancy him.'

'No, I don't.'

One couldn't go on denying hotly. She could only appeal to Louise to say nothing to Matthew of what she'd after all merely surmised.

Now she stared in the mirror, wanting so much to believe Louise's unintentional flattery, but the green eyes beneath the flaming hair merely gazed back in disparagement. Beautiful? Striking? What man, and by what man she knew she meant Matthew, would ever throw himself at *her* feet?

Jenny smiled grimly at her reflection, and turning from its cruelty, she snatched up her handbag from the bed and hurried downstairs to kiss her mother before leaving the house.

She found her on hands and knees in the kitchen, sleeves rolled to the elbows, one plump arm wearily describing soapy circles on the linoleum with a scrubbing brush. Disbelief sharpened Jenny's tone.

'Good God, Mumsy, what on earth are you doing?'

The soft rounded face looked up, downy cheeks flushed from her task, apologetic hazel eyes meeting her daughter's. To Jenny, gazing in horror, she looked much older than her fifty-two years as with a tremulous sigh she sank back on to her ankles. 'The floor looked a bit smeary, dear. I . . .'

'But I washed it all over this morning, Mumsy, before I left for work.'

Whatever possessed her mother? She was forever pottering around the house, doing things that never needed to be done, often after Jenny herself had done them. It made a mockery of all the help she gave.

'I just thought a small wipe-over.'

'With soap and scrubbing brush?' It was hard to mask irritation, only too aware of what lay behind all this. 'How can I go out while you're tiring yourself out completely, doing things like this?' It was a way to keep her here, and if she wasn't careful, it would.

'Leave it, Mumsy. Go and rest.'

Mrs Ross drew the back of a wet hand limply across her brow. 'I do really feel I must. I'm so hot.'

'I don't wonder.' Jenny moderated her tone, under-standing replacing annoyance. Two years was far too short a span to expect her mother to get over losing Daddy. She herself hadn't yet quite got over it. But she had a job to go to, lots of diversion, friends in the evenings. Mummy had nothing. The woman next door was as deaf as a post. The young couple on the other side had their parents, brothers and sisters, a host of friends, all of them visiting and in turn to be visited, too absorbed in their own pursuits to bother with a woman who tended to wrap herself in her self-imposed shroud of isolation. As for those in their big new houses lining the park, they with their bridge parties and their bowling and tennis and their theatres, to them those in the smaller houses were a world away, seldom encountered for long enough to exchange a word or two. Mumsy was a lonely woman. It was cruel to go off and desert her right now, and Jenny would quite readily have given up her evening to keep her company in normal circumstances, but tonight Matthew was drawing her as a lodestone attracts iron.

Relieving her mother of the scrubbing brush, Jenny tipped the pail of suds down the sink. 'Go and sit in the back garden, Mumsy. Take a book with you,' she ordered, feeling a pang of sorrow at the feeble ploy to keep her here. 'It's still lovely and sunny by the back door.'

Installed in a deckchair in front of the small border of bright annuals which Jenny herself had planted, Mrs Ross gazed up at her. 'You won't be too late home, will you, dear?'

'No, Mumsy, I won't.'

She was rarely late home – usually eleven at the latest, knowing her mother's dread of being alone, but the regularity of the query irked a little.

'I wish you didn't have to go out, dear.'

'I always go out on Friday night.'

'I suppose you'll be out tomorrow as well.'

'Just swimming, that's all. I'll have the rest of the weekend with you.'

Mrs Ross heaved a sigh that said how quickly the weekend would go before she must spend the coming week on her own until Jenny came home of an evening. But before the matter could develop further, Jenny dropped a hasty kiss on the flaccid cheek and went back into the kitchen to mop up the suds on the floor.

It hardly seemed worth going out now. Matthew would already be there. What if he'd taken it into his head to go off somewhere else? She'd have no idea where, and without him, the dance would go down for her like a soggy bun.

She had to at least try. Fraught with anxiety she called goodbye to her mother and hurried off. Turning into Cambridge Heath Road, she caught her breath in a huge gulp of relief. Jean Summerfield was just in front of her, sauntering along as though she had all the time in the world to spare. Breaking into a run, Jenny caught her up.

'Gosh, am I glad to see you,' she burst out, falling into step, already flushed from her short spurt on this hot evening. 'I did think I was going to be late. Matthew's already left. You know what he's like. He could go off anywhere without waiting for us.'

'Oh, he'll wait for me.'

Jean was a willowy brunette. Looking cool as a cucumber, she turned an extremely pretty oval face to Jenny, her voice a purr of self-assurance. She'd been going out with Matthew for nearly two months, a long time for any girl where he was concerned.

Jenny wasn't so sure he'd wait. He might be going out with Jean but he'd been seen on two occasions with that blonde Middleton girl from St Anne's Close, a fact Jean shrugged off with affected nonchalance. Jenny reflected that had she been treated like that, she would have given Matthew his marching orders long ago no matter how it broke her heart. Trouble was, Matthew's dreamy brown eyes hardly ever strayed in her direction, not in *that way*, so there'd never be a chance of her putting that valiant promise to the test.

'Marie Middleton told me yesterday she'd be there,' she remarked, more from the need to move Jean along faster than from any sort of spite, but Jean flicked her a look saturated with venom.

'For your information, she's not his sort. He doesn't care for blondes. Or *redheads* for that matter, if you want to know.'

The dig wasn't lost on Jenny and she felt ruffled. She was no competition. 'I just happened to see him eyeing her at the dance last week, that's all.'

She found herself rewarded by another glare, the small pretty face with its retroussé nose and bright red lips waspish. 'You keep your eyes to yourself. Dennis Cox is your partner. Anyway, Matthew told me he thinks I'm the tops. So there!'

Even so, her stride had quickened, past the Council offices, past the Bethnal Green Children's Museum set back from the road, on their right a train travelling the viaduct above the small shabby shops, filling the air with smoke and a sooty smell. They covered the half-mile to their destination far more quickly than Jenny ever guessed a small-built girl could, and she had to hurry to keep up with Jean, who was rattled.

Finally reaching St John's church at the Salmon and Ball crossroads, they were both hot, Jean's cheeks glowing prettily, Jenny's a fiery flush. In the hall, the pianist, drummer and saxophonist on the tiny stage, with its brown curtains hanging limp and dusty with East End smoke, were still sorting out their arrangements. The hall, with its faded religious prints around the walls and its small grimy windows, echoed with the garbled conversation of young people perched on splintery bentwood chairs waiting for the dance to start, girls in bright dresses, boys with hair slicked back with Brylcreem, their suits well pressed, jackets already hanging on chairbacks to reveal well-ironed white shirts.

Early arrivals had already commandeered the few folding tables on which to put their soft drinks and crisps. Jenny's gaze flicked anxiously to each one, knowing that if Matthew was still here, he would certainly have got himself a table. He had, of course – one of the better tables at the far end of the hall, near the band.

Sharing the table were Freddy Perry and Eileen Wilcox, who only had eyes for each other these days, and Dennis Cox. The latecomers were immediately spotted by Matthew who was instantly up from his seat, beckoning, his handsome face alive with welcome as they came over, his lips parting in a wide smile that revealed even white teeth.

'Thought you two would never arrive.' It was a full-toned voice that reflected a zest for life and the natural impatience of a soul seldom in need of rest. 'We got our drinks before it got busy.' He eyed the bar at the far end with its two ladies serving a growing queue. 'What would you like?'

Jean dropped into the seat he'd vacated, very sure of

herself. 'God, it's hot! A nice long cool lemonade, darling, large as they can make it.'

Jenny hesitated, wondering if she should offer to pay for herself or not. She heard him chuckle wickedly.

'Come on, Jenny, make up your mind.'

His well-spoken accent made the playful quip sound flippant. Those living in such as Victoria Park Road tended not to have the accents of the East End. Matthew had once said that his mother had been a lady's maid before she'd married. Jenny supposed that the mannerisms of her then upper-class employers must have rubbed off on her, though to her mind Mrs Ward boasted just too many airs and graces. Not that it bothered Jenny. She was well spoken too, her family as good as any. And all her friends spoke very much the same, so there was really nothing for his mother to be snobbish about. Thank God Matthew wasn't. He even joked about it, apparently to his mother's face as well as behind her back. Still, the quip took Jenny a little off guard.

Her already bright flush deepened. 'Can I have lemonade too?' Her thin enquiry annoyed her. His ringing laugh made her wince.

'What makes you think you can't?'

It wasn't his fault. She was an idiot. It was being so close to those velvet-brown eyes. Flustered, she hurriedly sat down next to Dennis Cox.

Dennis immediately began to monopolise her with an account of his new job. Coming straight from college armed with diplomas and bags of hope, he had landed himself a position in a firm of London solicitors. Listening to him, Jenny could well imagine him in years to come, bustling from court to court, bundles of legal briefs under his arm, probably having grown much plumper than he was now.

He was still expounding on his future when Matthew returned with two glasses of lemonade for the girls and two of ginger beer for himself and Dennis. Jenny smirked covertly. She'd seen the drill before. He probably had a tiny flask of whisky in the inside pocket of his jacket now hanging over the chairback. The moment the ginger beer was gone, empty glasses would be surreptitiously replenished by the contents of that flask, the same colour as the soft drink. Lots of the boys did it, not enough to get drunk on, but enough to be lively. If St John's vicar were to know, he would have a fit.

Matthew was lifting a mocking eyebrow at Dennis. 'Why don't you give the mouth a rest, Cox, and do some work for your living? There's two more drinks on the counter, and some crisps. Go and get them for us, eh?'

Dennis looked affronted. 'See here – I've been sweltering all day in the City.' The amiable laugh at his protest provoked even more indignation from him. 'All right for some. All you do is drive about in your dad's van all day. So what happened to that smashing job you were offered by Marconi's when you left college last year? I thought you were going to be big in radio communications or something.'

If he had hoped to rattle his opponent, he was disappointed. 'Turned it down in the end, old man. Dad's shop takes priority. His chest plays him up sometimes and there's only him to run it. He's not getting any younger.'

'And of course it'll be yours one day, won't it?'

The remark had an insinuating ring to it and although Matthew's easy grin did not alter, the dark eyes adopted a fractionally harsher glow. 'I don't need to prove I've more brains than you by sweating in some office.'

'You're just plain lazy,' Dennis sneered.

'I probably am.' The good humour had returned. 'Come on, Cox, get cracking. It's on the counter, all paid for.'

Slipping into a spare seat beside Jean, he left the peevish Dennis no option but to do as ordered. Eileen and Freddy, lost in each other, hadn't caught the small note of dissension, their hands hidden under the table.

Matthew grinned. 'Now then, you two. You're in company, remember? There's a time and place for everything, you know.' As their hands came back into sight, the pair looking sheepish, he turned his gaze on Jenny.

'You look nice tonight, Jenny. Blue suits that hair of yours.' The impish grin seemed to her to belie the compliment.

'You mean ginger?' she corrected, but was halted by the unexpected change in his expression.

'Some girls would give their eye teeth for that colour,' he said slowly, his scrutiny of her so deep and personal that she felt her cheeks flush and her heart give a leap. But Jean's brittle voice cut in.

'Matthew, I'm still waiting for my lemonade.'

The glass was within arm's reach, but he must have realised it was the only way she could get his attention at this moment for as he pushed the glass towards her, he treated her to a low 'mee-ow'. Jenny wanted to laugh out loud as Jean tossed her short dark curls in pique, a pout spoiling her pretty face. It was good to know she wasn't alone in getting the raw edge of Matthew's sometimes far too caustic wit.

When Dennis returned with the remaining refreshments, vague hostilities faded. The hall was growing uncomfortably hotter by the minute with so few windows capable of being opened. The band was still warming up, sheet music was being turned, scales on the sax being tentatively tested, the drums tapped at intervals. Dennis turned his attention to studying his already half-drunk ginger beer, eager for the small tot of whisky to liven it up.

'What do you think of this Hitler lark then? Me, I think he'll go into Poland, whatever Chamberlain says. If you ask me, we're being cocked a snook at. I don't relish giving up a brand-new job, but I'd be willing to go and fight him. The RAF for me. What about you, Matthew?'

'Haven't given it much thought.' Matthew's tone was airy.

'You should, old man. Don't want to sit by too long and get roped into any old thing when they start conscripting. Get in quick, I say. We're all officer material, you know, with our education.'

Jean gave a little giggle, pique forgotten, and squeezed her partner's arm. 'You'd make a spiffing officer, darling.'

'Will it be the RAF for you too?' Dennis was looking at him, waiting for a reply. 'It's the only service to be in. Great uniforms.'

His quarry leaned back in his chair, squinting through the shafts of dust-laden sunlight at the yellowed windows. It was as though he hadn't heard a word of anything that had been said.

'Ye gods,' he sighed, his favourite expression. 'It's bloody hot in here.'

'It's been a hot summer all round,' Jenny offered quickly, all she could think to say with an uncomfortable sense of embarrassment at the way he seemed to have neatly evaded Dennis's question.

But Dennis appeared to have forgotten his own question. 'Where's that flask then? You did bring it?'

'Does it matter?' Matthew grimaced as the band at last sprang into action with a ragged tempo that echoed tinnily around the hall. 'Who wants to bother with this rubbish anyway?'

'I do, Matthew,' Jean protested. 'Listen, darling, it's a waltz.'

He was an excellent dancer, as he was excellent at most things, and Jean was aching to show off in his arms. But he continued to frown at the tempo that would fail to allow him full enjoyment of his skill.

'I know.' His face brightened on a flash of inspiration. 'Why don't we go swimming?'

'Swimming?' There was an echo of disbelief from everyone except the couple still locked in each other's gaze.

'Victoria Park Lido. This time of year it's open till late. We could pop home, pick up our togs and be there inside fifteen minutes. Who's game?'

'Me.' If there was a sport Jenny felt happy with, it was swimming. But Jean was pouting again. Water would spoil those tramline Marcel waves of hers, even under a swimming cap. But rather than lose him this evening as she might well do, she grudgingly agreed. Dennis too had little love of water, but he agreed, not wanting to appear soft.

Matthew regarded the two lovers. 'A dash of cold water wouldn't do you two any harm. Fancy going for a swim?'

'What?' They looked blank.

'We're going to the lido. You two want to come?'

For a moment they regarded each other, coming to a silent mutual agreement. 'No . . . Not really.'

Matthew's laugh dismissed them. 'Right then, it's us four.'

It was a dash to get swimming costumes and towels, then back to meet at the park gates. Matthew, with one arm around Jean's shoulders, led the way, Jenny and Dennis following behind.

The evening belonged to Jenny, with Jean, eager to preserve her Marcel waves, sitting on the side of the pool, just her feet stirring the water as she posed hopefully for Matthew's attention.

Dennis, after lowering himself tentatively to his well-fleshed waist in the shallow end, pulled himself out again, shivering with the shock of cold water after the heat outside, then went and sat beside Jean. Matthew was unsympathetic.

'Come on, Cox, shut your eyes and jump. There's enough flesh on you to keep you warm on an iceberg!'

He himself had taken a flying header into the deep end, surfacing among the other swimmers to flick water from his dark hair with a brisk toss of his head before making it the length of the baths with a fast crawl to confront the shivering Dennis, his taunting laugh echoing over the surrounding tree tops above the cries and shouts of the other bathers.

Dennis declined to join him so he swam off again, deftly avoiding those around him, Jenny close behind matching stroke for stroke, until he hoisted himself out at the far end and made for the diving boards. Treading water, she watched the lean figure appear on the top board, poised, waiting for a clear space below before launching itself off, piercing the surface like an arrow. The skill and grace took her breath away. At the same time she felt a small sense of foreboding take hold. He took his physical assets so much for granted, that slim tireless body fashioned to perfection, that abundance of health, that quick alert brain. War was coming, unavoidable. Young men like him would be taken to fight for their country. She had heard her own father's account of the last war, the trenches, the mud, death from disease, bullets, shells, gas; men blinded, maimed, the rest of their lives ruined.

As a child she had shuddered from her own imaginings after listening to such talk. Now she shuddered again, seeing perfect bodies reduced to utter wrecks, bodies like Matthew's. She swam slowly now, trying to push away such visions, but they persisted. Men with such bright promise to their lives, so many blessings to look forward to, plucked off the fair tree like ripe fruit. True, there were those who had, and those who had not. Matthew was one to whom everything had been given; it seemed almost unfair that so many blessings should be heaped on one person while another knew little but ill health and hard luck. Yet how much worse would it be for someone like Matthew, with everything, if his happy world should crumble than for another already equipped for adversity? With no experience of how cruel this world could be, couldn't Matthew be more stricken than the already ill-fated should he come face to face with the worst aspects of this world?

Jenny pulled her thoughts up sharply. It was this threat of war. It might even yet be averted and there'd be no more need for morbid reflection. Matthew was climbing the diving board again. This time she turned away, again plunging into her own pool of dejection. War was no respecter of the beautiful and Matthew was indeed . . .

Her feet were suddenly tugged from below and she instinctively gulped air before going under, surfacing again to see him grinning into her face.

'You . . . you . . .' she spluttered at him.

Dejection swept away, she grabbed for his hair, a move he easily evaded. Together they wrestled, spluttered, yelled, laughed. His hands were cool on her body, his arms strong, hoisting her from the water as the whistle sounded for the lido to close. Jean was jealous, purposefully ignoring her. No doubt Matthew would kiss her into a better frame of mind when he took her to her door to caress her in a way Jenny could only dream of. But this evening had been hers. She was content, even to the point of allowing Dennis to drop a kiss on her cheek without shrugging him off, but no more than that.

They dawdled across the park, taking their time with the air still warm, lounging on a bench talking, giggling, Matthew bent on petting Jean into a forgiving mood. Then they went on in the last crimson glow of this midsummer evening which promised another fine day tomorrow. Matthew cocked a weather eye at the darkening red streaks, remarking, 'Red sky at night, shepherds alight!' His humour was whimsical as always, his mind on the rewards Jean would bestow on him for all the attention he intended to shower on her at her door.

When the friends parted company, Jenny glanced at the purpling sky promising its fine tomorrow. How many tomorrows before the sky darkened forever with Matthew far away? She firmed her lips and shrugged away the thought.

Chapter 2

With the metallic voice of Prime Minister Neville Chamberlain fading away, followed by a defiant rendering of 'God Save the King,' Jenny turned her gaze to her mother's face. It was chalk-white.

'What are we going to do?' For some reason the futile question got under Jenny's skin. She got up from the armchair where she had been sitting taking in what the sad, disillusioned, somewhat quavering voice had to say, hardly able to believe its message no matter that they'd seen it coming for weeks and especially these last few days, and switched off the radio.

'Not much we can do, is there? Sit tight, I suppose.'

'It won't be like the last war.' Mrs Ross, still huddled in her armchair, looked like a plump little elf amid the silence that seemed to have closed in around them now the wireless had been turned off. 'That was the first time ordinary English civilians had ever been bombed. We can expect them to do it again. And this time they'll use gas on us. Why were we issued with those horrible gas masks last year if they didn't think it would be used against ordinary people? Evil-smelling rubber thing, it smells like gas itself.'

'For goodness' sake, Mumsy.' She tried to be flippant. 'How would you know how gas smells? Except what comes out of the stove. It's all a storm in a teacup. Everyone says that once England has shown her teeth and stopped appeasing him, Hitler will back down. It's a show of strength, that's all. In a month this will all be behind us. Now I'm going to make a cup of tea. I think we both need it.'

Wishing she felt as certain as she hoped she sounded, Jenny went into the kitchen to put the kettle on, followed by her mother who had herself into gear at last. She was sure there'd be more alarmist sounds from her, but thankfully she said nothing, going about the task of setting out the teacups and saucers, the clink of china unreal in the odd sort of silence that lay over them. It was far too beautiful a sunny Sunday morning for such news.

She was on the point of emptying the teapot of its dregs from the last brew made just before Chamberlain's awaited announcement when there came a strange sound, a distant wailing, followed by another, much closer. For a second it was unidentifiable. Then Jenny realised.

'Oh, God, Mumsy, it's an air-raid siren.'

They stared at each other, her mother with fingertips bent against her lips as though to stop their sudden trembling, Jenny with the teapot hanging loose by its handle from her momentarily paralysed fingers.

Her flesh had gone cold, the rising goose pimples conveyed an actual sensation, the fear that clutched at Jenny's heart was like cold fingers attempting to restrict its pumping, pumping so heavy that it felt as though it were in her throat.

It was her mother who first came to life, swinging away from her with a cry, making for the hallway and the front door. She had flung it open before Jenny could collect herself enough to chase after her, catching her halfway down the few stone steps to the street.

'No, not that way. We must go down into the Anderson shelter.'

A man's voice was calling to them from across the road. 'Over here – into our shelter.'

It was Mr Ward standing at his gate beckoning to them. After a brief hesitation, Jenny took her mother's arm, hurrying her diagonally across the road. It would be far more comforting and, even though erroneously, it felt safer to be with others than the two of them all alone in the darkness of the newly built shelter put in for them by a paid man, having to sit by candlelight with the dank shelter's earthy smell all around them. Mr Ward would never know the relief with which she hurried towards him.

He was a tall man, in his early fifties she reckoned, who must have been an extremely handsome man in his youth – still was, she supposed. He looked very much like Matthew except that he was very thin and looked drawn. Matthew said his father had received a touch of mustard gas in the last war, leaving him with a slightly weak chest. He seemed a kindly man, and always nodded to her or her mother when passing them in the street, not like his wife who, though she would always nod too, left one with a feeling of inferiority. However, Jenny was sure she had no idea of the effect she had on others. She struck Jenny as somehow being older than her husband though she probably wasn't: it was just her attitude that made her seem so. Thirty years ago one might have called her a handsome woman and she still carried herself like a duchess. Jenny was sure she had a kind heart for all that but she had never felt at ease meeting her in the street. And now she was being asked to enter her home – or at least her Anderson shelter.

'We do have our own,' she explained as she came up to Mr Ward. 'We had it put in for us last week.'

He held an arm out as though shepherding them. 'Even so, we can't see two women alone down one of them. This is a time for us all to help each other. Come along.'

They followed him nervously through a narrow side gate into a small, neatly laid out town garden surrounded by trees and bushes whose dusty leaves screened it from neighbours' eyes. Mrs Ward liked privacy.

'Will Mrs Ward mind?' Jenny queried behind him.

'Why should she mind? We should all stick together in these times.' He sounded so like Matthew. Jenny fell silent as she followed him to the mound at the end of the garden that now covered the raw corrugated iron structure half sunk into the ground, its straight sides and curved top precisely fitted together, the soil already made a little less unsightly by a transplantation of geraniums and Michaelmas daisies. Her own, so far covered only by bare earth, had more the appearance of a wallowing elephant as it awaited a few plants to disguise its grimly utilitarian purpose.

She watched as he handed her mother down the four wooden steps to below ground, then herself. There was a curtain across the square entrance covering a small door already fitted. Hers so far had just a curtain. The door stood open and as she entered Mr Ward let the curtain fall back to its proper position, to shut out any light that might be seen at night by enemy bombers looking for a target. She was amazed at the light there actually was. An electric bulb in the centre of the curved roof, shaded by a small but beautiful orange lampshade, cast a cosy glow. But then, Mr Ward knew all about electricity, didn't he? The interior, measuring six foot by eight, was made to seem much narrower by double bunks lining either side to accommodate this family of four. At the far end a small table with a red chequered cloth held a decorative oil lamp; a square mirror propped against the back wall reflected everything back to give the illusion of a less cramped space. Above it a shelf bolted to the corrugated iron held provisions for a night's stay. The cold iron was painted pink, and a pink brocade curtain partly shielded the back wall for an extra sense of snugness. Thus a cosy retreat had been fashioned from what could have been an uncomfortable hole in the ground. Even the pervading mustiness of damp earth was allayed somewhat by a large bowl of home-made pot-pourri beside the lamp.

Mrs Ward was standing by the table, her posture very upright, her expression stiff, the unwilling hostess compelled to receive uninvited guests, which Jenny felt she and her mother must be. They were intruders into this extension of her home, which this musty-smelling underground shelter with its effort to appear cosy indeed was. Yet behind the stiffness lay an attempt to hide her fear for the moment, the air-raid warning having now faded away to leave an eerie silence outside.

'Thank you so much for having us,' Mrs Ross began in a small voice, she too feeling the tension, not just because of this impending air raid. In return she received a wintry smile but no word of welcome.

Jenny stood uncertain, wishing they hadn't accepted Mr Ward's invitation. In their own damp, half-finished shelter they'd at least have felt at ease, if isolated. She was glad Louise was also there.

Crouched forward on a lower bunk so that her head wouldn't knock against the one above her, her arms clasped about her chest in foreboding, Louise looked as though she were making some sort of obeisance at her mother's feet. But there the impression of humility ended. A younger version of her mother in many ways, Louise at seventeen bore all the hallmarks of becoming a staid, strait-laced woman by her forties. Already she had a tendency to bossiness and certainly a way of managing people whether they liked it or not. She was nevertheless a generous-hearted person, which Jenny imagined she owed to her father, and she had found herself liking Louise from the very start. Mumsy said once, when she had mentioned it, that Louise was rather like a black widow spider! But Jenny considered Louise's way of calling a spade a spade very commendable and people could not be held responsible for who they took after at birth. She was heartily glad, though, that Matthew took after his father rather than his mother.

'Not made a bad job of it, have we?' Mr Ward was

saying with pride in his voice. 'Me and Matthew put it up between us, but the titivating bits his mother did, and a great job she's made of it too. Never know how long we might have to stay down here if things get really bad.'

He gestured to the other lower bunk. 'Well, sit down then, both of you. Make yourselves at home.'

'Where is Matthew?' Jenny asked as she sat.

'Out with a friend, apparently.' Mrs Ward's reply was chilly, sharp, it seemed to Jenny, disapproving of her son's absence at such a perilous time. Jenny fell quiet. She might feel safe here, yet in the chill that had descended she wished she could be anywhere but here.

Her mother ventured, 'Young people seldom under-stand,' only to be met with more bleak silence, and in this vein the five sat facing each other, the Wards on one side, Miss and Mrs Ross on the other, each with their own thoughts, waiting for the first distant roar from swarms of enemy bombers they were sure were coming to annihilate them all.

Every now and again, her mother sighed, 'Oh, dear.' Mr Ward cleared his throat quite a lot, now and again smiling encouragement at them as they waited. Mrs Ward's face remained stony, but Jenny noticed how she twisted her hands together at one or two unguarded moments, and despite her own fear that persisted in clutching at her stomach, she found herself looking on the woman as being capable of human emotions after all. She knew so little about her, wondered how Matthew and his sister could live with such an unapproachable woman, except that she was their mother and they were used to her, she supposed.

But over and above her fear of the unknown beyond this shelter, she counted the minutes when she could be away from here.

Relief was a surge of joy in more ways than one when after only ten minutes – though it had seemed like an hour – the sweet single note of the all clear sounded. Everything that a moment before had seemed suspended in a sort of bubble of waiting, sprang back into life. Voices could be heard beyond the shelter. The whole street seemed to be alive with people as Jenny and her mother emerged to go back home.

She had never seen Victoria Park Road like this before, neighbours standing about in groups discussing where they'd been and what they had been doing at the moment of the siren sounding, speculating if it had been just a false alarm or not.

For Jenny it was an event she felt she'd never forget, not so much because of the fright as the camaraderie that appeared after it. Also it had been her first-ever glimpse into Matthew's home, at least as near as she imagined she'd ever be to it. A little like an eavesdropper, she had watched those twisting hands of Mrs Ward as she'd sat on the edge of one of the lower bunks, had been given an ever-so-brief peep behind the barrier she appeared to put up between herself and everyone else. Although Matthew hadn't been there, just being in the Wards' Anderson shelter had made Jenny feel closer to him than she had ever felt before.

*

Everyone had grown closer that Sunday. Men who would hardly have nodded the time of day to each other on their way to business, their privacy a virtual barbed wire fence, now passed on their observations of what the next few months might have in store for everyone. Women from the larger houses were even nodding more often to those in the smaller ones, snobbery magically put aside. Only on the bus going each day into the City were people still reserved, minding their own business, reading their paper, staring out of the window, perhaps smoking their pipes and cigarettes a little more reflectively, isolated from each other, apart from those riding together, Cockney vowels ringing loud, and of course the cheery voice of the bus or tram conductor calling for fares and pinging his ticket machine.

Everything was changing. The instant blackout extinguished all light but for the dimmest of blueish light in buses and trains. London's main railway stations were alive with men and women in uniform, with loved ones saying goodbye, husbands embracing wives, fathers kissing their children, mothers clinging to their sons, sweethearts interlocked. For some reason public transport became erratic; no one could be sure of getting to their destination on time any more. Not that civilians had many destinations to go to other than to work, since access to the coast just for pleasure was now forbidden unless one had a relation living there or specific reason to go. Seaside holidays stopped.

Everything stopped. On the wireless the BBC closed down its regional services, sticking to just one, the Home Service; schools closed, places of entertainment shut down to dissuade people from gathering in any one place for fear of hundreds being killed at once in an air raid.

St John's Girl Guide and Brownie troop and its Boys' Brigade ceased to meet, most of the children evacuated anyway from the East End to the country, away from bombs expected to fall on the population in a matter of days or weeks. The second wave of children to go since the Munich scare of 1938, they toddled off with their gas masks and their packets of sandwiches for their journey into the safe heart of the countryside, labels fastened to coat collars, mothers anxiously watching them go and wondering if they would ever see them again. Witnessing the scenes at Liverpool Street Station, and the looks on those mothers' faces as she passed on her way to work, Jenny could almost feel the heaviness of their hearts.

'It all seems so strange. I still can't get used to all this.'

Mrs Ross was helping paste strips of gummed brown paper tape in the recommended criss-cross pattern on the window panes, supposedly to help stop flying glass from the effect of a bomb blast.

'It makes the windows look so horrible. I don't like it at all.'

'It doesn't matter if we like it or not.' The gum tasted awful; Jenny pulled a face as she licked. She had tried resorting to a saucer of water to dip the gummed side in, but it was awkward, far quicker to steel herself to licking. 'They say it's safer. They say just one shard of flying glass can kill. I don't fancy being slashed by something like that, not even in a small way.'

Not that there had been any air raids since that first false alarm, a stray French plane at the time unidentified over the Channel, they had been told. But it was better to be safe than sorry.

Mumsy had already complained about the blackout regulations. Their own efforts were still temporary, made with flimsy frames of batten wood and cardboard with black paper pinned to them, and they had draped their shades with thick material for the time being to lessen any light that might escape. The result was having to sit in a dingy room and that in itself lowered the spirits. In time they would get proper heavy material instead of the present light curtains that let out a little too much light.

Of all the deprivations and inconveniences that had arisen, blackout was the worst. Air-raid wardens already knocked on doors ordering erring occupants in superior tones to 'Put out that light!' A lot of things irked, not the least of them, Jenny calculated, the total change in her social life.

With the departure of London's East End children the young men went off too. Of Jenny's little set Dennis Cox said goodbye and joined the RAF. He asked if he could write to her and Jenny had half nodded, rather hoping he might forget once he got out into the wide world and met other girls. She couldn't tell him she felt somewhat relieved to see him go. She had never really fancied him, but had just been naturally thrown together with him, and consequently was sometimes thought of as his partner.

Jean Summerfield's parents, deciding that London was

a dangerous place, went to relatives in Devon, to fulfil a longstanding dream of a cottage by the sea.

Jean's going was rather heartening. Although Jenny had never presented any competition for Jean where Matthew was concerned, Jean would nevertheless no longer be around to disconcert her.

Freddy, who'd enlisted as a part-time soldier during the Munich crisis before he had begun going seriously with Eileen, was called up immediately. Hastily, he and Eileen planned a registry office wedding, and leaving her pregnant, though neither knew that, he went off into the Pay Corps.

Of the group only she and Matthew remained. Obviously he was perfect for conscription under the new National Service Act, but unlike the other two he made no move to volunteer, much to Jenny's confusion. She had expected him to be the very first to do so but now she remembered the day when he had hurriedly and so noticeably – at least to her – changed the subject when Dennis had asked what service he had chosen to go into.

Already three weeks into this war, August and that particular Friday dance seemed years away. Yet every time she saw Matthew, that incident became like yesterday and the embarrassment she had felt then burned as acutely as ever, now also coupled with bewilderment. It was her mother, who like most meek souls always managed to extract a confidence from the most private of people, who treated Jenny to Mrs Ward's admission of dismay at her son's odd reluctance to join up.

'She really expected him to apply for a commission

by now,' Mrs Ross related to her daughter as she treadled away on her sewing machine, making blackout curtains to replace the black paper they'd had to use as an emergency measure.

'I don't actually expect it's cowardice, but I'm sure she feels a certain embarrassment about it. She's a person who needs to hold her head up in front of others but how can she while young Matthew is still hanging round? He *must* know he'll be called up sooner or later. I imagine he's thinking right now what a pity it was he didn't take that Marconi job as she wanted him to – he would have had a reserved occupation by now and no one to query his remaining at home.'

Jenny was threading tape through a finished curtain. She let it drop on to her lap. 'That's unfair, Mumsy.'

'I don't think so, dear.' Mrs Ross gave an extra push down on the foot treadle and with a final spurt pulled the fabric free of the machine needle, snipping off the cotton. 'If you ask me, I think he's quaking in his shoes in case he's called up.'

'That's not true, Mumsy!'

'True or not, I think he's being rather silly. He'll end up being pushed into any old thing – something quite unsavoury, with all the riffraff. All that education gone to waste. Unless of course he *is* hoping he'll be deferred. He could be, with his father not in good health and needing help with his business. But I think it unlikely. I hear there are some who are applying for deferment *and* getting away with it. Perhaps that is what's on his mind.'

Extracting the last curtain from the machine, she stood

up, stretching her back painfully. After she had laid the curtain across the chair she lifted the domed cover of the sewing machine back into place. 'There – that's done.'

'Matthew wouldn't do a thing like that,' Jenny said, even though her mother seemed no longer to be listening, apparently more anxious to measure her finished work against the upstairs windows. But her taciturn departure left behind waves of doubt pounding in Jenny's breast. What if her mother was right? Meek she might be. Indecisive and dependent she might be. Silly she wasn't.

Angrily, Jenny fought to push away the doubts her mother had sown. The curtain destined for this room idle in her lap, she gazed out of the living-room window at the warm blue of a late September sky. Each pane was criss-crossed by gummed strips of brown paper but she hardly noticed.

'He must have his reasons,' she said aloud several times to the blue sky beyond. 'He must have.' But it wasn't enough.

When the doubts her mother had voiced, innocently she was sure, began to bear down on her like a ton weight, she approached Louise. As his sister she must know more of the inner workings of Matthew's mind than anyone. Approaching his mother was unthinkable. His father would probably be very hurt by any reference to his son even being thought suspect; the last thing Jenny wanted to do was to hurt anyone with her prying. But she had to unburden her doubts on someone. Louise was the most likely candidate.

She caught her on Thursday evening in the church hall,

sorting out old Brownie uniforms for storing away for the duration. Louise looked up at her approach and smiled, a smile closely resembling that of Mrs Ward. 'Can I help you, Jenny?' Not 'Hello, what are you doing here?'

She smiled – there was no harm in Louise – and launched into her question. 'I was wondering about Matthew. Is he thinking of joining up yet?'

Louise's face went suddenly frosty. She seemed to age ten years, become Jenny's senior. 'Why don't you ask him? It's his business.'

That was all. Incapable of pursuing it, all she could do was say brightly, 'I suppose so – see you then, Louise,' and depart hurriedly, aware of Louise looking after her as she went.

Chapter 3

September twenty-ninth, Friday; Matthew's twenty-first birthday was two days off. He was to have thrown a party on the Saturday in Dennis Cox's home, his own mother declining to open hers to a troop of heavy-footed young people. But Dennis had joined up and so had most of Matthew's friends. So Jenny saw herself as a poor substitute when she accepted his invitation to help him celebrate his majority with a meal at a tiny restaurant by the Salmon and Ball pub in the Bethnal Green Road.

'Why me?' she'd asked, aware that had Jean still been around or the Middleton girl, now engaged to a young soldier, and had not declined, she would not have been so honoured.

'Why not?' he'd countered with a flippancy that didn't quite manage to hide a certain despondency in his voice.

He was missing everyone, that was certain, and again that insidious suspicion her mother had innocently planted plucked at her. Was he really scared behind that facade he'd put up? She kept telling herself that he must have some honourable reason for rejecting his mother's intentions for him to get himself a commission, but the more she tried to convince herself, the harder it was to believe it. What young man would scorn the chance of an officer's uniform? With his education he would certainly become an officer.

Sitting opposite him at a small table in the restaurant, gas masks in their square boxes hanging on the backs of their chairs, she forced herself to smile at him whenever his brown eyes met hers, knowing he was only using her as a bolster against his own loneliness.

It had been a wonderful meal, yet she had felt that every mouthful had to be forced down; Matthew too just picked at his food, although he had done a great job on the wine, even ordering a second bottle only to consume most of it himself.

Jenny fingered her liqueur glass of Tia Maria, gazing at the thick dark liquid in its narrow vessel. 'You're not enjoying this evening one scrap, are you?' she finally burst out.

He glanced up from the brandy he had ordered. 'Are you?'

'I was asking you, Matthew.'

'Me? I'm having a whale of a time.'

The remark, to her ear loaded with sarcasm, full of the implication that in normal circumstances she'd be his very last idea of a companion, struck at the very core of her being. She could find no reply to give him, and felt starkly aware how easily and suddenly adoration can be changed to vague hostility, no matter how temporary, for her heart told her that it could only be a short while before her secret feelings of love returned.

In silence she watched him lift the brandy glass, study

the amber liquid, swirling it thickly around the bowl. Bringing it to his lips he threw back his head, draining it in one gulp and coughing a little against its fiery taste. He signalled to the wine waiter for another.

'You'll get yourself plastered,' she warned, finding her voice again as the drink arrived moments later.

'Wouldn't be such a bad idea.'

'It would be a silly idea. You'll spoil your birthday.'

'Some birthday,' he muttered ruefully, taking a long swig.

Ignoring the connotation of her being poor company, Jenny opened her handbag and brought out a small oblong package wrapped in coloured paper. She laid it on the table in front of him.

'It's not much I'm afraid, but – happy birthday, Matthew.'

For a moment he stared at it, then his face lit up. 'You didn't have to do that, Jenny.'

He sounded suddenly like an excited schoolboy and she forgave him his shortened use of her name, her heart lifting as he began tearing off the wrapping with genuine pleasure as though this was the most important gift he had ever received. It was especially flattering as she knew of the presents he'd been given by his family. He had already shown her a monogrammed silver cigarette case from his sister. In fact Louise had asked Jenny's advice on what to get him.

'Matthew smokes,' she had told Louise. 'Why not get him a cigarette case? He hasn't got one.' So apparently that was what she had done.

He'd also mentioned getting a couple of hundred pounds in bonds from his grandparents, his father's people who lived in Finchley in north London – there were apparently no grandparents on his mother's side. Then there had been the main present, a Ford Eight from his parents, in which he had proudly driven her the half-mile or so to the Salmon and Ball.

'Well, open it then,' Jenny urged as he paused over the slim blue box she had given him, now stripped of its colourful wrapping. Carefully he lifted the lid to gaze down at the humble pen and pencil set.

'Jenny . . . that's really nice.'

She shrugged. 'It's just ordinary. I mean, it looks silver but it isn't really. I expect you already have a set.'

'No, I haven't.' He glanced up, giving her a long look. 'Thanks Jenny – it's the best present anyone could give me. I'll probably need something like this when . . .' Breaking off mid-sentence, leaving her to wonder what it was he had been about to say, he placed the box in his breast pocket with almost reverent care.

'What about your other presents?' she reminded him.

He gave a sardonic chuckle. 'Beware Greeks bearing gifts.'

'How do you mean?'

'I mean I feel I've been put under obligation by some people.'

'What obligation?'

'Oh . . .' He heaved a sigh, playing absently with a box of matches put on the table for smokers' convenience. 'Doesn't matter. Family business. But thanks, Jenny, for the gift.' He reached for his glass. 'Anyway, happy birthday, Matthew! May you have many more – God willing.'

Not waiting for her to lift her own slender glass, he drained his at a gulp, blinked, then grinned across at her. 'I think I'll have another.'

Jenny gnawed at her lip. 'No, don't, Matthew.'

'It's my birthday,' he stated truculently, then grinned again. 'Good old Libra, that's me. Stuck in the balance. Death of summer, birth of darker days. God! I wish I'd been born in spring, years from now.'

He was talking nonsense. He'd definitely had enough. But apparently he wasn't of the same opinion as her. 'I'm going to have another.'

Frowning, he clicked a finger and thumb rudely at a passing waiter. 'I want another brandy.'

'Please, Matthew,' Jenny hissed, embarrassed. 'You mustn't.'

His frown deepened. 'Christ! Not you as well.'

'Me?'

'Telling me what to do. Making decisions for me. Jus' like my mother. She does that, all the time. Louise and I, we jus' laugh, but sometimes . . . Time I was allowed to make decisions for m'self. Where's that waiter? Ah.'

The man stood beside him, polite yet superior, his elderly face lined and wise, his tone conveying the faintest hint of disapproval. 'You ordered another brandy, sir.'

'I did,' snapped Matthew, but the wind had gone out of his sails. He sat slumped a little as the drink was placed before him. Listlessly he pulled out the new cigarette case, offered one to Jenny which she declined, took one himself, lit it from a gold lighter, a present from an uncle, and drew in a deep lungful of smoke.

She had never seen him like this. It was as though she was looking at a totally different person to the buoyant carefree spirit of only a few weeks earlier. It made her heart ache.

'It's getting late,' she urged, and when he shrugged, continuing to smoke, his brandy untouched, she added, 'My mother doesn't like me to be out too late. She gets lonely. She'll be anxious.'

At last he spoke. 'You too?'

'What do you mean, me too?'

'Parent trouble.'

'No, not really. It's just that now there's a war on, she worries.' But a glimmer of his problem had begun to show itself. She leaned towards him. 'Matthew. What's the matter?'

'Who says anything's the matter? I'm fine. Couldn't be better. I've got my future nicely cut and dried, no worries, nothing. Life's grand. Just sit back and let my dear mother do the worrying for me, the arranging, the thinking. Who cares?'

He cut off abruptly, stared down at his untouched drink as though unsure how it came to be there, then he grimaced and sucked in his breath, pushing the glass from him and stubbing out his cigarette.

'Ye gods! Jenny – let's get out of here.'

Gathering up her coat, her handbag, the unsightly square box on its cord, while he paid the bill, she hurried after him, thankful that he seemed to be walking from the restaurant more steadily than she had dared to hope. But once outside on the pavement the air hit him and he swayed.

She took his arm firmly. 'You can't drive back in this state.'

'It's only a mile.'

'It's so dark. You'll have us hitting a lamppost. We could walk. I've got my torch. So long as we don't collide with a wall of sandbags.' She tried to make a joke of the sandbags surrounding the council offices. 'You can get your car tomorrow. And you must clear your head before you get home.'

'*Must?*'

She realised she had probably sounded slightly domineering. His earlier words spoken against his mother's efforts to sort out his future ought to have warned her. She hurried to repair the damage, giving a light laugh.

'Your mother will hit the roof if she sees you. You'll never hear the last of it.'

'You can say that again.' He chuckled too, his tenseness easing a little as, falling silent, he leaned on her, letting her guide him. Neither spoke as they negotiated the quiet crossroads under the railway bridge.

It was darker than they had anticipated after the restaurant lights, dim as they had been. Not a chink of light shone anywhere. Jenny's small torch, itself covered by black sticky paper with just two tiny holes cut in it, gave hardly a beam and they needed to walk slowly, cautiously, in case they bumped into something hard like a pillar box or a lamppost, none of them lit, all of them obsolete. The bowl of the sky these days was dead-black from horizon to horizon as no one in town had ever seen it; stars looked as large and bright as sequins and the Milky Way stood out like a solid path of frozen mist in the enveloping silence up there.

'Isn't it beautiful?' Jenny breathed, glancing upwards in wonder at it as they felt their way along. Time stretched out in silence between them; she judged that soon they would come upon that unevenly built wall of sandbags round the council chambers, so she moved even slower. Suddenly Matthew came to an abrupt halt, dragging on her arm.

'What is it?'

She heard his sigh. 'It's . . . not been a very successful evening, has it?'

There was a slur to his words which she tried to ignore and she attempted to make yet another joke. 'My fault, or yours?'

'Mine.'

'You've not been the jolliest of people tonight,' she admitted candidly.

'And of course, you know why.' Again that sarcastic ring, but at whom she did not know.

'I don't think I do.'

'Yes you do. It's what's been hanging over my head these last few weeks. I know my mother means well, but she rather jumped the gun telling people her son was going to be an officer. Let her down, didn't I? And now everyone thinks I'm scared to join up, yellow, because I've not made any move to do anything. I can see it in their faces. I can see it in yours.'

'Not mine, Matthew! I don't think that.' But she did think that, had battled with her conscience, tried to ignore the thoughts that assailed her. It had to show in her face, in her voice, no matter how she tried to disguise it, even from herself, as she told herself that Matthew was no coward.

She heard his explosive laugh. 'There's blind faith for you! Real true loyalty. No doubts at all.'

He shrugged away from her, supporting himself with one hand against a lamppost. 'Don't you have jus' one small doubt, Jenny, in that great big heart of yours? Aren't you just a little curious to know why I . . . why I didn't volunteer, like Dennis and Freddy and half the country?'

His attitude confused her, put her at odds with herself. Her entire evening with him had been spent struggling with that malignant tumour of doubt, not knowing for a moment that he'd perceived the cracks in her armour. Now he was accusing her and she had no defence. She reached out and took his arm. 'I don't know why, Matthew. You're making me feel very unhappy.'

'I'm sorry.' She wasn't sure if the apology was genuine or spoken in anger. 'Seems it's the fashion t'be unhappy.' His body seemed to sag a little against the lamppost.

'All I know is I've got to tell *someone.*' For a moment he fell silent while Jenny waited, then quietly, as though ashamed of himself, he said, 'Someone I can trust. I trust you, Jenny. Above anyone else I know, I trust you. I wish . . . I jus' wish . . . God, I feel a bit sick.'

She waited while he rested his head against the iron

post. In the utter darkness, but for the pinprick of light from her torch, she could hardly see him. Standing there, she stared into the black night, the chill of autumn creeping about her shoulders all the more chill for there being no light anywhere. It felt as though they were the only two people in the whole world; East London was preparing for sleep, no buses, no vehicles of any kind drove past them, just a low hum of which she was only just aware could be heard, so low it was, of some distant flicker of life in this darkened city. Silence, the silence of a metropolis waiting for that something it knew would happen eventually.

She shivered, not from cold, but from foreboding, thankful for the presence of Matthew, even if a little the worse for wine and brandy. Yet if she hadn't gone out with him this evening, she wouldn't be here now to feel this fear of the dark, this ominous dark with its low distant rumbling like the warning of a storm yet to break but still unseen. And again she shivered.

Matthew's voice made her jump, even though it was so low that had a breeze ruffled the still air, she would have missed his words.

'All my life . . .' He paused as though thinking it out, then began again. 'All my life Louise and I have been nursed along, protected, pampered. Our parents have always been there to fight our fights, solve our problems, especially my mother. I know she always meant well so I let her get on with it. I even thought it funny. But I took it all for granted. My fault. But there comes a time . . . I've just begun to realise the harm it's done. It's like being smothered by a blanket, warm and safe, but – well, suffocating if it's pulled too close. Throw it off and you realise just how fresh the air can be. D'you know what I'm trying to say, Jenny?'

He didn't wait for her reply. 'I've got to break away. Make my own life. But how the hell do you say to someone you love, someone who loves you: "Thanks for everything, but I'm off"? She does love me, but so, I don't know, so selfishly, and she doesn't even realise it.'

His words trailed off as he became lost in his thoughts while Jenny stood by not knowing what to say.

He began to talk again. 'This war. It seemed my chance to get away without hurting her feelings. But she's cheated me even out of that. And she can't see it. Had it all worked out for me, trying to help, holding my hand yet again, making enquiries to get me into some officer cadet training unit or other. I don't know what she had in mind or thought she could do – I've not been listening that much. All I know is that this time I want to do things for myself. I'm twenty-one. I don't want her to keep holding my hand.'

Jenny found her voice. 'Can't you explain to her how you feel?'

'Explain!' His voice was still slurred. 'Don't think she'd understand. Only hears what she wants to hear. Diff'rent for Louise. She's a girl. She's nat'rally happy to cling to her mother. But me. Got to let go. Let it go on too long. Should've volunteered for the Territorials last year, but she talked me out of it. Scared then at me going off and getting m'self killed. Everyone was panicking a bit at that time. But now she can see it's inev . . . inevitable she's doing her damnedest to see me in the best possible situation, going into an officer cadet training college, getting a safe job. But I don't want a safe job. I'd have liked to become an officer, but *I* wanted to sort it out. *I* wanted to. She's spoiled that for me. Now, Freddy's got married and joined up. Dennis – that soft idiot – is having a go. Suddenly I'm still a boy in a world of men, and it's shaken me. I decided I wouldn't sign on under her rules – thinking she can sort it all out for me. I'm going to wait 'til I'm called up, take my chances.'

'That could be rough on you,' Jenny said. 'You'd just be in the ranks.'

'Exactly. I want to rough it, start from the first rung for a change, on my own. If I get a couple of stripes, it'll be on my own merit. If I get as far as a commission, it'll be my own doing. I probably will get a commission – my education – but it won't be my mother getting me there. I want to do it all on my own, and if . . . if . . .'

He broke off. 'Oh, God, I feel sick.'

In sudden urgency, he leaned towards the kerb and retched quietly.

'You see, Mumsy?' Jenny cried first thing next morning at breakfast after relating Matthew's explanation for not apparently leaping headlong into the forces, her faith in his intentions now unshakeable. 'He isn't a coward. He simply wants to do things his way.'

Mrs Ross's smile was one of sad experience. 'Doing things his way could be biting off more than he can chew. He's always been used to the soft life by all accounts. He'll be in for a shock, I should imagine.'

'So will a lot of men,' Jenny said firmly. 'They'll have to get used to it. I can't see why he should be any different. He'll learn to adapt, like most people do when there's no going back. I'm sure we'll be seeing a side of Matthew no one ever saw before.'

'Well, we shall see, I suppose.'

'Yes, we shall,' Jenny stated with conviction, rising from the breakfast table to start clearing away, confident in the eventual fulfilment of her conviction. She didn't have to wait for long.

Two weeks prior to Christmas, the autumn having been so uneventful it hardly seemed they were having a war at all – people were calling it the phoney war, the funny war, even the bore war, and some evacuees were even returning home – Jenny opened the door to a knock. There he stood, one leather-gloved hand clutching a small suitcase, his overcoat collar turned up against the chill wind, the well-cut suit beneath soon to be exchanged for the rough khaki of a private in the Royal Corps of Signals. His smile was wide, his long narrow eyes bright. He looked as though he had been given a birthday present.

'Thought I'd pop over to say cheerio.'

Not knowing what to say, all she said was, 'Come in out of the cold for a second,' and all but dragged him across the doorstep as her mother came from the living room to wish him well and invite him to come and sit by the fire for a moment.

'It's warm in there, Matthew. There's such a draught from the door.'

'No thanks, Mrs Ross,' he said as Jenny dutifully closed the door a little. 'Got a train to catch. Just thought I'd say a quick goodbye to Jen . . . Jenny.'

Despite the miserable feeling inside her at Matthew's going, Jenny couldn't help but smile at the hasty correction before her mother as the woman melted discreetly back into the living room, leaving the pair of them to say their goodbyes. She wondered if her mother suspected the feelings she had for Matthew. If she did, she had never betrayed it.

Alone with him, she still couldn't come up with anything wise or clever to say.

'So you're off then.' It was the only thing she could find, obvious, inane, feeble, betraying nothing of the desolation churning in the pit of her stomach.

'Yes.'

'I hope you get by all right.'

'I hope so too.'

'Nice of you to come over to say goodbye.'

At this he gave her one of those searching looks that never failed to set her heart racing with useless hope. 'Well, I would, wouldn't I?'

'Why?'

'Because . . . it's you. My best friend.'

It wrung her heart. She would always be his best friend, no more than that. That was obvious now.

'I'll miss you, Matthew,' was all she could find to say, a catch in her throat that she hadn't wanted to be there, to her annoyance quite audible.

On impulse she reached up and touched his smooth

cheek, then with the same spontaneity, leaned forward and planted a kiss where her hand had momentarily touched. The flesh felt cold from the biting wind outside but the spicy fragrance of his skin warmly filled her nostrils. She stood back, alarmed by her own temerity. For fear of ridicule she had never before dared kiss him. What would he think now?

'Take care of yourself, won't you?' she heard herself say.

His smile was not at all taunting. 'Don't worry, I will.'

Some of her composure returned. 'I'm glad you got your own way in the end.'

'Don't know about that,' he laughed, the laugh light and confident in a way she'd never heard before; before it had always been touched by a tinge of defiance. 'It's up to me now to prove myself right. Anyway, if I don't swim, I can only sink.'

The old defiance coming back, the caustic quip.

'Don't say that.' She experienced a shudder of sudden apprehension, a premonition, dread, so light that it went as quickly as it had come. His was a charmed life, bright with promise. He'd be all right. People like him always were. He had to be.

The easy expression had faded to be replaced by a thoughtful, almost affectionate regard. 'I'd like to thank you, Jenny, for making up my mind for me – the night we had that dinner together.'

Her face grew hot. 'I did nothing . . .'

'You listened. It was enough.'

She was startled by his arm coming around her waist,

pulling her gently towards him; then he kissed her full on the mouth. It was a long lingering kiss, revealing the passionate core of him that she had always imagined yet thought she would never be invited to probe. Even now she knew it came purely from regret at leaving a dear friend, or perhaps from his trepidation at the unknown into which he was about to step, but no more than that.

Curiously dizzy, she felt herself put gently from him. When she spoke she was annoyed to find that her voice shook. 'Lots of luck, Matthew.'

'You too, Jenny. I'll write, let you know where I am. Although God knows where I . . . where any of us will end up. But things will never be the same again.'

'I suppose not,' she replied lamely, her shaken nerves calming at last.

For a moment he looked searchingly at her. Then he held out his hand, unaware of anything behind her candid grey-green eyes but what she knew she dared convey – a friendly regret of his going. Yet, oh, how she wished it possible to show him how she truly felt as she took the offered hand, the cool slim fingers closing over hers in a firm and steady grip that had the essence of real friendship in it. How she wished it was love rather than friendship, but she wasn't prepared to fool herself.

'I don't know when our paths will cross again,' he said, his tone low and full, 'if they ever do. But whatever happens, Jenny, I want you to know that you'll always be one of my nicer memories.'

'Perhaps we could keep in touch,' she said quickly and he smiled, almost gratefully.

'Perhaps we will. I'll try and write to you, Jenny. Look after yourself.'

Then he was gone, out of the door and down the steps to the street, turning towards Cambridge Heath Road and the nearest bus stop, moving on swiftly with that fast springy step of his.

The fierce wind battered at his trilby on which one hand was keeping a tight hold. Perhaps that was why he didn't turn and wave, she thought as she stood watching him going out of her life.

Whether his own family had stood at their door to see him go on his way, she had no idea. Her eyes had become too misted to see that far, which she blamed on tears caused by the bitter wind. She couldn't recall when she had cried last, apart from when her father had died, of course. She wasn't really crying now, except that the wind touched a little colder against a small part of her cheek where a rivulet had begun to trickle down as finally she turned and came back into the house.

Chapter 4

A few weeks later, as promised, came a letter from Matthew, from Catterick in Yorkshire, full of his traumatic introduction to the regimental sergeant major, to his platoon sergeant, to square bashing and to evil food and hard beds.

Slowly getting to be a proper soldier – in hot water all the time. Uniform fits where it touches. The chaps in my hut took the mickey out of my accent at first. I never knew I had one. Said I sounded a bloody snob (their words) and damned arrogant, which I didn't like that much. They started to call me College Boy, but after I had a set-to with one of them and duffed him up, and got seven days C.B. – not College Boy, but Confined to Barracks, they have started calling me Matt and sometimes Wardy after my surname because there's another Matthew in the platoon. So I suppose being called that must stand for something. They're not a bad bunch once you get to know them. I still can't get used to being bawled at . . .

There were two pages of cheerful grousing. He seemed quite genuinely happy, a vastly different man to the one who had said goodbye to her that day. If anything, he seemed happier than he had been in his carefree days before war had broken out, despite the restrictions of army life. Jenny could only think poetically of a bird released.

He had concluded his letter by writing that he was off down the local with a few mates for a couple of jars.

Jenny wrote back, heartened by his writing to her, but he did not reply. In his usual careless fashion he had written as promised and had already forgotten her. She could imagine him skipping through her reply, thinking he'd answer it when he had the time, but with his thoughts on other things he had probably put it away and lost track of it, his promise pushed further back into the corner of his mind, eventually to die altogether.

Taking what struck her as an obvious hint, she didn't write again, so that the only news she gleaned of him was what filtered through from his mother to others and thence now and again to her mother.

The only one left at home out of the old crowd she'd once gone about with, Jenny began to experience a very real dread of being tied to her home forever, staying in night after night after work, keeping her mother company through the long dreary winter days stretching ahead.

Her whole life had become dreary. Coming home on slow buses in the blue glow that enabled the conductor to see the coins he was given, masked headlamps just penetrating a stygian winter evening although street lamps gave out a tiny downward pinprick of light with the slight relaxing of blackout regulations now that no air raids seemed forthcoming, all made for a miserable existence. There was no point her going out for an evening. The West End was no longer lit up like a Christmas tree. And although cinemas, theatres, dance halls and restaurants had all reopened, football stadiums following suit, what fun could be had going anywhere alone?

Even Matthew's sister had gone away to stay with relatives in Surrey. True, Jenny was again helping run the Girl Guides, the vicar of St John's having restarted all its groups, but it wasn't the same any more. There now seemed just her and Mumsy, the two of them even spending their Christmas alone.

She nurtured wild thoughts of joining one of the women's services – anything to escape this purposeless role of companion to a parent who was prone to seeing herself as already approaching old age. Sympathise with her as she did, Jenny longed for something to give her life meaning, to be somewhere where she didn't have to make understanding noises or give her mother comforting pats on the hand. It was unkind to think like that but she couldn't help it. Everyone was off somewhere. She alone was stuck at home. But when it came down to brass tacks, how could she be so cruel as to desert Mumsy who'd always had a need to lean on her as she had leaned on her husband? Yet were circumstances to call on her to stand on her own two feet Mumsy might surprise everyone by coping admirably, as people often do when forced to battle on alone.

She was slowly coming to know the dilemma that had

faced Matthew, but it was her mother who solved her
problem, quite by chance.

'I wish you didn't have to work in the City,' she said
towards the end of May. 'What if they do start bombing
London?'

The papers had reported an air raid on industrial
Middlesborough and earlier that month bombs had been
dropped near Canterbury, without casualties, but too near
for comfort; she was alarmed for her daughter's safety.

'Perhaps you could find yourself something local, away
from the City.'

Something local? And be even more at her mother's
beck and call? Again came that desire to escape.

'I really should be thinking of doing something towards
helping the war effort,' she ventured, immediately crushed
by the alarm on her mother's face.

'You mean war work? Oh, no, dear, you couldn't go
working in a *factory*. Not a nicely brought up young girl
like you.'

'Lots of *nicely* brought up young girls are doing heavy,
dirty jobs. I don't see why I should be any different.'

She thought again of Matthew, her heart going out
to him for that time of his dilemma. But again it was
her mother, mind working on possible ways to have her
daughter closer to home, who came to the rescue.

'I was wondering, dear. Perhaps you're right about
helping with the war effort. What if you applied for a job in
some local hospital? They are crying out for help. There's
the chest hospital just the other side of the park. All in the
open air. You could go along there and make enquiries.'

With mixed feelings, just to appease her mother, Jenny went along to 'make enquiries'. It was even nearer home but at least she'd be meeting people, new people, instead of the same old faces in the same old stuffy Leadenhall Street office. It would be nice to get out of it and into someone else's world for a while. She had little idea how one went about applying for jobs in hospitals but assumed it to be much the same as anywhere else. The middle-aged, prim-faced woman who had probably never seen any other application to her shiny well-scrubbed cheeks than soap, looked up at Jenny from her desk, her gaze full of disparagement.

'I am afraid there are no places at the moment for untrained girls. If you care to register in the proper manner you can go to a training hospital if you seriously wish to become a nurse.'

She hadn't for a second thought of becoming a nurse. All she'd come for was a job nearer home. The woman seemed to glare at her.

'If you are looking for romance and excitement, young lady, you will be sadly disillusioned. This is a *demanding* profession, physically, mentally, suited only for the most dedicated women and entailing sheer hard slog and long hours for precious little reward other than the satisfaction of seeing a patient recover under quiet, efficient, selfless nursing.'

'That's all the reward one needs,' Jenny said without thinking, carried along on the woman's zeal. She saw the thin lips compress at her audacity in adding her opinion.

'All too often it is not. After giving oneself until one is

drained utterly, and then to be required to do extra duty, one begins to wonder. Such doubts can often form in the mind of a nurse pushed beyond endurance when she grows weary. It is those who find that little extra strength to push aside such doubts who make true nurses. I regret they are all too few.'

Rather than risk another comment that would most certainly be ripe for criticism by the look of this woman, Jenny held her tongue, not sure if she actually wanted all this. Yet she felt herself already being absorbed, the idea of hard unrewarding work an answer, even preferable to the boring, barren futility that had lately become her life.

Refusing to give herself time to think, she filled in the application form under the stern, sceptical eye of her interviewer, if only to show her that she wasn't afraid of hard work.

It was not long after, wondering just what she had got herself into, that she was bidding goodbye to a tearful parent to commence training at a hospital in the heart of Hampshire. She had escaped.

'I don't think I'm cut out for this.'

The fair-haired girl's plaintive sigh reached Jenny from the other side of the bed as they removed the soiled bottom sheet from underneath an incontinent elderly patient.

Trying to ignore the smell wafting up from the stained sheet, Jenny smiled across at her fellow student nurse. 'We were told to expect this, you know.'

'One thing bein' told what to expect, another 'aving

it right up your nose. I think I'd sooner 'ave joined the WAACs than this.'

'What, with bombs dropping all over the place around London?' The girl was a Londoner and had been glad to be here in Hampshire. 'Sooner or later London will become a target and you could be stuck with a searchlight unit. That's what they go for first, you know, searchlights. I would sooner be here and safe, with all the slops and bedpans, for all the hard work we have to do.'

All too soon after being sent to Hampshire, Jenny had discovered what real mental exhaustion was as she strove to absorb what the demonstrators and lecturers were telling her. Her ankles had ached from endless bed-making, scrubbing miles of floors, interminable polishing of bed springs and scouring what seemed like millions of metal bedpans until they shone again after being emptied down the sluice.

But for all the headaches: trying to cram six months' training into six weeks, a wartime necessity; the drudgery, being saddled with the distasteful chores second-year nurses passed on to student nurses; all the cleaning up of incontinent patients, emptying slops and bedpans, mopping soiled floors, she had discovered that caring for those unable to care for themselves had its rewards. She really did feel she was doing something worthwhile at last. Often Jenny could hardly believe it was really she who now trod the wards in the uniform of a nurse – not that the uniform enhanced her appearance.

In lisle stockings and flat leather lace-ups, a white apron so starched that it practically stood up by itself, and indeed stood out from the blue striped dress like a bell-tent, she spent hours before a mirror battling with the piece of snow-white material that would eventually form her cap – at least once she had mastered the technique of folding it correctly so that the pinched pleats lay flat enough not to flap about over the crown of her head like some wayward seagull.

Like a true nurse she worked hard to aspire to the art of moving swiftly yet quietly, but with all that quantity of starch, quietly was virtually an impossibility. Her starched uniform heralded her approach with all the subtlety of an oncoming express train.

There was scant opportunity for going home. In this she felt a little guilty. Poor Mumsy, all alone because she had been selfish enough to want to get away. Well she *had* got away, and she *would* have gone home, but a train packed to suffocation with servicemen and women could take three times as long as in peacetime, incessantly stopping and starting and then crawling along between times. Too much of a chunk out of one's day off. Such a thing as a whole weekend off hardly existed. And after working twelve hours at a stretch, she was only too glad to 'live in', falling into bed utterly exhausted to sleep away her day off.

With the beautiful early summer of 1940 she spent many a free day in the corner of some field with a friend or two, dozing in the hot sunshine pouring from a cloudless sky, only too glad to think about absolutely nothing, least of all guilt at not going to see Mumsy.

That year she got home twice, the first occasion in August, the second occasion in the autumn when she ran into Matthew Ward on his way back to his unit after a week's leave. She was amazed at the change in him. In one short year he had become more broad-shouldered, more steady-eyed. He looked taller, older, yet the ring of devilment still echoed in his voice as he greeted her.

'Ye gods! Jenny! And every inch a nurse. You look a picture.'

'So do you,' she returned lightly. She wasn't about to upbraid him for not ever writing to her again. The feeling she'd long thought dead now rose again like a bird as she regarded him.

His uniform, although still the rough khaki of rank-and-file, gave him a debonair appearance, and on his sleeve he bore the twin stripes of a corporal. He was making it there, Jenny thought with a small leap of pride in her heart for him, his own way.

'Not yet an officer, I see,' she said with a brave attempt at flippancy and he gave her a grin, crooked and rueful.

'My CO suggested I put in for it. Went up before the Selection Board but got cheesed off with the stupid questions they asked. Afraid I got a bit bolshie with some silly arse of a psychiatrist there and they chucked me out. Not literally, but well, turned me down – at least for the time being.'

As he chatted, Jenny couldn't help but notice how some of the edges of that 'college-boy' accent had blunted. Listening to him now, each word had a rough-and-ready tinge to it. Oddly enough, it rounded off this new Matthew to perfection – a man of action, certain of himself, a man able to fight his own fights without help from anyone. She wondered as he went on talking how his mother viewed this new person. Did it pull at her heartstrings for the boy he had once been? It didn't pull at her own, that was certain, except to make her heart swell with pride and love for this man who stood chatting lightly, without a care in the world because he had been able to surmount each obstacle as it had come his way.

'I expect the Selection Board will have another bash at me before long,' he was saying. 'The CO was damned disappointed, though God knows why. Me – I'm not sure I want to bother now. I've got a great crowd of mates and just now we're too busy playing soldiers on some godforsaken Yorkshire moor for me to worry just yet about trying to become an officer.'

'What do you do?' she asked.

For an answer he placed a finger against his lips in a playful gesture. 'Careless talk costs lives. Really, we just muck about out in the field with walkie-talkies, practise radio relay, get wet and tired and lost. Usually end up in the right place, eventually, then all go back to the schoolroom to learn where we went wrong. Then we all go off to the pub and forget it. It really is a load of old bull. I don't think any of us bother to take it in except enough to keep our sergeant happy. Don't know as I want to start seriously studying again just to be an officer. Had enough of that at college.'

He paused to regard her closely. 'But what about you? I bet you do enough of it. A nurse, eh? Always thought you were cut out to be something like that. I think that's why I admired you so much, Jenny. Got anyone in tow yet?

Some handsome young doctor?' There was a look in his eye that made a spark of hope leap inside her.

'No one at the moment,' she said, smiling, then she said something utterly stupid before she could stop herself. 'I don't have the time.'

'Me too.' He gave a low chuckle. Had she disappointed him? 'Having too good a war to get roped in. Women tell you too much what and what not to do. I'm free for the time being. But you never know, do you?'

He broke off and on a sudden thought crooked his arm and tugged back the sleeve of his overcoat to glance down at his wristwatch, the gold one which he had told her last year had been given him by his father's sister for his twenty-first. 'Ye gods! Got to go, Jenny. If I miss my connection I'll get put on a charge for being late. Cheerio then. And take care of yourself.'

'You too.' Dismally, she was aware she had blown the one chance she might have had of his asking her for a date, or even if he could write to her. On sheer impulse born out of desperation she leaned forward and laid a kiss full on his lips. Expecting him to pull away she was surprised by his arm coming around her, the kiss being held, and it was she who broke away in a fluster, taken off guard by the strength of his lips on hers, there in the street.

'Like you said,' she burst out idiotically, 'you'll be late.'

He nodded, seeming to gather his wits. 'Yes, I will. I'll write to you, Jenny.'

He seemed so tremendously happy as he went on his way. Rosy from his promise, the pressure of his lips still felt on hers while her own foolish confusion mocked her,

she watched him go, shouldering his small pack, his step
jaunty. War hadn't touched him at all. The terrible events
of Dunkirk, of desperate men with their backs to the sea
until the armada of small boats had come to their rescue,
had passed him by. If anything, she had seen more of
conflict than he.

A fleeting vision of her part in it passed through her mind,
days and weeks compressed into seconds as she watched
Matthew's departing figure. A once-quiet, smoothly running hospital suddenly filled with a consignment of
casualties from those beaches. A first-year student nurse
thrown into the deep end trying to cope with a picture of
defeat, the exhausted, the filthy, the torn bodies, her first-
ever experience of war at its most vicious, all the worse
because her life as a student nurse only the previous day
had been so sedate.

Surrounded by that upheaval, she had cooked porridge,
cut mounds of bread and butter, helped undress those who
passed out into sleep the moment they were left alone,
sometimes just where they stood. She had washed the
wounded, tried not to weep over the dying or turn away as
gangrenous or maggot-infested wounds were uncovered,
and had wished to God she had been qualified to do more
than just assist and cut bread while those skilled medical
teams operated on the suffering. And the June sun had
shone on.

She saw Matthew turn, throw her a careless wave. She
waved back, smiled. No ghosts of dead and dying comrades, no splattered bodies and shattered limbs haunted his
vision. He had continued, as he'd said, to play at soldiers

in the safe environs of a Yorkshire moor. Pray God, Jenny
thought as she waved, heartened by his promise to write to
her, there would never be need for it to be otherwise.

For a week as he took orders, drilled, cleaned his equipment and uniform free of moorland mud and grass
knowing that next day they'd need cleaning all over again,
Matthew thought of Jenny Ross and the kiss she had given
him. No mere friendly one. He'd always had a sneaking
suspicion that underneath that touch-me-not exterior she'd
always presented, she had been in love with him. That kiss
had proved it, but even then she had broken away before it
had had a chance to develop, becoming all formal again,
telling him he'd be late back.

Each time he thought about it, he found himself shaking
his head in disbelief, found himself wondering about the
feeling it had promoted, musing about the girl herself.

Her nurse's navy-blue coat had suited her colouring.
Hair, burnished to old gold by August sunshine, still flared
despite being drawn into a neat roll behind her ears; it made
her look pretty really. He'd never noticed before. Probably
the uniform? Not as leggy as he'd once thought her, not
so overwhelming and always ready to help everyone. That
had always been her trouble. She'd seemed more at ease.
She'd make someone a wonderful wife one day.

The thought brought an unexpected pang deep inside
him, rather like a longing. He'd write to her again, definitely.
In the past she'd always been too much of a managing
person to be thought of in any other way than as a friend.
Back in those careless days he had much preferred girls

who liked to lean on a man rather than have a man lean on them. Jenny had never leaned on anyone. Perhaps she'd changed, had grown less independent. Perhaps it would be nice to find out. At the thought a small ripple of excitement made itself felt in the pit of his stomach.

Sitting on his bed cleaning his equipment after a day on some muddy moor, he found himself wanting to find out, thinking about her, her life. Yes, when this bloody training allowed him a moment to himself, he would write. Good to have a girl to write to. He hadn't got her hospital address but her mother could forward it on. And when he next came home on leave . . .

Chapter 5

He had meant to write. But that weekend, with the Army's usual lack of forewarning, his whole unit found itself transferred to a camp just outside Birmingham. With all the excitement that went with it, writing to Jenny had to be put to one side. That week he had a lot to do, settling in, and the following Saturday when he and a few mates wangled an evening pass into Birmingham, it was shelved again. But he would write, he told himself as he picked up his pass. He still felt good about her.

Cadging a lift in the back of an Army truck to save a bus fare, the group split up to find their own way to whatever part of the city they sought for a few hours' pleasure. Matthew found a dance hall near the town centre. Obviously popular, it was packed, the floor crammed with couples, girls in bright dresses, men in uniform, a tight kaleidoscopic mass gyrating slowly to a strict-tempo waltz by a top-quality band.

'We'll slope off then, see what talent there is.' Once the last two mates with him moved away, Matthew found himself alone, already losing interest.

'See you later,' he muttered to himself, for they had already melted into the crowd. He didn't know why he felt so despondent. Jenny crossed his mind briefly, though why, he couldn't say. She had never excelled as a ballroom dancer. She knew how to dance, but she was better at sports like swimming and badminton and tennis. So why this odd pang thinking of her here in this unfamiliar dance hall? Yes, he was feeling at a loose end at this moment. He would write to her when he got back to camp.

What he needed now was someone to take away this unaccustomed loneliness he was experiencing. With an effort he perked himself up and surveyed the crowd, as his mates were doing a little way off.

Not much was here except for one petite dark-haired girl at one of the far tables, visible now that the floor was clearing from the waltz just ended and the lights were coming back up. She was with a Marine. Yet the way they were leaning away from each other, not talking, conveyed that she might not be with the Marine for much longer. Matthew took heart, began to feel better. She'd do.

'Found anyone yet, Matt?' Dave, one of his mates, was back, himself still looking for a likely partner.

Matthew nodded towards the girl and drew a knowing chuckle from Dave as he followed the direction of the nod. With the remark, 'Didn't take you long, then,' the stockily built Dave prowled off on another search.

Alone again, but this time feeling somewhat better, he fished into the breast pocket of his khaki battle blouse and pulled out the silver cigarette case his sister had given him; he had almost forgotten his twenty-first, it seemed so far away. Lighting a cigarette, he leaned against one of the pillars at the entrance to the large hall and inhaled slowly.

He needed to summon up some sense of nonchalance, and, surrounded by a protective cloud of smoke which he was exhaling, he found it.

He seldom needed courage to approach any girl, even when she was with a partner. One could soon calculate whether the partner was steady or merely casual and act accordingly. But that pale oval face set in a mass of luxurious dark hair, hair that even from here contrasted startlingly against the simple yellow dress she wore, brought an odd trepidation that he could not shake off. Suddenly it seemed very important that he should. Jenny, with her fiery hair and her straightforward manner, faded a little as he began his slow walk towards the girl with the Marine.

As if sensing his approach, hardly had he taken half a dozen steps than the girl turned her head towards him. Her lips broadened into a tiny smile, its message unmistakable. She had been looking thoroughly bored, but already the bored look had fled, leaving hope in its place. Matthew's heart lifted. It might not be such a bad evening after all. He threw a glance at her partner as he drew nearer. No wonder she was bored. The guy's face sported a mass of ripening acne. Other than that he could probably be classed good-looking, but in his present condition he couldn't be very savoury to her.

Matthew stubbed out his cigarette in an ashtray on one of the tables he passed, bringing a surge of interest from the hopeful ring of girls around it, each young eager face looking up in brief anticipation of being asked for the quickstep now being struck up by the band.

The dark-haired girl had turned away from him, seeing him bend forward towards the table, assuming she hadn't been the object of his desire after all. He saw a small upward-tilted nose and lips carrying just a little too much bright red lipstick but which now possessed a most becoming little pout. Why did he suddenly feel so shaky?

Matthew took a deep breath and walked the last few paces as nonchalantly as he could. It was the fate of all faced with the prospect of asking the girl of their choice for a dance, especially if she struck them as ravishing, to feel at least a fraction nervous, alive to the possibility of an abrupt turndown, having to walk away as though it hadn't mattered to them in the least. He had hardly ever suffered from that, but this time, inexplicably, he had joined the ranks of the nervous, at the last minute losing his nerve.

Pausing in front of a wide-eyed blonde, her hair dragged into what was currently called a victory roll, he offered her his hand, at the same time executing a casual tilt of his head towards the rapidly filling dance floor. In a trice the blonde was on her feet, almost knocking over her port and lemon in her haste. Seconds later he was winging her away across the floor, choosing one of the gaps that still remained between the fast-moving couples. To his relief the blonde danced well. Conscious of the eyes of the dark-haired girl following his progress, he couldn't have borne someone who might have hampered his steps.

'You're ever such a good dancer,' came the light words whispered into his ear, to which he nodded absently.

He had no need to be told he was a good dancer. He'd

always gained pleasure from it, from being watched, stretching his talents to the full. Yet it had become imperative to put his present partner through every intricate movement of the quickstep he knew, so that those dark eyes watching him would know he was good. Though God knows why that should matter.

A disconcerting thought came. What if she were only mediocre? All this weaving and twirling could frighten her off. Immediately he moderated his steps – the floor was becoming too crowded for showing off anyway – and fell to making occasional light-hearted smalltalk with his partner.

The ending of the quickstep came as something of a relief. Escorting the blonde back to her seat, he made for the bar and the safety of those hovering males who, despite the romance of their various uniforms, hadn't yet felt inclined to leave their kind and ask for dances, and couples having already found a partner for the evening – perhaps, he grinned, for life.

Yet for all the press of people, he could still sense the dark-haired girl's eyes watching him, and he found his need to know more about her pushing away that last-minute reluctance he had felt.

For the past half-hour the dark-haired girl had sat out through dance after dance, feet tapping under the table as she watched the couples, uniforms and dresses melting together as one, moving around the floor.

Susan Hopkins cast her escort a contemptuous glance. Apart from one visit to the bar for a pint of black-and-tan for himself and a small port and lemon for her, he hadn't moved out of his seat the entire evening.

He had cut such a dashing figure in his dark blue Marines uniform when she'd first met him last week: tall, broad, the briefest scarring on his face from an old outbreak of acne giving it a certain rugged look. She had felt proud to be on his arm. They had gone to the pictures, the cheapest seats, but he'd explained he hadn't drawn his pay yet and she was ready to forgive him. He had asked to see her again, but this evening instead of his gorgeous dress uniform, he had turned up in this horrid khaki thing. It diminished the aura of romance, of the debonair. Not only that, but the dormant acne had run riot during the past week she hadn't seen him.

She'd never been endowed with a strong stomach for unsightly things like suppurating pimples or nasty-looking cuts and bruises. Any physical defect aroused squeamish sensations. It was just as well, she thought watching the dancers, that he hadn't taken her on to that floor – being so close to those yellow-headed pimples would have made her positively sick. Most certainly there'd be no goodnight kiss, that's if she could get out of his taking her home at all. Already she was rehearsing a polite farewell, this date definitely their last.

The previous waltz had been in full swing, the lights dimmed, the faceted crystal orb in the centre of the ceiling flicking sensuous rainbow flecks over the dancers. Suddenly, she had felt an explicable compulsion to turn her eyes towards the hall entrance.

Among the slick RAF uniforms, the rakish body-hugging

navy blue, the officers' smooth attire, the soldier's khaki battle dress was unspectacular. The man it clothed, however, made it look as superior as any officer's as he leaned with casual grace against one of the dance hall's pillars. She saw him reach into his breast pocket, extract a cigarette case; with growing interest watched him light a cigarette, his head bent for a moment over the flame. It was then he looked at her, directly, just as she was sure he'd done earlier, which had caused in her that odd need to turn. It was as though he had actually spoken to her. When their gaze met across the clearing dance floor, she had looked quickly away, filled with embarrassment.

The band had struck up with a quickstep. The man by the entrance stubbed out his cigarette and began walking towards her, making her heart start to pound against her ribs with excited anticipation. But as she composed herself to rise casually at his invitation to dance, ignoring her Marine, the soldier had paused just a few steps away, bending towards a common blonde in a red dress sitting nearby. Seconds later he had whisked her away.

Pique had replaced embarrassment. How dare he? Susan watched him move with supple grace across the filling dance floor with the girl, looking quickly away every time he glanced briefly in her direction. But she didn't miss his expression. What was it? Appraisal? Amusement? Taunting, perhaps. When the quickstep ended with a final flourishing crash of cymbals and a flamboyant twirl of female partners, she pretended not to look as he conducted the blonde back to her friends. But at least, instead of lingering, the soldier turned and sauntered away to the bar.

In that instant, Susan Hopkins made her decision. 'Oh, look!' she burst out to the practically lifeless Jack, 'I've just seen a friend of mine. Must pop over and have a word. Won't be a tick.'

Giving him no time to reply, she was off, skirting the vacated dance floor, timing it perfectly so as to collide with her quarry as if by accident. It worked, even if in the process she trod on his foot, something she had not planned, almost taking herself off balance. Instinctively he caught her, held her steady with firm hands on her shoulders. 'Careful there!'

Deep brown eyes fringed by thick lashes gazed down at her in open amusement. Her embarrassment was more real than she had intended.

'Oh, golly! I'm sorry. I didn't mean to . . . Did I hurt you, like?'

'You?' He laughed, taking stock of her diminutive figure. 'I don't think you've broken any toes.'

'Oh I'm ever so glad.'

She was instantly conscious of her Birmingham accent against the refined tones of this man. Yes, he was a corporal, but his speech sounded so incongruous with the mere two stripes on his arm. His smile gently mocked her.

'What, that you didn't hurt me, or that you stepped on my foot?'

Susan fell silent. He must have seen through her ruse. Her face felt hot. Whatever possessed her to embark on this silly idea in the first place?

'You came at me like an express train,' he was chuckling. 'A fraction more weight on you and you could really have done me an injury. There have to be subtler ways to start up a conversation.'

Indignation finally rescued her from embarrassment. 'Fancy yourself, don't you?'

The grin diminished a little. A momentary look of sadness, loneliness perhaps, crossed his face, and she had a strong feeling he was about to play it down as if she almost heard his words form in her head: I'd be the only one that does. But instantly he brightened, his tone teasing. 'Don't tell me you've not been watching me right from the moment I came in. Actually, I'm flattered.'

Now she was embarrassed again – that look that had passed so briefly across his eyes had gone. 'Well, I might've looked at you. You're a good dancer. Everybody looks at good dancers, don't they?' She wriggled a little in the grasp he still had on her. 'I've got to go back to my friend.'

He released his grip. 'The chap you were sitting with? Is that all he is – a friend? And there was I thinking, the prettiest girl in the hall and she's already spoken for.'

That was why he hadn't asked her to dance. She felt a surge of anger towards her innocent escort for spoiling her chances.

'I'm not *spoken for*, if that's what you call it. I just came in with him. Just a date, like, for this evening, that's all.'

'So you're free to dance with whoever you please?'

Why did she feel he was mocking her? If it hadn't been for that look that had flicked past his eyes, she'd have walked away by now. She had to put up some resistance so as not to look cheap. He mustn't think she had engineered this meeting. 'Not with you,' she said, trying to appear in control.

'Remember it was you who got in touch with me first, to coin a phrase,' he laughed. He *did* think she'd engineered it all. 'Well, you win. Would you care to dance?' He gave an explosive laugh as she tossed her head in sulky refusal. 'Ye gods! How kaleidoscopic can you get?'

She wasn't sure what that meant but it didn't sound very flattering, and in a huff she swung away. He caught her arm lightly.

'I'm sorry. Don't go.' There was genuine contrition in his dark eyes as she turned to look at him, immediately replaced by a look of enthusiasm as the band struck up. 'Listen. It's a foxtrot, the best dance there is, even better than a tango. You foxtrot?'

She loved nothing more. Moreover he seemed to her so like a young boy in his own delight at it that she nodded despite herself; instantly he caught her up and whisked her away on to the dance floor to the delightful slow and regular beat of a rendering of Glenn Miller's 'Moonlight Serenade'.

It was like gliding on clouds. Guided with swaying grace through each intricate movement, she floated. Small though her limbs were, she followed his long steps without faltering, each change of direction, each smooth turn, each measured pause. He was so easy to dance with it was as though they were one person. He didn't speak, seemed conscious only of the variety of moves, practically turning them into an exhibition with not too many on the floor for this rather specialised number, unlike the popular easy-to-do waltz that always filled the floor to crush proportions.

At first she felt uncomfortably conscious of being seen so on display, especially by her former companion. But there was no need to worry. A glance towards where she had left him revealed him looking as though he'd fallen asleep. She was sure that had her handbag not been in his keeping he'd have left. Well, as soon as the number finished she'd retrieve her bag and leave him to it. If the man she was now with chose not to see her home after the dance, she'd see herself home, though she hoped it would not be that way. But either way, at least she would escape those horrid pimples.

The music ending, a ragged clap came from those who'd attempted the dance. Susan smiled up at her partner, awaiting his next move.

It came as she had hoped. 'Do you fancy a drink?'

Susan thought quickly. 'Have to get me handbag first. I left it on the table. I could see you at the bar if that's okay. Won't be a tick.' Somehow her accent no longer mattered. He smiled.

'I'll see you there, then.'

She was off. 'My friend's asked me to see her home afterwards,' she told her Marine with a play at urgency as he looked up with an apathetic grin. 'She's frightened of going home on her own. Hope you don't mind. I am sorry about that.'

There was little he could do as she whisked up her hand-bag. After all, he was only a casual date. A one-evening date. No doubt he'd slide off and find himself someone else and no harm done. It happened all the time, had once happened to her, annoyingly. But not tonight, she prayed as she made her way back to the bar.

She found her corporal, slim, tanned fingers curled around a pint of bitter, the other hand holding a small glass which he offered her with a grin. 'Thought you'd be a gin and orange person. Am I right?'

'Ooh, loverly. Thanks.' She smiled up at him, taking the glass and sipping at it carefully. 'I hadn't better get myself sozzled, had I?'

'You've probably never been sozzled in your life,' he said solemnly.

'I've bin a bit woozy, like. A couple of times.'

He produced his cigarette case and flipped it open towards her.

She regarded it with admiration as she shook her head. 'I don't smoke. Real silver, in'it?'

He shrugged as though her comment had touched a raw spot, but she didn't interest herself beyond that. The orchestra had reached an interval after a jive that had jammed the floor to suffocation; it was the bar that was now crowded, the babble deafening. But between her and her new partner an awkward silence had fallen, threatening to drag on if she didn't find something to say soon. She gazed about, racking her brain and sipping her drink far too quickly. It was he who broke the hiatus. She saw his lips move but couldn't make out what he said above the noise.

'What?'

He raised his voice. 'I said I still don't know your name.'

'Sue Hopkins,' she yelled back.

'Sorry?'

'Sue . . . Susan Hopkins.' No one ever called her Susan, but announcing her name in full above the din helped make it clearer.

Quite audibly, in one of those odd pauses that can occur in the midst of a dozen conversations, she heard him repeat her name, savouring it as though he thought it the finest in the world. Had it been Cleopatra it could not have sounded more romantic to her ears, the way he pronounced it.

She looked up at him, shouting over a new wave of babble. 'What's yours?' For a moment she thought he hadn't heard; his head tilted slightly as though considering her, then with a glance around the crush of people he grimaced.

'I've had enough of this. Shall we get out of here – go for a walk?'

Just catching the words, not knowing what to say, she nodded. He shouldered his way through the crowd to place her glass together with his own on the bar. Then he was back, tilting his head at her, and she could only follow him, an odd excitement taking hold somewhere deep inside her. The dance didn't matter any more.

Outside, enveloped in the pitch dark of blackout regulations, it was like entering another world. People moving cautiously, heralded by the merest pinprick of torchlight, came at them out of total darkness, to disappear just as totally. Vehicles, few and far between, lights all but obscured by black paint, faintly showed the kerb for a moment to leave it even more dark and dangerous to the pedestrian after they had driven by. Susan huddled close to her companion.

'You've not yet told me your name,' she reminded him as they took their first few steps, slow and measured in the fitful light of the tiny hand torch she'd produced from her handbag. The reminder was whispered, for their surroundings seemed to demand muted voices, muted sounds.

'Do you want all my name?' she heard him chuckle.

'Why not?' she challenged.

There was a pause, then he said, 'Matthew Leonard Ward.'

'Sounds posh,' she breathed, awed, and tucked her arm more firmly through his.

'Not really. Leonard's my father's name. My mates in my unit call me Matt. My mother would have a fit if she heard. She's always insisted on me being called Matthew. She's a stickler for respectability and . . .'

The tale, bordering upon tongue in cheek, was interrupted by a body colliding softly with them and a mumbled apology as it continued on its way through the blackout. But Susan was wondering about this mother – she sounded a right dragon.

'Damned stupid blackout,' Matthew was saying. 'Nothing happening and they black everything out. When there's a raid, they light everything up, switch on all the searchlights. That's what I'm on at present – searchlights. I'm in the Signals and they stick us on searchlights. Now that's what I call great thinking.'

'Got any brothers or sisters?' she asked, changing the subject from what he did in the Army. He was a corporal and that was all that mattered. She wished he'd been an officer but officers didn't look at girls like her. They went to better places than the Troc.

'One sister, Louise. Reminds me of our mother.'

It seemed he said it a little too tersely for comfort and she hurried to put some lightness back in their conversation. Nasty moments, like nasty cuts, even small ones, unnerved her, made her shudder. There were plenty of arguments in her house but she was used to them. Quickly healed, easily got over. It was with strangers that she cringed at moments like this.

'I've got lots,' she said in an effort to sound bright. 'Two sisters and three brothers. It must be funny having a whole bedroom to yourself. Sort of lonely, like.' This she said with a small pang of sadness for him. Perhaps it was the way he had said 'one sister', as though he regretted not having a brother or something. She'd always been told that only children were lonely children, and two wasn't much more than one. He and his sister were probably spoiled, where she'd never been, and it was still probably lonely and quiet. She hated quiet in a house, never having known it.

He didn't reply. They walked on in silence, uncomfortable silence it now seemed to her.

'It's getting late, I think I'm going to have to be going 'ome soon,' she burst out in a fast gabble, far too loudly, her voice sounding high and thin, lacking sophistication. He, the soft-spoken, refined man-of-the-world from down south would be jolted to his senses, seeing her as just a local girl from Birmingham, without education, the product of a crowded family. The spell had been broken.

'It must be nearly eleven,' she ploughed on, hating herself, the way she spoke, the way she acted. She had ruined the evening for herself. 'It's the air raids we've bin havin-g . . .' The accent fell on the 'g'. He didn't sound his at all, the 'ing' soft and alluring. She should have tried to copy it. Too late now. 'Me mum and dad like me home before anything starts. They worry about me, y'see. And I do have to think of them, don't I? It's only right.'

'Yes, it is only right,' he agreed with a deep sigh which dispirited her even more though she didn't know why. 'Do you live far from here?'

'Not far.' She could in fact walk home from here, which appeared now to be what she was going to do. 'Only walking distance.'

That damned 'g' again. *Walking,* she said in her head, walking. 'I sometimes catch a bus if it's raining,' she finished aloud, forgetting again.

'Well, it's not raining, so may I walk you home?'

Susan held back the gasp of joy. He wasn't disapproving of her after all. But she mustn't sound too eager. 'I suppose you could, if y'like. To the top of my road? I can go on from there. But you don't have to.' She had suddenly remembered what her turning would present to him. No doubt he came from a posh part of the south. 'Don't you have to be getting back to where you're stationed?'

'I've enough time to see you home, I'm sure.' How

beautifully he spoke, his tone soft, seductive. He took her arm. 'I'll let you show me the way.'

And, she hoped, the picture of the road where she lived fading into obscurity, he'd kiss her goodnight, and ask to see her again. Oh, please, God, let him.

Chapter 6

It took ages to get to sleep for thinking about her evening's success. Lying in bed in the cramped little bedroom she shared with her two younger sisters at the top of the house, she tried to imagine the world Matthew had described to her as he walked her home. How different it was. The bedroom he had all to himself sounded as though it could swallow this one twice over and still have space to spare.

Hers, measuring four long paces each way, held her single bed and one, three and a half foot wide, for Beryl and June. Hers stood tight against the window wall, theirs against the opposite one, with just space enough between the two to shuffle into bed, going sideways. The wall where the door was had a single wardrobe and a three-drawer chest. Not one drawer or the door to the wardrobe could be opened fully because the beds got in the way. What couldn't be got into drawers or wardrobe went under the bed; every morning in this room resembled a public jumble sale, all three girls squeezing past each other to dress.

The only wash basin was downstairs by the back door in a tiny recess. It meant moving aside to let pass anyone wanting the toilet which stood in a block of six in the communal back yard. It all made for hot tempers when three boys, three girls and two adults were trying to manoeuvre around each other to go their separate ways for the day. Their father moreover did not look kindly on a girl trying to put on her make-up when he wanted to get to the mirror to shave.

Across from her bedroom was the room, even smaller, of her three young brothers, still just boys. Below theirs was her parents' bedroom, below that the living room with an area at one end for cooking. This, their only family room, had five doors: one for the recess where they washed, one to the cellar, one to the yard; a fourth to the street was never used because of a settee in the way – the back door served as the only exit in this place – the last leading to the stairs winding up to the upper rooms.

This was her home, each room atop the other. But for the block of exactly similarly designed houses on either side, each propping the other up like something built from a pack of playing cards, Susan was sure it would have fallen over. Built at the turn of the century for factory workers, the houses were dark, dingy, featureless, all looking as if they had been accidentally leaned on at some time by a careless giant who had concertinaed them, squeezing them upwards like toothpaste from a tube.

She had never considered her home this way before. She'd been born here. All her friends lived in similar places. Some day when she married she had expected to move in to something much like them. But tonight she had peeped into an environment Matthew Ward had described as they walked home, and now she saw these surroundings through a veil of angry discontent, for the first time in her life feeling ashamed of where she lived.

His home might be in London but it sat in a tree-lined road. There were no trees in her street. His overlooked a park. Birmingham had its share of parks and open spaces but not where she lived. His house had hot water, and a bathroom. Her bath hung on the back door, her lav was one of a block of six in the communal yard, with doors so warped anyone emptying rubbish in the dustbins alongside could peep through if they felt that nosy.

Filled with resentment, Susan found herself listening for sounds she had never really noticed before: Beryl, sixteen, eighteen months younger than her, sighing in slumber, probably dreaming; June, fourteen and just left school, a restless girl even in her sleep; her father coughing – too many cigarettes made him bronchial. The back door opening then closing gave a little shake to the house – her mother was coming in from the Red Lion at the end of the street where she was barmaid five evenings a week. Soon came the whistling of the kettle, rising rapidly to a thin scream, fading away, like a soul dying, as it was lifted from the gas stove to make her mother's cocoa.

Susan was still awake when the house vibrated to her mother wearily mounting the stairs. The bedroom door below scraped over the lino, then scraped again as it closed. Complaining bedsprings. The intermittent cough ceased. The springs squeaked afresh as Jack Hopkins humped himself over his wife. After urgent whisperings and a giggle, the springs were soon going like a park seesaw, her mother's mounting joy evident. Then, after a while, silence. Later came heavy snoring – there were no secrets in this house.

Outside sounded the small noises of the night: the mewling cat near at hand, a dog barking further off; an urgent click of high heels on the pavement below, the clink of a milk bottle being put out for the morning; a low distant growl of a solitary lorry, perhaps an army truck, passing a few streets away on its way through the city towards some barracks or other. She thought of Matthew, probably asleep in his. Dreaming of her? Or was she forgotten? She didn't think so. He had asked her for a kiss on the corner of her street, hadn't taken it as his right but had asked permission. He'd asked to see her again. He would write to her when he next got a pass. He had even stood watching her go on along her road, given a brief wave as she turned reaching her door, and gone on his way.

At the recollection a tingle passed through her and in a sudden bout of ecstasy, Susan drummed her heels up and down beneath the bedcover and, taking the sheet between her small teeth, bit hard to relieve the pent-up joy. What did he look like in his sleep? Trying to imagine him, the sounds of the sleeping world went unheeded.

From far away came another sound, faint, but its message already understood, tensing the muscles, plucking at nerves. Rigid, Susan lay listening, waiting though instinct told her to get up and run, though where she was not sure.

The thin lone voice was joined by another, slightly nearer, then another, nearer still, each rising and falling in its own time. The first, hardly discernible now with those nearer wails taking up the cry. That first and the second and the third had died away, their message complete, but their relay was still advancing like a relentless tide.

Her parents' door opened. Her mother called up, 'Sue! Get the gals up. Robert! Les! John! Come on!' Her tone was one of piercing urgency. But Susan was already up, shaking the girls awake.

'Warning's gone. Come on – hurry up.' She dared not put on a light. The blackout curtains were a flimsy affair that needed time to check before one could be sure no chink gleamed out into the night. There was no time to check.

Transition from deep sleep to alert wakefulness was immediate, a gift given only to animals and those in peril. They were on their feet feeling for top clothes – like herself, these times they went to bed in their undies, the easier to dress in an air raid.

Beryl was shivering. 'Brr! I'm cold.'

In the darkness, June's voice: 'I think I've got Beryl's dress on.'

'It don't matter – just hurry up.'

'It does. She'll tear the seams.'

'Then hurry up and change over. We've got to get down the cellar.'

The boys were already racing past the door, boots clumping down the stairs. Grabbing handbag and warm coat, Susan pushed the girls ahead of her, hearing the first crump of anti-aircraft guns.

'Where's the gals?' came her mother's anxious call.

'Sod the gals!' came her father's grating voice. 'Where's my fags?'

'Blow your soppy fags – there's some in the cellar.'
'Tailor-made make me cough. I don't like 'em.'
'You'll have to lump 'em! Where're you gals?'
'Coming, Mum.'

The siren on the roof of the police station in the next street broke into its frantic exchange with an ear-splitting wailing. At the same time the ack-ack gun situated on a piece of waste ground at the far end of the road began cracking. The Hopkins family, like every family around them, all but fell down the four concrete steps into the cellar to be cocooned in comparative safety for the next several hours among the junk of a lifetime spent living in one house. The junk was now pushed to one end to accommodate an ancient double bed, a sagging put-u-up, two camp beds, an oil stove for warmth and a portable electric ring to brew tea, the concrete floor sporting a tattered rug to give a semblance of comfort while age-old cobwebs made grey curtains against the walls.

In this underground environment they sorted themselves out a little more calmly but no less tensely beneath the cold glare of a single electric bulb while above them the night began to rage.

As anti-aircraft guns began whacking away at laden German bombers droning above with their deep-throated, throbbing engine note, most likely caught in a web of searchlights, Susan sat thinking of Matthew. He had said he was in a searchlight unit. Was he on duty tonight? Searchlights were always vulnerable to attack. What if . . .

A noise, like the tearing of canvas, made the family

start. It seemed to be in the very cellar. The explosion sent them cowering to the floor as the light bulb swung madly on its flex to send the shadows of the camp beds flying wildly across the bare brick walls.

When nothing more happened they got to their feet, their hearts still racing, to sit back on the edge of the beds or on one of the old kitchen chairs long since consigned to the cellar.

'Sounded like it fell right in this street,' Vi Hopkins said. 'Jack, you ought to go and look. They might need some help.'

Shakily Jack reached for a tailor-made cigarette. 'There'll be others helping, I expect. Better not get in the way, like.'

'Long as it wasn't our house.'

'We'd know if it was, with dust and stuff. And the roof would've come in on us.'

'So much for being safe,' Vi remarked, looking up at the still-intact basement ceiling. But even if the house suffered, cellars would stand up to anything so long as it wasn't a direct hit. 'Someone in this street must have got it though,' she mused sadly. 'Hope no one was hurt.'

'We'll know in the morning,' Jack said as the worst of the raid drifted off. The bombers might come back, or they might not. It all depended. But while there was a lull, it was best to sleep. He climbed into the ancient double bed, fully dressed, pulling the blanket over his head.

Susan looked at him, contempt a dull, wordless emotion inside her, and thought of Matthew out there amid falling, jagged-edged, razor-sharp shrapnel from anti-aircraft guns, a tin helmet his only protection as he did whatever people did with searchlights.

With morning and the all clear, the sun shining as though in mockery of last night's devastation, her father returned from his reconnoitre to say the near-miss had flattened two houses at the end of the road opposite the Red Lion.

'Hope it's not put paid to my job,' Vi sighed. 'I need that money.'

'They said one landed in Lile Street.' He worked in Lile Street in a small factory making the springs that went inside the chin straps of steel helmets. War work and his bronchitis had kept him out of the forces.

'Anyone hurt on our street?' Susan asked.

'One of the families was in someone else's basement. But they can't find the woman as lives in the other one. You know, that one with the frizzy hair. Husband's in the Merchant Navy.'

'Mrs Norton. She often comes into the Red Lion for half a pint. Oh, not her.'

'Old Hardwick said he asked her into his basement, but she wanted to stay in her own place, like. She must be under all the rubble. They're digging now.'

'Oh, that's terrible.' Susan rather liked the plump little woman who always smiled at her when they passed each other. To think of her dead, bleeding limbs all broken and crooked . . . Shuddering violently, Susan thrust away the horrific injuries her imaginative brain conjured up. She was going to have to pass that house this morning on her way to Cotterels, just off Broad Street where she worked behind the counter selling underwear. What if the broken bleeding body was brought out just as she was passing? She'd be sick there on the spot.

The gap where the two houses had stood towards the end of the long row just like hers struck Susan as she passed as being like two missing teeth in a previously unbroken set, albeit that the set was full of decay, their stumps a pile of rubble. The roofs of the houses on either side were gone, and the windows in all the others were gone too. So were several windows in Susan's own home. She had left her parents clearing up the glass and her father re-hanging the front door, blown off in the blast, leaving the back of the settee and the living room beyond open to the street.

The Red Lion was minus all its windows, doors and most of its tiles. Already men were spreading a tarpaulin over the roof, the publican having erected a hastily painted sign: 'More Open than Usual.'

Susan tried not to look as she passed the ARP and Auxiliary Fire Service men working among the rubble, faces white with dust, their sweat for all the chill of the bright March morning tracing sepia rivulets down their cheeks.

'Watch that wall!' The warning made Susan stop, but the caller was talking to a comrade. 'Looks dodgy. There's a gap down here. Hang on a minute. Listen.'

She wanted to walk on, but found herself standing mesmerised as the man shone a torch into a hole for another to peer in. 'See anything?' He shouted into the hole. 'Anyone there? Are – you – all – right?' Then to the other man, 'What's the old girl's name?' The name supplied, he called, 'Mrs NORTON!'

'There,' he broke off. 'Is that a leg? Can you see?'

'Only a bit of wood.'

'MRS NORTON! It's no good – someone'll have to get down there.'

It was impossible to tear herself away as a slim man began to squeeze himself through the aperture, careful not to dislodge loose bricks, splintered beams, and broken furniture balanced so delicately. What would they bring out? Susan wanted to run but couldn't. It was like being a rabbit hypnotised by a snake's stare. Her stomach churned with a sick feeling.

The AFS man was halfway in when a shout came. 'There she is!'

Heads swivelled. Turning into Calvert Street, the small round figure, seeing her home in ruins, had broken into a run. Old Mr Hardwick caught her in his arms as she came abreast of him. 'Where've you been, love? We thought you were . . .'

Over his shoulder her eyes surveyed the destruction. 'It's all gone. All my nice furniture . . .'

'Never mind your furniture. 'S long as you're safe.'

'All my John's stamp collection. What's he gonna say?'

'He'll be only too glad to know you're safe when you write to him. You come into my house now and I'll make a cup of tea. You probably need it.'

Being guided across the road towards his own window-less home with its patches of missing tiles, ('Thank God it fell at the back of them places, or I'd of had nothing

left either,' he'd said earlier) her gaze still clung to the
wreckage.

'Sorry I didn't take up your offer,' she was apologising,
as though that mattered now. 'I ran round to my daughter's
place as soon as the siren went off round here. I had to be
with her. She's on her own too – him in the Navy. I didn't
want her to be alone. I shouldn't of gone.'

'If you hadn't of, you'd of been down there,' soothed
Mr Hardwick as they passed Susan without seeing her.

The diggers were brushing themselves down. Neighbours waiting in the wings had come out with cups of tea
for them as Susan went on her way, leaving them standing
in groups, sipping gratefully. She had much happier
thoughts now, eager to tell Marie who worked with her
behind the counter on ladies' and men's underwear all
about the new chap she had found.

A week went by. A fortnight. Disappointed, Susan had
given up expecting to hear from him. Then came a letter.
There was a Hollywood musical on at the Odeon. Would
she care to meet him outside at six thirty?

Would she *care*? She took so long with her make-up,
getting her long dark hair just right, choosing what dress to
wear, that she made herself late, finally arriving to find him
pacing up and down outside. But his face brightened as he
saw her; taking her arm, he conducted her inside.

It was wonderful walking into the cinema on his arm,
her small figure making him seem taller than he was.
Wonderful standing in the foyer, its dull blue lights, in
recognition of blackout regulations despite the two lots of

dense velvet curtains shielding the line of doors, giving the sumptuous decor a strange wan look as she stood aside for him to pay at the kiosk – tickets to the balcony, of all things. Wonderful going up the wide, carpeted stairs that muffled their footsteps and then sitting with his arm about her shoulders in the comfortable plush seats as they watched Eleanor Powell dance across the screen in typical Hollywood splendour. Afterwards they had taken a long saunter while he told her more about himself and she in turn told him something, not too much, of her life. His arm had been about her the whole time and the warm September night had wrapped itself about them both, a light warm breeze playing with her hair and the hem of her summer frock, and they might have been somewhere on a high mountain top rather than a crowded, dirty, smelly, bombed city.

In a quiet dark corner away from homeward-bound cinema and theatre crowds, he had drawn her to him and kissed her, a long lingering kiss that had set her blood tingling. He had asked no more of her than that, but she knew that they would meet again, and again, and she couldn't wait to get to work on the Monday to tell her two workmates there all about it. She was his girl. It was almost too good to be true, unbelievable. Susan prayed that night for this thing to last forever.

Chapter 7

His back against the unlit mobile searchlight, Matthew stood beside the as-yet mute field telephone, his companions waiting, watching. Nothing doing yet but there soon would be. Thin clouds scudding across a full moon would soon disperse, leaving sky and earth bright from what had become known as a bomber's moon – ideal for Jerry who had already checked the weather and knew he could enjoy good hunting tonight.

Which city would Jerry go for? Birmingham? Coventry? Callous to hope it would be Coventry, but Susan lived in Birmingham. What if she suffered a direct hit? It didn't bear thinking about.

They had been writing to each other for two months now. Each time he thought of her, which seemed to him to be every other second, a flood of warmth swept through his insides followed by cold fear for her safety. He'd never felt like this before. If he were to lose her now . . .

The man beside him chuckled. 'What's that great big sigh for, Matt? Not that girl you go to see every time you get a pass?'

Bob Howlett was a close mate, of a similar background to his own. Their accents often drew smirks from the mix of Welsh, Scots, Midlanders and Cockneys, especially their rough-tongued sergeant, Pegg, constantly and vociferously cursing his luck in being saddled with a couple of junior NCOs whose education put them far above him, except for his military dedication, though theirs, according to him, was nil. Both had been before the selection board. Both had been rejected, one for his flippancy, the other for his apathy. Bob possessed no ambition whatsoever. Six feet tall and thin as a pole, propped at the moment against the sandbagged parapet he looked like a loose bag of bones with a stoop that resisted all the Army's attempts to straighten him up. Nose aquiline, chin long and narrow, physically he was the most unprepossessing man Matthew had ever known, yet he displayed the sweetest disposition and an agonisingly mild temper. People didn't come any better than Bob Howlett. Too good ever to become an officer.

Matthew grinned at him, laying aside thoughts of Susan for a little moment to follow this second train of thought. 'I wonder what old Peggy would do if either of us ever did get a commission?'

'Follow us to the ends of the earth probably,' Bob said with lethargic sagacity. 'It won't be me though. I'm no leader of men. Don't want to be. All I want is this war to end and me to be back with Phyllis and the kids.'

'Amen,' Matthew echoed fervently, at the same time hoping that Bob wouldn't suddenly bring out his latest photos of his blonde-haired wife and three children as he was wont to do.

From far away came an almost inaudible eerie wail of

a civilian air-raid siren. But for the stillness of the country around, it would not have been detected at all. Their own klaxon had sounded a short while before, sending men running to their stations. As though in obedience to that faint wail, the moonlight poured out from its shielding of cloud to throw every object on the earth beneath into stark relief. From the direction of distant Coventry tiny dull flashes silhouetted the black horizon. Thin cones of light, made squat by distance, began to play back and forth, crossing and re-crossing the sky in slow motion, low down, like flat furtive ghosts. Hardly discernibly came a low and ominous crump-crump, crump-crump-crump of a far-off barrage. Coventry was getting it. Matthew found himself offering up silent prayers of thanks, his radio set still quiet, their own searchlight still in darkness. Not Birmingham tonight, thank God.

The field radio crackled. Suddenly sick at heart, Matthew unhooked the earphones and put them on to note the coordinates they conveyed. A shape materialised from the darkness of the field around to stand beside him.

'Why are we still in darkness, sonny?' Sergeant Pegg's voice filled the night air, making the nearby mobile parabaloid sound indicators tremble.

Matthew sprang to his job. 'They're going on now, Serg.'

To his barked command, the huge disc clonked. A shaft of blinding light pierced the sky, here picking out remnants of fagged cloud in fleeting, flat and fuzzy patches, moving hastily on, there the cone's vortex swallowed up eerily by the immensity of space. But Sergeant Pegg was not happy.

Stepping close, he put his lips close to his quarry's ear to be heard over its messages.

''Alf asleep was we, Corp'ral?'

'No, sir.'

'Well, I suggest yer get yer finger out a bit more sharpish, next time, an' stop bloody daydreamin'. Fine example you are. Whatever'd 'appen to us if you ever got a commission? The day you do, my arse'll turn into a bleedin' pumpkin, that's wot. Now keep yer mind on yer job or I'll 'ave them stripes orf yer before yer can say, "Oh bloody my!"'

For twenty minutes Matthew kept his mind on his job, the sound indicator booming and roaring, amplifying every sound of any plane overhead, pinpointing its direction. On one occasion his searchlight trapped a plane, prompting others to sweep over and join it in a perfect star of beams, the ack-ack guns in a nearby sandbagged pit consequently opening up in an energetic earsplitting barrage. The plane swopped east, then north, finally managing to evade the deadly nucleus of light by slipping behind a low cloud and no doubt veering off to rejoin its fellows over Coventry.

One by one the searchlights were doused. Matthew's radio went quiet. Bob and the rest of the crew fell to rolling cigarettes.

'Tell you what,' he said, his tone low and confidential, recalling the sigh Matthew had given earlier and interpreting it correctly as only a gentle, perceptive soul could. 'Why don't you propose to this girl of yours? In a letter. See what she says.'

Matthew looked up with a frown from the cigarette

he too was rolling. On a corporal's pay, packet cigarettes ran away with money and he did his best to discourage his parents sending cheques; telling them in no uncertain terms that it made him look bad before his hut-mates and that he was managing adequately enough.

'I've only known her two or three months. I can't go mad.'

'If you feel about her the way you appear to me to, I would say you wouldn't want to lose her to someone else. Better now than never.'

That was true. But marriage. Matthew gave Bob a nod to placate him and told himself he'd have to think about that one. The more he thought about it, the more it seemed it was what he wanted. He remembered having the same feeling about Jenny, strange little twinges of excitement in the pit of his stomach when he thought of her, but Susan had come along and the sensation had transferred itself to her, fourfold. He knew now who he wanted, that it was Susan for whom he would further his career, making her proud of him. Perhaps he'd take Bob's advice, re-apply to the selection board. A man should do all he could to support his intended.

Sitting on his bed, a book on his knee for support, he absorbed himself in putting down on paper all he wanted to say. But reading it back, he cringed. The worst drivel he'd ever read – she'd laugh her head off. Better to tear it up before he did any damage and made a complete fool of himself.

But he didn't tear it up. Instead he folded the flimsy wartime paper and laid it carefully inside his pay book.

Finding a fresh sheet of paper he penned another letter, full of the things he normally wrote to her, his hut-mates, their doings, the smelly Eddie Nutt whose socks stank the place out every time he opened his locker, the lecherous clown Taffy Thomas, the foul-mouthed Bert Farrell, Bob and his family, Sergeant Pegg, the rotten food, the hard beds, how much he looked forward to seeing her again and hoped it would be soon, and how was she, and what had she been doing?

'Ward, M.L.C. 092.' Matthew shouldered through the waiting men to receive two letters. Perched on a wall in the weak sunlight of the November morning that threatened rain, he put aside the one from his parents and opened the other with its large childish handwriting.

The letter was short, two small ruled pages, laboriously written, with several words misspelt, which evoked a surge of compassion . . . no, more one of tenderness. It was little more than an outline of her activities since he'd last seen her – pictures with a girlfriend, a dance or two. A twinge of panic smote him that she could so easily meet someone else during one of those dances, someone more conveniently to hand than he.

'Damn this bloody war!' he uttered so vehemently that Bob looked up and grinned.

Hastily scanning the second page of writing which didn't quite reach to its foot, it was the last line that brought relief flooding through his chest in a hot glow: 'I've been worried you might get fed up of riting to me. I cant wait to here from you.' A thousand words penned by the world's greatest poet could not have conveyed as much meaning as he read into that one artless sentence.

Life took on new meaning; time was a most precious commodity. But it was one the Army seemed perversely set on spinning out into an eternity of misery, for just as he was settling down after his day's duty to write to her the beefy bulk of Sergeant Pegg appeared to announce that the whole unit was on the morrow being sent to the wilds of Wales on an exercise, duration not divulged, all passes cancelled. Matthew, who had planned on wheedling a few hours' pass for himself, suffered an intense sense of loss hardly to be borne.

'Damn this bloody war!' he uttered for the second time that day as he fought to rush off a letter to Susan.

The Blitz was a tyrant. Begun in September and still going strong, there was no chance for Jenny to be at home for Christmas or New Year. Her mother had either to spend both on her own or go to her sister in Leicester. That she wouldn't do, fearing to travel alone. Daddy had always done everything and she, used to following him around like a small puppy, had still not learned independence.

'Can't you *try* to get away, dear,' she asked when after the sixth or seventh attempt Jenny got through on the telephone to the couple next door – well, the girl next door now that her husband had been called up.

Her mother sounded out of breath from hurrying into the other house, shouting down the mouthpiece as though distance made this obligatory although there'd not been a lot of static crackling over the wires.

'I'm on duty, Mumsy. I can't just get time off. It's terrible here. So many people being brought in injured.'

'I don't like us being apart.' The voice filled with consternation. 'I'll have to spend all night Christmas down the shelter all on my own. We've had a bomb come down near here. Some of the tiles are off. It's only a matter of time before this place is hit. I wish you were here. I feel so . . . so . . . isolated. Can't you come home?'

'They need every nurse they can get here at the moment, Mumsy.'

'Well, it's terrible. They should allow you home for New Year at least.'

'German bombers don't worry about holidays, Mumsy. They'll drop them whatever day it is.'

'I don't think I can stand being here all on my own.'

'Can't Joan next door come into our shelter with you?'

'I couldn't ask her that, dear.' Her mother's voice had dropped to a whisper lest the girl overhear. 'I couldn't open my house to *strangers*.'

'She's not a stranger. You're in her house right now. Now she's on her own too, you could both become quite good friends and help each other. We need to help each other these days.' The Blitz had made everyone conscious of the need for people to help each other.

'She won't be here at Christmas or New Year. She's spending the holiday with her family or her husband's family.'

Jenny tried not to let her sigh echo down the line. 'Well, I can't come home. The hospital's bulging. There are even beds in the corridors. And during an air raid we have to get as many as we can under the beds or down into the basement. It's like another hospital down there.'

'If you asked them nicely, they'd let you have just *one* day?'

'I can't, Mum.' She'd not been listening. 'This line's going funny. I'll have to ring off.'

'But Jenny . . .'

'I'll try to get home for a few nights after New Year, but it's impossible at the moment. You'll be all right, Mumsy.' She wanted to say that her being at home wouldn't stop a bomb dropping on it. 'I'll get time off eventually. I shall need it to get over all that we're going through here.'

'What, dear? What?' The crackling was growing noisier; impossible to hear anything now. And her time was almost up, her money running out. Moreover, she knew she was taking liberties during work time.

'I've got to ring off, Mumsy. Love you.'

'What?'

'Love you, Mumsy. I must go.' A sturdy, starched blue figure was approaching. 'I'm on duty. I'm wanted. Try to get home as soon as I can.'

She replaced the receiver on its hook, goodbyes cut short by the glare from the stone-grey eyes of Miss Grenville, approaching with a few attendant senior staff.

'Have you not enough to do, nurse?' The question was quietly authoritative. Jenny's reply was hasty, unrehearsed.

'My mother, Matron, asking if I'd be spending Christmas with her.'

In truth she had no real wish to go home. Christmas here would be far more exciting if she could believe what the nurses who'd been here last Christmas told her: wards decorated with paperchains fashioned from whatever coloured paper they could get hold of, spending any off-duty hours in each other's rooms to make them; going round the wards on Christmas Eve, their blue capes drawn close around them as they sang carols in muted voices, each nurse holding a lit candle; later sitting in the nurses' quarters all cosy and warm by a fire while others piled in to roast chestnuts and eat the mince pies someone's mother had sent, swapping jokes and stories of latest conquests with junior doctors.

That had been last year's. Jenny looked forward to this year's but wondered if it would have changed since the Blitz started. But anything was better than just sitting at home with Mumsy, even if there was an air raid on Christmas Day itself. She wouldn't even put that past the enemy.

She had been transferred to the London Hospital from her teaching hospital in October, a month after the Blitz had started. Eight weeks on and night bombing was still going on, not a single night free of it, remorseless, dominating all else. As darkness fell, she, like everyone else, merely prepared herself for the wail of sirens, the drone of bombers, and the horrible tearing sound and crash of falling bombs when the very air shook and dust drifted in from everywhere. The sky turned lurid to the mad clanging of fire engines, ambulance bells that heralded another stream of casualties. She and everyone felt it would go on until the war was finally won, all steadfastly refusing to imagine it could be Britain who might lose. Such a prospect remained so preposterous it was unthinkable.

Jenny stood aside for Matron's entourage to pass, waiting to make her escape back to her ward, but the woman halted, eyes fixed on her. 'If you are on duty, nurse, then you should know that telephone calls are not permissible. If you are not on duty, then you are off limits. I shall see you in my office at six thirty.'

'Yes, Matron.' Jenny watched miserably as she and her staff moved on. Six thirty. Well planned. Two days remained before Christmas and the evening had only just grown dark because of the introduction of British Summer Time. Clocks were now kept one hour forward the whole year round to confuse an enemy whose own time remained as it had been prior to hostilities. The bombers would not arrive for a couple of hours yet. Plenty of time was left for civilians to get home from work, eat and get into shelters, and for her to endure a formal and uncomfortable dressing-down from Matron.

She had been through the drill before, standing in the centre of Miss Grenville's office, Miss Grenville walking around her with measured steps, quoting hospital rules to her in quiet tones as measured as her walk. No punishment had been meted out: humiliation constituted punishment enough. Jenny found herself almost wishing the bombers would come early, requiring her duties to take precedence over any visit to Matron. But that would come sooner or later.

The all clear sounded just before dawn; while the people of the East End sank back to pick over lost homes, grieve lost loved ones, or just feel glad that they had escaped unscathed, the doctors and nurses of the hospitals all around toiled on, endeavouring to repair often irreparable injuries. For Jenny, exhausted by morning, her talking-to from Matron was just added torture. She fell thankfully into her bed in the nurses' quarters to forget about everything for a few hours until night came again. A week of that and then it would be days, spent mopping up the dregs from the previous night.

By February, freezing and cheerless, it was a wonder there were any buildings left to be bombed. Even some already flattened received a second direct hit. Yet, emerging for a breather in the cold light of dawn, she was always amazed so many still stood, windowless, battered sentinels. How this hospital had got away with just glancing blows so far seemed a miracle. How those who worked within it kept going was a miracle. Exhausted nerves stretched like rubber bands, they remained professional amid unbelievable chaos. As for herself, she was just an efficient puppet in a starched apron; obedient, mechanical, quietening some hysterical parent while nearby a terribly injured child seemed far more in need of her help; a mind trained at last to say, 'Walk, nurse,' when the sight of a woman with broken legs going into labour screamed for her to run, maybe knocking someone over in the process. It was frustrating, while the injured poured in still, covered in dust and blood, to be required to make tea for overstrained doctors. Though often essential, keeping them going, more often than not the tea remained untouched. It was hard at times to be obedient.

She recalled resentment when, wanting to stand by for the injured to arrive, she'd be required instead to help transfer geriatric patients to the basement. Coaxing the frail and sometimes perverse elderly into wheelchairs to be trundled to safety could test obedience to breaking point and struck a poor second to the business of tending victims of bomb-blast and fire.

'I feel more like a maid-of-all-work than a nurse,' she complained in early March, the night bombing still going full blast, as they carried a dear old soul back up a flight of stone stairs after the all clear had sounded. The lift was again out of order. O'Brien gave a tinkling laugh.

'Dear Mother o' God, isn't that what we're here for?'

O'Brien was small, dark and Irish, a bundle of smiles and dedication whose upbringing had endowed her with the unquestioning obedience of a nun. At times Jenny envied as well as admired her. When it seemed impossible the hospital could continue after broken gas mains cut off the cooking facilities and all they had to cope with was a portable paraffin stove, O'Brien's tranquillity as they fought with the thing reduced Jenny to a state of humility. With no running water for days on end, O'Brien took it all in her stride, emptying bottles of disinfectant into basins of cold water for washing hands after each dressing until the liquid turned cloudy grey, all the while praising God for the blessings of disinfectant.

At these times, Jenny yearned for the smooth routine of that teaching hospital in Basingstoke. She had learned her skills there, but East London was the acid test of a nurse's stamina. Here, controlling fatigue meant overcoming not the simple weariness of a few nights' lost sleep but the perfidious wearing down of her mental faculties, creeping up on her like a hooded assassin. The only hint of anything amiss would be a second or two of apparent sleep, yet coming back to herself to find she had accomplished her task as though she had been wide awake all the time.

More alarming were those longer moments of forget-fulness, as when she had taken a pile of bedpans, not to the sluice, but straight through the doors of an operating theatre without any recollection of how she had got there. Beating a hasty retreat, she had felt flustered and very much awake.

Much more recent had been that strange hallucination when she had looked up from taking a blood pressure to see a haggard and terribly emaciated young man standing at her elbow.

She remembered saying, quite loudly, 'I'll be with you in just one minute,' and wondering vaguely at the astonished look from her female patient. She had turned again to find the young man was not there. He never had been. Recognising her mistake for what it was, a figment of total exhaustion, it had taken a while to shake off a belief that it had been a premonition of some sort, for what really alarmed her was that every time she thought of it, the young face hovering before her seemed to be that of Matthew Ward.

It left her wondering for days how he was, where he was. In fact she could hardly wait for her next time off duty and she sacrificed a night out with the girls to pop home instead. The air-raid sirens hadn't yet sounded and after sitting for a while in the back garden with Mumsy in the improving April weather, she wandered down to the shops in Mare Street where Mr Ward had his electrical shop, with the precise aim of casually asking how his son was doing.

'Stationed in Wales at the moment,' she was informed as he handed a customer a repaired radio. Such things these days were either repaired or second-hand, most things not on ration having vanished from sight.

'He was near Birmingham,' Mr Ward went on. 'But like always, being trooped all around the country.'

'He's okay then?' she pressed, still unable to get her hallucination out of her mind. At least he hadn't been sent overseas.

'Fine. Had a letter from him a few days back.' How like Matthew he spoke. 'Found himself a girl. Don't know how serious it is, but he seems smitten by her. That's how it goes. In the forces, you meet all sorts. His mother's not pleased. Says it probably won't last as she's in Birmingham and he's in Wales.'

And Jenny's heart had sunk as she smiled and left, although it had been inevitable he would meet someone. She thought of herself, out of sight and out of mind. She should stop thinking about him and get on with her own life. But at least he was safe.

In no mood to go home just yet to have Mumsy defining the bleakness she knew must show on her face, she wandered down to St John's church. She needed time to think. Of what, she had no real notion, but she had to sort out her thoughts of the future. It was imperative to stop dreaming of Matthew and get on with her own life.

St John's stood closed on this early Saturday evening but did not look quite so isolated and remote as it once had behind its tall iron railings. They had gone now, as had all iron railings, to be melted down into guns and tanks in the fight for victory over the enemy. It now stood amid the open space looking slightly vulnerable, its sooty brick bathed a dirty gold from the slanting sun, its once-proud stained glass windows now war damaged and mostly boarded up, no longer reflecting back the golden glow.

For a while Jenny stood there, contemplating whether she should go back home now, but she let her feet carry her towards the church itself and into the neatly laid out gardens behind it, still known locally as Barmy Park from the asylum for the insane that had once stood there. Sinking down on a bench with the low sun full on her, she watched people wander past, their thoughts most likely on enjoying a little fresh air before consigning themselves to the communal shelters and Bethnal Green Underground to await the arrival of the night bombers. All these people were passing yet she saw herself as quite alone, not because they ignored her but because she wanted it, so that she could think in peace of Matthew, of herself, of how she stood with him and he with her. Once again she decided to stop thinking about him and get on with her own life.

With that in mind, she got up and resolutely turned her face towards home. A voice hailed her as she passed the church again. Louise Ward ran up to her, slightly out of breath, cheeks flushed, her mousy hair rolled up primly in a style known as a victory roll, unflattering for anyone with the broad jaw line which she had inherited from her mother.

She looked excited. 'What're you doing here, Jenny? I thought you were nursing.'

'I've got a day off,' Jenny supplied but Louise could hardly contain herself.

'I'm only home for the weekend. Guess what, Jenny, I've gone and joined the Wrens.'

'You've what?' Jenny stopped walking.

But nothing could diminish the enthusiasm shining on Louise's face. She looked transformed. Gone was the prudish strait-laced mien. This girl glowed, and Jenny recalled the exact look on her brother's face when he'd come to say goodbye that cold winter day. It was like looking at a bird newly released from a cage and she realised that Louise, for all she would never have admitted it, had been as trapped as he had been once she blossomed into her teens. Without warning she had broken loose from all the old ties that had bound her. Because of the war she was suddenly her own person. 'I'm eighteen now, eligible to join up. I signed on and they took me. I had a medical and I passed A-one. I want to see the world.'

See the world. Perhaps dangerously so. Jenny eyed her dubiously. 'Did you tell your parents what you intended to do? What do they think?'

Louise gave a giddy laugh. 'Mother was shocked rigid. Dad hasn't said much. I sprang it on them. If I had told them what I was going to do Mother would have stopped me, I know. It took me being evacuated . . . well, not exactly evacuated but more or less . . . to give me a taste of what could be had. So I signed on for the WRNS. I'm leaving next week for Portsmouth.'

Walking home with Louise chatting incessantly at her side about her medical, how girls were needed to relieve Royal Navy personnel from office duties, how she had been told that they could be sent anywhere in the world and all the countries she might see, Jenny found it impossible to broach the subject of her brother's involvement with the anonymous Birmingham girl and if she thought it could be serious. Yet again she told herself to put it out of her mind, that their lives had gone their separate ways. But how nice it would be had it been otherwise.

Chapter 8

The coming of spring found Matthew still crouching in ditches in the wet wilderness of Fforest Fawr in the heart of Wales, trying to keep a crackling field radio dry under a gas cape.

'One thing's obvious,' he muttered to Bob Howlett beside him. 'She's no letter writer.'

In four months he had written Susan one letter a week as regularly as clockwork, each one several pages long. In return he had received just five letters from her, each hardly more than two sides of a piece of Woolworth's notepaper. Her bad spelling, he understood, perhaps made her slow to reply, but if she had any feelings for him, surely she'd write more frequently.

'She's lost all interest in me,' he said miserably. 'Bound to happen, she there and me here, and Birmingham full of uniforms.'

'Is that what you think?' Bob asked, scanning the rain-soaked peaty moorland. 'That she's just uniform crazy and nothing else?'

'No, of course I don't. But no girl is going to wait for months.'

'Lots do, in wartime. They'll wait for years.'

'Yes, if they've been going steady long enough. We hardly met above a couple of times. I wouldn't blame her.'

Beside them, Taffy Thomas shifted his uncomfortable position on his haunches. A Welshman he was, but from sunny, civilised Aberystwyth on the coast. This part of the country with its sopping heather wasn't his cup of tea at all.

'What you need is to get it out of your system, boyo. A bit of diversion. Two sisters I know of. Real beauties, the pair of 'em. Met 'em a week or two ago. One for me, one for you, eh? Make you forget your poor broken heart, that will.'

'No thanks, Taff,' Matthew murmured. Taffy looked mildly spurned.

'There's a terrible waste. Just have to do the best I can with both of 'em, then, won't I?' Grinning, he went back to scanning the horizon and misty forms of men scurrying about on manoeuvres, what could be seen of them through fine rain and the smoke of the thunder flashes going off.

Returning to camp, Taffy was off to the farmhouse where the sisters apparently lived; their father was in the Army, their mother working late in some nearby town. He returned later that evening, a little the worse for wear and very triumphant.

'Missed a treat, you did,' he stated, flinging himself on his camp bed in the tent he shared with Matthew and Bob. 'Damned stupid, you, mooning after a girl that don't want to know, as far as I can see.'

Having spent the entire day trying to put Susan out of his mind and annoyed that she refused to go, Matthew allowed his curiosity to arouse itself, if only moderately. 'What's she like then, this sister?'

Taffy let out an odd sound that passed for a knowing laugh, rather like a lion grunting. 'Big. Would eat you for breakfast, boyo. Put the blood back in your veins for you though. I could take you next time, if there is a next time. And if you was to get a letter from your girl, then no need to tell her, is there?'

'Might take you up on that, Taff.' Defiance held him in a vice. Two weeks waiting for a response to his last letter to her, and still nothing.

'You're on then,' said Taffy, and Matthew's mood loosened enough for him to give way to a terse chuckle.

'You're a lecherous swine, Taff.' But at this moment Taffy was a tonic to an aching heart.

A few days later he was glad he hadn't been led into temptation, with fatigues preventing him sneaking out of camp with Taffy to the infamous farmhouse. Handed a letter from Susan, he read what seemed to be the usual dutiful scribble, except for one short badly spelt paragraph:

I hope you don't think I'm not intrested, Matthew. I don't know how to put my feelings down on paper because when I read it it sounds so silly so I just tare it up. But I do need to tell you that I reelly do . . .

The next two words had been crossed out, obliterated so completely that a diviner couldn't have read them, after which she had continued:

I won't half be glad to see you again so I can tell you
how I reelly feel.

All at once it seemed his luck changed. Before he had a
chance to reply, the whole unit was returned to Northwood
and with a forty-eight-hour pass to boot. On wings of
joy he rushed to the phone box on his arrival, finding a
lengthening queue of Army personnel eager to tell families
of the chance to be with them for the weekend.

In a fever of impatience he tagged on to the end of
it, cursing the time the one already in the phone box
was taking. At last, the receiver in his grasp, he gave the
exchange the telephone number of the shop where Susan
worked, having long ago looked it up after she had told
him where she was employed.

'Hello?' A high, piercing voice spoke loudly in his ear
as he asked for Susan. And then, querulously, 'Who is
this?'

'Can I speak to Miss Susan Hopkins?' he repeated.

'I'm sorry,' came the voice, quite tersely. 'Staff aren't
allowed to take private calls.'

'But this is urgent.'

'I'm very sorry, sir. This telephone is for customer
enquiries only.' She wasn't a bit sorry, in fact she sounded
highly pleased to refuse his request. 'Only if the call is
from the family of one of our staff with dire news do we
allow them to take a call.'

'Then could you give her a message?' he intercepted.
'Could you tell her I'll see her tonight – on the corner of
her road – at six-thirty?'

The voice had become filled with exasperation. 'Really, sir, I am far too busy to relay messages from every Tom, Dick and Harry arranging dates with members of my staff.'

'Please – just this once. We're – we're . . .' He thought quickly. 'We're engaged, and . . .'

He broke off as the phone-box door was yanked open. The voices outside came instantly loud, the speaker even louder.

'Git a bleedin' move on, mate. There're others out 'ere, y'know.'

Matthew shot out a hand and jerked the phone-box door shut again. 'Please . . . I've been away on a training course.'

'Engaged, you say?' There was now lively curiosity in the voice on the other end of the phone, and for an instant he hesitated. What had he said? Then he came to an instant decision. 'That's right. And I need to speak to Miss Hopkins. It is very important.'

He waited while the faceless one ruminated on this piece of news.

'Well,' it deliberated at length, 'I really cannot alter our rules, but on this occasion I will pass on your message. What name?'

'Matthew Ward.'

'Very well. But I sincerely hope you are not making a fool of me, Mr Ward. And please keep in mind that my staff are *not* allowed to make use of this telephone for private purposes unless in an emergency.'

'I'll remember. And thank you.'

Thoughtfully he replaced the receiver. Engaged, he'd said, in fear of being cut off. Engaged. Well, why not? All that fretting, all that longing, the tone of her last letter – he was sure now that those obliterated words had been 'love you'. And didn't he want this relationship to last? And hadn't he spent these past four months pining, if he really admitted to it? Well then . . .

The prospect of being engaged sent a thrill of excitement through his veins he hadn't expected. Lost in thought, he opened the door of the phone box to be almost pushed against the edge of it by a soldier squeezing by to get in, throwing Matthew a baleful glance as he did so.

"'Bout bloody time too, mate! Got *my* missus ter phone too, y'know.'

The stress lay on 'my'. The man assumed he was married. He would be, soon. And again a thrill coursed through his veins.

He hadn't expected Susan to be there on the stroke of six thirty, but not finding her there on the dot, irrational anxieties began instantly to manifest themselves. Had the manageress not passed on his message? Had he in fact frightened her off with his damned silly proposal? Wouldn't any girl be? She'd never said she loved him, apart from that crossed-out bit in her latest letter which could have been anything, just a spelling mistake too bad to let by. That bit in her letter about wanting to tell him how she really felt, one could read all sorts of meaning into such a line. In retrospect he had kidded himself. He was a fool.

It occurred to him as he waited in the damp warmth of this still-light mid-April evening that he didn't really know anything about her. He *felt* that he knew her, but it wasn't the same thing.

Staring along her street that teemed with grubby children at play, their shouts echoing from the flat, scabrous walls on either side set with endless doors and windows, not a tree, a plant, a blade of grass to be seen, he realised how unlike was her life to his. He had to be honest with himself. Because he thought himself in love was he seeing all this and her too through rose-tinted glass? Perhaps, as well as love, did he feel some sadness and pity for her too? Without that he would be viewing these slums with utter distaste, eager only to get away.

Where he stood was a pub, its blown-out windows and frames covered by sheets of waterproof-painted cardboard, its walls, door and sign pockmarked from flying shrapnel. Across the road, a little way down, a gash in the previously unbroken row of terraced houses held a pile of rubble, a result of the bomb Susan had told him about. The slanting evening sun picking out the interior walls that had once been private pitilessly exposed the wallpaper, the poor fireplaces, the smallness of the rooms that had once been, and almost touching the rubble, the houses of the next street, hitherto unseen from here, now peeped through like people surprised at being caught in the open.

He glanced at his watch. Six thirty-five. Was that all? A breathless voice called his name, light footsteps from behind him came running, and there she was, almost falling into his arms as he turned, her tone gabbling with panic.

'Oh, Matthew. I had to stay behind at work. Stock-taking.

I got your message but I only just got away and nearly missed the bus. I was so scared you wouldn't wait. I thought you might think I didn't care and give up and go away . . .'

She was reaching up, kissing him, here in the street for everyone passing by to see. 'Oh, Matthew, did you mean what you said? On the phone? You did mean it, didn't you?'

He nodded, gently stopping her frantic embrace, aware people were grinning as they went past. 'It wasn't a very romantic way to propose . . .'

'Oh, it was!' she broke in, still holding tightly to him. 'I never dreamed I'd get such a romantic proposal. And to think that bitch didn't tell me until it was time to close and then said we had to do stock-taking. She let me go a bit earlier, but I hate her.'

'Doesn't matter. You're here.' She'd never know how relieved he felt. 'I want to take you out, Susan, to celebrate. I can't afford much in the way of a posh restaurant, but . . .'

'I couldn't eat. I'm too excited,' she burst in. 'I want to go somewhere quiet with you, darling. Just us two, and we can talk all about *things*. We've got to discuss things.'

'Yes.' Her closeness was making him feel worked up inside, a sort of churning making it hard to breathe properly. They had to get away from here. 'Where do you want to go?'

At last she broke away, thought for a moment. 'It's still light. It'll stay light for ages yet. Let's get some sandwiches and take them up on Beacon Hill. We can watch the sunset and be all romantic – just you and me. It only takes half an hour to get there.'

On the rounded promontory called Beacon Hill, more or less deserted but for one or two people walking dogs, they reclined on Matthew's greatcoat on the rabbit-nibbled turf to eat a couple of meagrely filled off-ration chicken sandwiches as the sun sank lower.

'On a clear day you can see ten counties from here,' Susan said, huddled inside her coat against the rapidly cooling air. The sun had become a red ball in the smoky haze of the city, outlining the rim of their world. She pointed southwest. 'That's the Malvern Hills.'

Matthew looked, then laughed. 'Clouds.'

'They're hills, Matthew.'

'All right, hills,' he laughed and she turned a petulant face towards him.

'Don't make fun of me.' Her lips were so close that he leaned forward and kissed them, tasting the sweetness that was her lipstick but which he was sure must also be her lips. Forgetting her pique she returned the kiss, nestled against him, lying quiet now and watching the rim of the sun finally sink out of sight, leaving its reflection to tint the clouds orange and pink, that in turn bathed the earth in ruddy glow.

'Matthew,' she said quietly, slowly, relaxing against him. 'You did mean it, about us being engaged? Only it was so casual. It was romantic, being said over the phone, but . . . well, you know, if you said it again now.'

He tightened his arm around her. 'Darling, I'm saying it now. Shall we get engaged?' Yes, this was what he wanted.

Couldn't imagine life now without her. She would be his wife. He felt his insides leap with the joy the thought brought. 'Susan, I want to marry you.'

He heard her deep intake of breath, her reply exhaled in a series of long sighs. 'Oh . . . Oh, Matthew. Oh . . .' She seemed incapable of saying anything else. It meant yes, he knew. But there were material things to think about too, unwanted material things. 'I'll have to tell my mam and dad.'

'Will they object?' She was still not twenty-one. She must have their consent. His heart fell a little. But he needn't have been anxious.

'No. They'll be glad to see me go and make a bit more room. I've got three brothers and two sisters and we've only got three bedrooms. They'll be thrilled, especially as you're someone really nice with enough money . . .'

'Hold on,' he curbed her, laughing. 'I'm not Rockefeller, you know. I'm existing on a corporal's pay.'

'But your family's well off, aren't they?'

'They're nothing to do with me.' He hoped he hadn't sounded a bit grim but he didn't want to think about them at this moment. 'You'll be marrying me, not them.'

'I know. Oh, Matthew, of course I know. Married. I'm going to have to pinch myself to make sure this is me.' She had turned, lifting her face to his. 'I shall love you always, Matthew. Always and always.'

And on her cue he kissed her with a pressing need for her bursting inside him like a radiant explosion. Consumed by its heat he let his weight bear her down beneath him and on the warmth of his greatcoat they made love, she in trusting joy of his promise and he in the knowledge that they would be together till all eternity. And it was beautiful.

He wrote home, cramming his letter with Susan's charms, and defiantly told them that he was engaged.

That Sunday he went dutifully to see Susan's family. Susan had already broken the news and her mother, fair, full-bosomed and not a bit like her trim daughter, planted a kiss on his cheek in a cloud of Evening in Paris perfume.

'She's right about you being so good-looking, love, ain't she, Dad?'

'She's right, yeah,' echoed Mr Hopkins.

Susan's two sisters sat on the arms of the settee, the air around them redolent of peardrops from nail varnish being applied as they both regarded Matthew with mute envy of their sister.

Two of her brothers were in the street, the youngest sprawled on a mat in front of an empty firegrate torturing a clockwork train with a screwdriver.

The place smelled of Sunday midday dinner and Matthew was glad he hadn't been invited to eat with them; the lingering odour of overboiled cabbage almost overwhelmed him so that it was difficult to draw a breath without feeling nauseated. Susan, sweet and fastidious Susan, deserved better than this. He would give it to her as soon as this war was over and they could find a place together. Meantime, as soon as they were married she might go to his parents and live in a far more wholesome atmosphere.

Mr Hopkins, a small man who looked as if he had once

been handsome, lounged in an armchair rolling a cigarette which he lit. The match was dropped in the empty grate, the matchbox replaced on an already cluttered mantelpiece. 'Wondered who she'd end up with,' he muttered.

'I'm very glad she's found herself a nice lad,' said Mrs Hopkins, handing Matthew a cup of tea while Susan, sitting beside him on the edge of the settee, smiled with satisfaction and cuddled nearer to him. Her teacup was on the floor at her feet, the liquid in it strong and muddy, as was his. He took a sip, tried not to grimace and put it down beside hers. Behind him a mound of well-thumbed magazines kept sliding forward, making his seat uncomfortable.

'When you planning to marry then?' Mr Hopkins asked.

Matthew glanced at Susan, saw her eyes, those deep blue eyes, full of trust. 'As soon as possible,' he answered.

Mr Hopkins coughed, a moist rumbling cough, and flicked the wet butt of his cigarette into the grate. 'Up the spout is she, then?'

'I'm sorry?' Matthew queried at once, hardly believing what he heard and appalled.

'Pregnant is she?'

Susan's two sisters giggled. The boy on the mat looked up, mildly interested. Mrs Hopkins gave a small embarrassed tut.

'No, Mr Hopkins, she isn't,' Matthew said tersely, wanting to be out of here as soon as he possibly could. Love Susan as he now did, beyond measure, he did not want to set foot in her parents' house ever again. This man

repelled him. But that Susan was small like her father, it
seemed incredible that he was indeed her father. With no
way to explain to him, a man who confused love with lust,
his feelings for his daughter, he said instead, 'If I'm posted
before we can be married, there might not be another
chance for a long time.'

Mrs Hopkins was giving him a scrutinising look.
She had quite large breasts. They strained at her sturdy
white brassiere, the top of which was visible above a blue
organdie blouse. Matthew looked quickly away, thinking
of Susan's small firm breasts. He longed to be out of here,
to be alone with her.

Mrs Hopkins was appraising him slowly. 'I must say,
though, it fair took us all by surprise, our Sue telling us last
night as you'd asked her to marry you. Came as a bit of a
shock, like. No wonder we thought you and her had been
up to a few tricks.' She gave a tinkling laugh at his look.
'Come on, love. We've all done it. But whether she is or
she ain't, I'm glad you're serious about her. And if it's all
right with her, then it's all right with us.'

The china-blue eyes followed him slowly as somehow
he got to his feet, his hand seeking Susan's and holding it
firmly. 'I'll have to be going now, Mrs Hopkins.'

She looked surprised. 'You ain't drunk your tea yet.'

'No, I've got to get back to camp. And Susan and I, well
we . . .'

She giggled at his awkward pause, her tone full of
feminine wisdom. 'Of course. You two want a bit of time
alone – to say goodbye, proper like.' She came over and
took his hand in her soft one. 'Now you come and see us

again as soon as you can. You're always welcome. I'm glad for you both. I know how hard it is for people in love to wait, but meeting you, I know you'll take care of her no matter what you two get up to. I reckon our Sue's a lucky girl and at least you've asked to marry her. So we can look forward to you both setting a proper date, eh? And soon, eh?'

'Well, as soon as the Army lets us.' He looked at Susan and saw her eyes shining. 'I don't know when that will be, but I'll try to get something sorted out. It will probably have to be at short notice, knowing the way they work – probably end up in a registry office. The Army doesn't give weddings top priority for leave.'

Again he looked at Susan, expecting to see disappointment in her face at the possible lack of a wedding without the trimmings, but her eyes were still glowing.

Chapter 9

The Blitz was over. The evening following that Saturday the tenth of May, the worst night of any that the enemy had dished out, people went to their places of safety as usual, nurses stood on alert to receive yet another influx of casualties as usual, but the bombers didn't come.

'I wonder what's wrong?' Jenny's question echoed that of many, almost as though they had been robbed of something. Quite silly really. But O'Brien, jolly as always, had an answer.

'Ah well, isn't it Sunday, an' all? And isn't it about time they'd be thinkin' of havin' a day of rest? Holy Mother o' God, I expect they need it.'

'If they don't, then we do,' Jenny said with just a twitch of a smile. 'But I don't think Hitler believes in Sundays or God.'

Like everyone else she was holding her breath. Come Monday, after lulling poor battered Londoners into a false sense of security, they'd be back again – part of Hitler's plan to demoralise them further, it had to be – and she would again form part of a team trying to patch up a new intake of victims. But after a fortnight and everything still quiet, Jenny felt she could at last let out her breath.

She was also given her first full weekend off in months.

'Now you'll have the whole weekend with your mother,' O'Brien said, a wistful lilt in her tone that there was no chance of her getting home to see her family, way off in Northern Ireland. She'd have been appalled to know that the prospect of spending the weekend with her own mother didn't fill Jenny with as much joy as she supposed.

All she wanted was to relax a little. Being with her mother, telling her how lonely she felt, was only swapping one tension for another. Of course it was uncharitable to think like that, but now that the worst of the air raids seemed to be over she felt she would have liked to spend this first weekend off in the company of the friends she had made. She needed a bit of fun, a bit of freedom, for who knew what lay around the corner?

The city's ruins had still continued to smoke ten days after the Blitz ended. Victims were still being dug out of the rubble, domestic services were still not working properly, thousands of families remained without homes, and streets still stayed blocked; sometimes a street had to be cordoned off where an unexploded bomb was being defused.

But slowly the intake of casualties was diminishing and this past fortnight had given Jenny a taste for a new freedom that had begun to be felt by her and her colleagues, a sense of adventure as after a night out she and a few others would clamber back into the nurses' home via a window surreptitiously left unlocked. The hospital's notion of keeping an eye on its vulnerable young nurses meant proper curfew being kept, with doors locked at ten thirty prompt. Anyone returning later than that must get past the superintendent's office, and if she didn't have an official pass, issued to very few for special circumstances only, a visit to Matron the next morning would ensue – a fate usually worse than death. But rules were made to be flouted. After months of air raids with hardly a moment for herself except to flop down exhausted on a makeshift bed in the safer basement after duty, Jenny felt happy to flout them with the rest.

'No, not this weekend,' she told O'Brien as they ate after-duty Bovril sandwiches in O'Brien's room. 'My mother's not expecting me. A few of us are going to a dance at the Palais in Hammersmith. I don't want to miss it.'

O'Brien stopped halfway to taking a bite from her sandwich. 'But I heard you once say you were not much of a dancer, did I not?'

'I'm not. But I'd still like to go. Be nice to let my hair down for once. Why don't you come too?'

'Me? Bejesus, I'd be no good. I've two left feet, so I have.'

'Me too. But it'll get us out of ourselves for a while. We'll keep each other company.' She wouldn't feel so out of it with O'Brien as her life raft, someone to talk to while the others were whirled off in the arms of those who picked them for partners.

It was with amazement that Jenny found herself among the chosen at the very first dance, a waltz, something she could do fairly well without falling over her or her partner's feet. She was in fact asked to dance several times and discovered she wasn't half as left-footed as she had once thought herself, so long as she concentrated on what her partner was doing, and so long as it was a waltz or a not-too-fast quickstep. She felt guilty leaving O'Brien, glad to sit out the more difficult dances, the foxtrots, the tangos and the seductive rumbas. O'Brien seemed quite content just to sit and watch, even pushing Jenny to dance with anyone who came up to them.

'I was niver a one for this,' she said brightly, her ready smile hardly leaving her round face. 'Now a good jig is more in my line, so it is.'

But as the evening wore on, she began to fidget and look at the clock high on the white and gold wall above the band.

'If we don't leave soon, Ross, we'll be back too late to get in properly and have to creep past the superintendent's office, so we will, and if we're caught it will be Matron's office in the morning.'

Jenny laughed. 'That's all solved. Bennett left a lavatory window open and a dustbin underneath.'

'And what if someone closes it?'

'They won't. She's given instruction to one of the night staff to keep an eye on it. But it's still early yet.'

Someone coming towards her with a purposeful expression which she was coming to recognise as an invitation – and the dance was a waltz, thank God – stopped her from saying any more. Not only that but she thought she recognised him as one of the young junior doctors from the London. He held his hand out to her and nodded enquiringly.

Whisked away, her feet by now adjusting to one or two

of the more intricate waltz steps, she was unsurprised but highly delighted when he said, 'I know your face.'

She leaned back from him to study him. 'I'm a nurse.' The floral dress she wore would not have betrayed her. 'I work at the London.'

'I thought I'd seen you somewhere. That's where I work.'

'Oh.' She felt him swing her and concentrated on matching the step and not squashing his toe in the process.

'I'm on Dr Farnborough's team. A junior doctor so far. But I hope to qualify next year. My father's a GP. In Bristol. I'm Ronald Whittaker.'

'Jenny Ross,' she reciprocated. 'I'm just a nurse. Studying hard.'

He chuckled as he swung her into a turn. 'Don't ever say just a nurse. You lot have been worth your weight in gold these last months of the Blitz. Couldn't have managed without a single one of you.'

'Not the mess I've been getting into during the worst of it,' she said with a small self-deprecating laugh. 'Dropping basins of water all over the place . . . Oops! Sorry.' She'd caught his toe, breaking his turn but he hardly noted it. He was staring at her, slowing his steps down more to a walk.

'I know you,' he burst out in revelation. 'Yes. During an air raid. In the basement.'

The basements had doubled as operating theatres and casualty. And now she definitely recognised him too, and the recollection made her blush. He had been assisting in stemming a haemorrhage. She had knocked into him as she hurried past with a basin of disinfection solution.

The liquid had tipped all over the floor so that she had been obliged to mop it all up, getting in the way while all around people cried out for relief from their pain. Later he had come over to ask how she was. All that had been going on around them and he had asked how *she* was.

By the end of the waltz, to her astonishment, he was asking her if he could see her again. 'I know we work in the same hospital, but I would like to see you on a social basis. Perhaps we could go across the road to the pub for a drink, when we're both off duty.'

Before she could stop herself, she said, 'I'd like that.' Seconds later that last kiss Matthew had given her flashed through her mind, a kiss that meant so much at the time. But that was it – *at the time.* Time had gone on. Their ways, which she'd thought might hold promise, had taken their own turnings and she'd vowed to get on with her own life. Maybe this man was her new life, her future. Matthew certainly wasn't. He was the past.

She found she and Ronald had something in common. He knew the Basingstoke teaching hospital where she had been. He had left just before her arrival. It seemed such a coincidence and only natural they should make a second date as soon as their off duty hours again matched. And when on their third date he told her he thought she was quite lovely, the understatement carrying a depth of honesty, she felt uplifted and indeed felt lovely for the first time ever. Even so, old habits tended to die hard; his admiration of her made her scoff.

'Don't be silly, of course I'm not. I wish I'd been born dark-haired.'

'You've got gorgeous hair, Jenny.'

They sat in darkness on one of the few market stalls operating in wartime, manned by older men and some women holding the fort for their own menfolk away at the war. Whitechapel's street market, a thriving place before the war, had become sparse, the variety of goods narrowed down to vegetables, second-hand clothing, bike parts, and so on. Perched on the empty stall between a skeleton of rusting tubular uprights, breathing in the dank odour of cabbage leaves trodden underfoot earlier and the sweet waft of beer from the pub they'd just left, he couldn't see her in the blackout, nor she him, but his hand moved up and in the inky blackness felt its way across her short curls. 'I do so love touching your hair, Jenny.' He leaned forward, gave her a kiss. 'I know this sounds sudden, but, Jenny, I love you.'

For a moment she was quiet, then she said softly, 'We've only seen each other three times. You can't. It's too early.'

'It's never too early, darling. I am, I'm in love with you.' He kissed her again, gently, and all she could do was kiss him back, telling herself that Matthew was another world, a closed chapter. She felt a little sad, but this was *her* life. And she had to take it with both hands.

Sitting in the sunshine of her tiny back garden, overlooked by all the other houses around that were beginning to cast lengthening shadows across it, Jenny let her mind move gently over that third date. It had been far too early for him to start professing love. Had she felt the same it would have been fine, but she hadn't. Nice as he was, she became angry with herself that even as he kissed her, Matthew with his quirky smile had floated into her head, making her merely suffer the kiss, thus allowing some past infatuation to spoil what could become something worthwhile.

She found herself telling Ronald that this weekend she had to spend some time with her mother. After all, duty came first. But was it really that there might be a slim chance of bumping into Matthew or at least finding out how he was? She needed time to think – about Ronald, about her life, to shake off this silly longing and grow up. Ronald was a nice person but it was early days yet. A day or two away from him might clear her head and let her see things as they stood. Too easy to end up an old maid in crying after something that couldn't be had when what could be had was maybe staring her right in the face.

'Jenny, dear, come in and have your tea.' Her mother, calling to her, interrupted her reverie.

'I thought we could take a little stroll in the park afterwards,' Mrs Ross continued as they sat together in the small dining room with the sun pouring in through the window. 'It's a lovely afternoon and I don't usually care for going for walks on my own. But now you're here it would be nice for us. They don't give you half enough time off at that hospital.'

Jenny held back a sigh of protest. She didn't want to stroll anywhere. It had been peaceful just sitting in the back garden relaxing in the gentle curve of the deckchair. So long since she'd been able to relax. Resigned, she went to gather up a cardigan.

'No one would dream there was a war on,' her mother

murmured as they passed the noisy Victorian drinking fountain with its usual cluster of children around it denying visitors a chance of peace or a sip of water.

'Let's take a walk over to the other end,' Mrs Ross suggested with a grimace towards the raucous, scruffy children. 'It's quieter over there. I like the grottos and rockeries with all the rhododendrons. They should be in bloom.'

It was a long walk; the park was vast. Jenny let her mother chatter on as they wandered past the wide lake with its twin islands designed as sanctuary for water fowl. There was another lake, an ornamental pond near the main entrance with fish and water lilies. But it was all beginning to look a little sad. Parts of the park had been turned over to allotments rented by local men too old to be called up. Jenny could see some of them hoeing around their spring cabbage, lettuce, onions, carrots, stringing up runner beans, all bent on their work, everything else around them going unnoticed. Men who no doubt had once only ever got their hands in the soil for a hobby, now dug like navvies. Tomorrow, Sunday, they would be at it again, bending their backs and trundling their wheelbarrows home laden with tools or green produce to help supplement the family rations for another week. People who had any sort of garden or back yard now kept chickens for their eggs and flesh – another boost to a larder slimmed by rationing.

The cricket field now had guns on it, multi-barrelled cannons that had made a terrible row during the Blitz. 'I'll be so glad to see the end of this terrible war,' her mother was saying. 'It would be so nice for you to go back to a nine to five thirty job and come home every night like you used to.'

'It can't last forever.' She didn't want to go back to some nine to five thirty job. Nursing, for all its restrictions, its rules and regulations, had given her in its own way a taste for freedom. She wanted more and by the time this war came to an end she hoped she would have moved on, living a life of her own. That could be a long way off; the war, the way it was going, seemed to have no end to it at all. Night bombing had ceased for the time being but that was no guarantee it wouldn't start up again. Everyone, for all they had breathed a sigh of relief, was still on edge. The Germans had all of Europe; only this island was left, with just a strip of water between it and the enemy. German invasion was all the talk. Meanwhile British merchant ships were being sunk, every day another one, tightening rationing still more. Even clothing had now gone on ration. The loss of seamen's lives meant it broke the heart to listen to the news. War in North Africa was now going badly, troops had been pulled out from Crete. No one knew what would come next. She could be thirty by the time it all ended.

'I know it won't last forever, dear,' her mother was saying, clinging to her arm as though needing support. 'It's just becoming too much for me, for all of us. Look at the bread we eat. Grainy, grey stuff, going stale almost as soon as it's cooled. Real white bread's a thing of the past. By the way, the tiles on our roof have been mended, by quite an elderly man who came. The bombing did such a lot of damage.'

'We're lucky. People have had it really bad elsewhere.' She thought of the injured brought into casualty, smothered in dust and grime and bits of brick, operated on hardly cleaned up. She thought of the gaping spaces left in blocks of tenements, just rubble now, still uncleared and beginning to settle and weather, greening with fast-growing weeds; places where people had once lived. All their possessions were now gone, perhaps they themselves were gone.

'Yes,' her mother agreed, sobered by much the same thoughts. 'We have been lucky. The times I've put my hands together and . . .'

A voice calling Jenny's name cut her short. They turned to see a fair-haired girl pushing a pram in which a child around a year old sat. At her side was a fresh-faced young man sporting a pencil moustache and wearing an officer's uniform. Instantly Jenny recognised them.

'Eileen! Freddy!' She grasped each in greeting as they came up to her. 'How are you?'

Eileen's voice hadn't changed, the same dreamy one she remembered. 'I thought it was you, Jenny. I said to Freddy, "I'm sure that's Jenny Ross," didn't I, Fred? How are you, Jenny. Are you still nursing?'

'I'm fine,' Jenny returned, formally now the surprise of seeing them had passed. 'Yes. In London now. I'm home for the weekend.'

They nodded without interest. 'Freddy's home on leave,' Eileen said while he smiled rather superciliously. If Eileen hadn't altered, he had, from the soft lovesick youth to a man with a bearing that suggested arrogant confidence.

Jenny turned her attention to the little boy in the pram. 'What's his name?'

'Simon. He'll be a year old in three weeks' time.'

'He's a handsome lad, Eileen.' She cooed at him but the boy merely stared back, solemn round eyes regarding her with that peculiar stare most one-year-olds adopt, their trusting baby smiles long since used up. 'You must be very proud of him.'

Freddy nodded and looked pleased while Eileen bent forward over the top of the pram and touched her offspring's fair head with a fond and possessive hand. But her face had clouded.

'I wonder sometimes if this is a world we should be bringing children into, what with our boys bombing Germany, and the Italians on their side, and the fighting in North Africa, and with all this bombing. My mum and dad's house got a direct hit you know. But they weren't in it at the time.'

'Oh, dear.' She didn't fancy conversing about the Blitz. It was past.

'And after all our RAF boys did last summer, fighting up there all alone in the air. You heard about poor Dennis Cox? Killed in his Spitfire.'

Jenny had heard. She nodded solemnly.

'Damned waste,' Freddy said abruptly.

'You used to be his girl at one time,' Eileen said, looking pityingly at her. 'It must have come as a terrible shock to you especially.'

'It was never serious between us,' Jenny said while her mother gave a sad sigh and murmured something about

Dennis Cox being such a nice boy too. 'We were just friends really.'

'Even so . . .' Eileen persisted lugubriously, making Jenny want to laugh. Like many who lead uneventful lives, which was how Eileen struck her, she seemed to need to feed, like a carrion crow, on the tragedy of others. 'It doesn't seem possible, though. Poor Dennis Cox – dead. It's terrible.'

'Yes, terrible,' Jenny echoed. So many people dead. So many lives spoiled by loss, by permanent injury, by sights they should never have seen. Men in battle, civilians who should never have been anywhere near a battle, children too young to be thrown into war, young people just leaving school with all their lives ahead of them, their eager lives consisting of but a few short years after all. They shall not grow old as we who are left grow old . . . Jenny felt tears prickle her nose and sniffed them back, probably sounding as though she was making light of Eileen's pet word, terrible, for the tragedy that hung about so many people. But it was true: having seen so much, tended so many dying and torn bodies, she couldn't find it in her to reserve sorrow for Dennis Cox alone.

'But have you heard about Matthew Ward?' Eileen had perked up.

Jenny's heart gave a sickening leap, fear for him pounding like a hammer in her throat. 'What about him?' It was all she could manage.

'Got himself engaged. To a Birmingham girl. They're getting married soon apparently. Now, he's the last person I'd ever have imagined would settle down. I said to you,

Fred, didn't I? "He'll end up a bachelor," I said, didn't I? And you said, "He'll still be chasing skirts at forty." You said, "Men like that who can get their pick of girls usually end up with no one. Far too choosy for their own good." Do you remember saying that, Fred?' And as he nodded, 'So you could have knocked me over with a feather when his father told me in his shop the other day. I don't think his parents are very keen. A girl from Birmingham. So far away, isn't it? He sounded as though Matthew was really in earnest about her.'

Jenny's heart, still reeling from her initial fear, now felt as though it was plummeting slowly, a broken-winged bird, spiralling down and down. 'I didn't know,' she said, trying to sound unconcerned, but her voice trembled.

'And so sudden,' Eileen was saying blithely. 'I wonder if he's had to. I wouldn't be a bit surprised, you know. I bet his parents feel terrible.'

In the lounge Lilian Ward glared at the letter which had arrived only moments ago.

'How could he? He hardly knows the girl. He's only just met her. And bringing her here this weekend. It gives me no time whatsoever to prepare and get some food in. I hope she'll be bringing her ration book. I'm not in the mood to feed strangers. He has no consideration at all. Doesn't even ask if I *want* to see this . . . whoever she is.'

Leonard Ward watched her stalking back and forth between the leather three-piece suite and the coffee table where he sat with his breakfast cup of tea by the open bay window of the front lounge before leaving to open up his shop.

In summer it was nice to sit a while here with the morning sunshine slanting in, warming his chest that played him up so in winter, the curtains moving gently in a breeze off the park that brought the sharp scent of cut grass. From here he had a fine vista of the park peeping between the large houses opposite. Even so he looked forward to being in the shop to smoke his pipe. No Lilian there to frown and order him into the back garden. He'd have liked his pipe now, but he could hardly get up and walk out with her so furious about Matthew's letter.

'He's already told us about her,' he reminded gently.

'Yes, absolute volumes in his last letter. Not one word asking how we are. Nothing but this . . . what's her name?' She consulted the letter again, then refrained from using it. 'This . . . girl. Now he wants *us* to meet her. Says he's serious about wanting to marry her. We'll see about that.'

'He's over twenty-one, Lilian. Not much you can do about it.'

She was not to be mollified. It would take quite a bit of patience and understanding, perhaps even firmness, to calm her down. She had always been a dominant person. Perhaps that was why he had married her, a woman who had known her own mind and stuck to it in an age when most women were mostly pliable, soft creatures looking to marriage and security. All that despite being in service when servants were expected to be servile.

Leonard smiled. He could forgive her domineering nature, which concealed a good and caring heart. And at the moment that good and caring heart was being tested to the limit. When all was said and done, Matthew was at fault.

'After all we have done for him,' she continued, still pacing, her back stiff, her indignation solid enough to be cut with a knife. 'This is how he rewards us, telling us he intends marrying some common thing from Birmingham, someone we don't even know, and actually bringing her here for us to meet. No warning whatsoever.'

Leonard allowed a little longer for effrontery to cool before getting up and saying he must be off before his customers began to wonder what had happened to him.

Opening up, his first customer had been Eileen Perry who used to be giggly Eileen Wilcox. In just two years she had now become a plain, staid, contented housewife and mother. Her husband was in the forces, but a quartermaster or something that didn't see combat, so she didn't bear that strained expression many wives had with husbands fighting somewhere far away.

Eileen had asked after Matthew and, glad of someone to talk to about it, he told her perhaps more than he should. Later he wondered if it had not been better kept to himself, for Eileen Perry loved a gossip and nothing displeased Lilian more than her private concerns being aired in public.

Ah, well, the deed was done now, he thought as he served customers with torches and fuse wire and round two-pin plugs and took in the odd wireless for repair, and wondered what this girl, this Susan from Birmingham, would be like. Utterly beautiful, stunning, marvellous,

Matthew's earlier letter had gone on among many other things, all of which his mother had dismissed with several sharp and disparaging snorts of disgust.

Chapter 10

Susan stared at the large bay-windowed house as Matthew held open the gate for her. She'd seen such houses in the better parts of Birmingham but had never been in one.

Ahead of her lay a wide gravel area bordered by small flower beds in full bloom, and shrubbery. The bay windows displayed white lace curtains, each so perfectly pleated that they resembled a regiment of soldiers. Susan saw a downstairs curtain twitch slightly and felt observed, rather like a fish in a glass tank. She shivered, hesitating in the gateway.

'Oh Matthew, I hope they'll like me.'

She strove hard to say like, rather than loik; strove to keep her voice from shaking. She'd been practising for this day ever since he had said he was taking her to meet his parents, but it was no less harrowing for all that. But Matthew had told her time and time again that he adored what he called her singsong accent, so surely they would like it as well and thus her.

'Of course they'll like you,' he laughed, taking her arm supportively as they went towards the door, a gesture for which she felt grateful. 'They'll fall in love with you at first sight, just as I did.'

Reaching the porch he planted a small encouraging kiss on her cheek, but in the state she was beginning to get herself into at the daunting prospect ahead, its message was lost on her, for as though by a given signal she saw an indistinct wavering shape distorted by the fluted glass of the door appear behind it, the door opening almost immediately. A slim, tall, upright woman with vivid blue eyes stood there looking at the two of them. An angular face, still with traces of beauty, topped by short greying hair whose stiff waves looked as regimental as the pleated curtains that had twitched earlier turned now to her, its smile of welcome seemingly chiselled from granite.

Matthew pushed Susan forward a fraction. 'Mum, this is Susan.'

Even in the midst of her fear of the brittle blue eyes, so different to Matthew's soft brown ones, Susan wondered at his use of Mum rather than Mother. Mrs Ward looked as though she should be called 'Mother' or even Mater; certainly not Mum.

The woman extended a hand in formal greeting rather in the manner of a pontiff suffering the touch of some unwashed layman. Obediently Susan took it, finding it stiff and cold. But with etiquette observed, Mrs Ward withdrew her hand and stepped back for them to enter.

'Was it a decent journey, Matthew, dear?' The voice was warm and took Susan completely by surprise. The woman was human after all. 'I did begin to think you were just a little late.'

'You know what travelling's like these days, Mum,' Matthew laughed easily and kissed her offered cheek.

'I never travel far these days,' she said as he put down his kit and Susan's small, slightly battered weekend suitcase in the wood-floored hall, a hall of such width that Susan felt her whole family could have almost lived in it. She thought briefly of her own cluttered living room with its old furniture and with its everlasting noise of argument and laughter. About this place there was a silence that seemed almost tangible, as if a cold ghost lived there.

'Dad home?' Matthew queried easily as he and Susan followed his mother into the lounge. Susan wished she could feel as easy, but then, he would feel easy, wouldn't he? This was his home.

The lounge was huge. The furniture looked lost in it, sparsely and tastefully laid out; a parquet floor bordered a large beautifully patterned carpet that looked sort of Turkish. Through the bay window, the high summer sun cast a minimal vertical strip of gold on to one tiny area of the wood floor, missing the carpet completely, which Susan imagined would never be allowed to be touched and consequently faded by any lengthening shaft of autumn sunshine. Mrs Ward probably had one of those posh blinds that well-off people used to keep damaging sunlight out.

'He'll be home for lunch,' his mother answered. 'As usual. But of course he must go back afterwards to open up for the afternoon, Matthew, whether you're here or not.'

'So you're the Susan we've heard so much about in Matthew's letters. He certainly didn't lie about you.'

Mr Ward's appearance prompted a surge of relief after an hour stiff and fraught with tension. She took to him the

moment he came in at the back door to immediately shake
her hand and utter his hearty comment before turning to
his son to ask how long he would be home.

'We go back Sunday night,' Matthew supplied with a
chuckle at the innocent, stock question asked nowadays of
every serviceman home on leave.

Mr Ward too gave a low chuckle not unlike his son's,
with a touch of mockery in it that could be taken the wrong
way if one missed the whimsical gleam in his eyes. They
were slightly lighter than his son's, more hazel than brown;
she could see who Matthew took after, glad that it wasn't
his mother. But if he'd taken after his mother, she knew
she wouldn't be here with him now.

'Don't give you long, do they? Well, we've got you for
the weekend at least. We promise to send you back all nice
and clean.'

She had a feeling that as a young man Mr Ward might
have possessed the same caustic humour as Matthew, but
that it had mellowed or been mellowed by life. She wasn't
usually clever enough to see inside people, but he was so
much like Matthew in looks and manner, she felt she could
guess at the person he'd once been because Matthew had
been a bit like that when she'd first met him.

It came to her that she still knew very little about
Matthew as they sat down to a small but beautifully set-out
cold lunch of salad and luncheon meat, all she supposed
the Wards' food ration would stretch to (dutifully she
had handed over her ration book which Mrs Ward had
not waved away). They were making conversation from
which she began to feel excluded. At ease with his family,

he was a stranger to her. Why had she consented to come here, when his way of life was so removed from hers? There came a dull feeling that once back in Birmingham, it would be the end of her and Matthew. She didn't fit in here. She was yet to meet his sister. If she was anything like Mrs Ward . . .

Susan felt most uncomfortable, smiling when she thought she ought to, answering the odd question put to her mostly by the friendly Mr Ward. The afternoon when he would disappear back to his shop loomed before her like a prison sentence. To sit looking at Mrs Ward's chilly expression all afternoon was not to be contemplated. She dreaded the moments when Matthew, quite at home among his own, would blithely wander off on some pursuit and leave her alone with this woman.

Mr Ward left, saying he would see her later that evening. Mrs Ward led them upstairs for Susan to put her case in the room allotted to her and freshen up. Freshen up sounded so posh.

'The bathroom is there.' She indicated a door at the end of a long landing which curved slightly at the end.

Susan nodded wordlessly. She had never seen a bathroom. The sort of people she knew in Birmingham did not have them. At least this would be a small refuge for her where she could escape this woman's penetrating eyes.

The landing had six other doors. Six. Susan had never seen such a thing. Surely, other than the bathroom, the rest couldn't be all bedrooms. Matthew said his was a four-bedroom house, so the one at the opposite end to the bathroom might be a cupboard.

'And this is your room.'

The door she had assumed to be to a cupboard was opened for her to inspect her quarters. And what quarters. Everything became a pink and white blur as, blindly, Susan stepped within as she had been bidden, a faint smell of lavender greeting her. It was neat and modest in size, though not what Susan would have called small by any means, with a single bed, a dressing table with delicate white and pink jars on it, and a mirror, a cupboard and a chair. The walls, curtains, bedspread and a fluffy rug by the bed were pink, all the furniture white, and the linoleum brown, the only contrast. Susan stifled a gasp of awe; tried to behave as though she were used to this sort of room.

'Thank you very much, Mrs Ward,' she managed in a whisper, while Matthew grinned and said loudly:

'My room, of course, is that end, by the bathroom.' In other words he and she would be separated by two doors, but only she was meant to detect the amused connotation he was conveying, his mother quite oblivious as she left them to go into their separate rooms to unpack what they'd brought with them.

He did indeed go to his door and open it, but as his mother went on out of sight down the stairs, he stepped back and came towards Susan, moving silently.

'I'll help you unpack,' he whispered purposefully and instantly she knew what he meant.

A knot of excitement formed deep in her stomach as she went into her room. Matthew followed quietly, no longer the stranger he had seemed during lunch.

For the sake of propriety as he pressed her down on the

bed with the sun shining bright through the window, she whispered, 'What if your mother comes up and catches us?'

He was bending over her, his mouth ready to close upon hers. 'She won't. As far as she's aware, you'll be unpacking in your room and I in mine and good manners will prevent her intruding into either.'

'But if she hears . . .' But Matthew's lips closing over hers smothered any further protest as, his weight upon her, her body responded with waves of longing surging through it.

'She doesn't like Susan, does she?'

Matthew leaned with his back against the bench in the work room behind his father's shop. The question was a foregone conclusion, but he had to ask it. Now was the time.

The shop was quiet for the moment. Saturday afternoon shopping took many people up west now that they felt safer with the Blitz failing to return. Not that there was much to buy; coupons, ration books, points, had put paid to casual spending. People were forced to save up a certain amount of points to buy a dress or a pair of shoes, so all the joy had long gone out of buying. But it was an excuse to get out, wander around the main shops, perhaps take in a cinema or theatre afterwards to forget shortages, loved ones overseas, the war itself.

With the shop quiet, the opportunity for a heart to heart with his father presented itself nicely. Susan had popped out to get some sweets with the coupons she had been saving for this weekend. She'd be back within a short while and in that time Matthew intended to tax his father on his mother's reaction to Susan. No good asking her how she felt. She'd merely have given him a blank stare and remarked that it was his business at whom he threw his hat, the remark full of disapproval. And he already knew by her attitude that she disapproved, so why ask? Yet he needed to ask, and now his father leaned back in his creaking swivel chair and, pressing dark, pungent tobacco into the bowl of his pipe with his thumbs, frowned in deep thought.

'You know your mother,' he said after a while, effectively avoiding a direct reply. 'Never been one to show her feelings.'

'That's what I told Susan. She's dead scared of her.' He saw the knowing half-smile his father gave and anger rose up inside him. 'Why the hell can't she be normal, like other people?'

'You mean she doesn't conform to your idea of normal, all sugar and spice.' There was reprimand in the quiet tone. 'Does that mean she should be discredited? She is honest and upright and has always done her best for you and Louise – in her own way, the only way she knows.'

'Yes, I know. I'm sorry.' He felt chastened. No one could accuse his mother of under-handedness or paying lip service to anyone. If she called a spade a spade, everyone could be certain it was nothing else. But if only she had one gentle streak in her, let the rules be bent ever so slightly; if only she was capable of letting people down lightly with a little white lie now and again. Timid people like Susan needed a little gentle understanding.

His intention had been to come out this afternoon to see his father, leaving Susan and his mother together to get to know each other without his having to hold Susan's hand, but she had begged to be allowed to come with him. Looking into the pleading in those blue eyes, he knew that to refuse her would have been like leaving a lamb in a lion's den.

His father lit his pipe, its acrid smell mixing with that of solder and flux and dust. It brought a sense of nostalgia, of belonging, that Matthew had once taken for granted, had thought would last forever, but now made his thoughts keen-edged with the knowledge that at any time he could be sent away to God-knows-where, perhaps never to come back. He felt his heart grow pinched and small with the fear of all this being taken from him.

'Your mother,' Leonard was saying, puffing a cloud of blue smoke into the air. 'She has always had high principles, from the day I first saw her. She frightened the life out of me, you know. Me, who always saw girls as soft, pretty creatures with no brains, whom men could command, to see a young woman come striding into my father's draper's shop as though she owned it, really got up my nose at the time. But I couldn't get my mind off her. She fascinated me. She was a beautiful woman, your mother, beautiful and straight-backed, and she held her head high. I used to look for her coming in. But I couldn't get up the courage to tell her how I felt about her. When I did, she turned me down flat.'

Leonard gave a small quirky grin at the recollection, his pipe gripped firmly between his teeth. 'You could never know what that's like, to open up your heart to a woman when it's not in your nature to do so and be turned down the way she turned me down. But finally we did start walking out together. She's a woman in a million, Matthew, believe me.'

'I didn't mean to discredit her,' Matthew said, shame-faced. 'But she's got to understand that I intend to marry Susan. I don't want her resenting Susan. I know she does already and I don't know why she should. She's only just met her, and Susan's the most likeable person I know. She's sweet-natured and loving. She's not pushy and loud. So why?'

The old chair creaked as Leonard leaned back into it again. 'Maybe she considers you both a little young and hasty. You and Susan have known each other only a few months. You've hardly had much chance to see each other regularly. Perhaps if you both waited a while longer.'

'What's there to wait for?' This was his life. They had theirs to look back on, had been fortunate, but what had he got to look back on so far, and how much future would be allowed to him? 'This isn't peacetime with long, well-arranged white weddings and strings of bridesmaids and a fine honeymoon afterwards. We might not have tomorrow and forever. I could be sent overseas at any time. I might not see her for years. I might even be . . .' He checked the words quickly, then reverted to the hackneyed idiom of defiance: 'We have to have something to cling to in this war.'

'Yes.' The pipe stem clicked audibly against Leonard's teeth. 'This bloody war.'

The shop bell tinkled. To its peremptory summons, he hoisted himself out of the chair, knocking the pipe out on the bench.

Matthew listened to the murmur of voices beyond the opaque glass of the dividing door, the conclusive note of a customer departing. The bell tinkled again, fell silent. Leonard came back into the back room bearing a domed, fretwork-fronted wireless set which he set down on the bench. He chuckled, making a joke against himself.

'Look what I've come down to. My father loved his little drapery shop and said I would inherit, but he died in debt and lost nearly all of it. It was your mother who was my widowed mother's mainstay. She made her sink what little was left into another shop after the last war, saying that electrical goods would be the coming thing. She was right. We did well. That's how we came to live in a nice area like Victoria Park Road. I'm no snob and I know where I came from, but your mother wanted better things for you and your sister. That and her love of the old order of things makes her seem to act above herself, but her heart's in the right place where you and Louise are concerned. I've got a lot to thank your mother for.'

The last words had a ring of finality about them. There was no more to be said on that score. Besides, any minute Susan would come running in, waving her few ounces of sweets in triumph. Matthew changed the subject, nodding towards the wireless come in for repair.

'Bloody ancient thing, that one. Looks a bit beyond it to me.'

Leonard grinned compassionately. 'She's a widow.

Can't afford much. Asked if I could do anything with it before Tuesday. Doesn't want to miss ITMA. Tommy Handley's her only bit of pleasure these days. God knows, she needs someone to cheer her up, if only on the wireless. There's little to cheer anyone up lately. Every time you tune in there's another setback – what with Rommel and Tobruk. And Crete, us having to pull out, five thousand killed . . .'

'I heard,' Matthew said tersely.

'Enough to make anyone lose heart. But it comes to something when you hear people say we might have to negotiate peace terms with Germany.'

'Rumours,' Matthew snorted. 'Like the bomb that chases people around corners – the German secret weapon. Some are actually believing it.'

'Everyone's on edge, that's why.' Leonard began unscrewing the casing of the wireless cabinet, lifting it up to reveal coloured wires and oblong valves. 'London blitzed to buggery, Coventry too, then suddenly, silence, everyone wondering what Hitler has up his sleeve next. Invasion probably. I don't know.'

Matthew nodded glumly. He'd seen the scenes of devastation as he and Susan took a bus from Euston railway station to home. He had rejected taking the underground, not wishing to subject Susan to the wretched bits and pieces of the thousands who had used the platforms as shelters during the nightly air raids and who still stubbornly went down there at nightfall, refusing to believe the Blitz would not return.

Above ground had looked just as dismal, pitiful.

Through the bus windows they had gazed at acres of blackened ruin still uncleared, walls precariously hanging, charred timbers, twisted girders pointing skyward with accusing fingers, the air still heavy with an acrid effluvium of burning that remained in their nostrils long afterwards, a memento of all London had suffered. And even in his own long road fronting an open park some houses had gone. After those guns and searchlights sited in the park itself, he supposed.

He watched his father extract a valve from the set. Testing it, he shook his head with tacit sympathy, then replaced it with one salvaged from another old set already beyond repair. Plugged in, the set crackled into life with tinny music.

'Ah, she'll be pleased,' he breathed. 'Defeated by a dud valve. I won't charge her for that. Husband died two years ago and she hasn't a soul to turn to. Though she keeps telling me her son is serving on the *Royal Oak*.'

'*Is*?' Matthew queried. 'The *Royal Oak* was sunk at Scapa Flow at the beginning of the war. All hands lost.'

'Exactly.' Leonard nodded, replacing the casing. 'Not a soul to turn to. I'll get this back to her this evening. She'll be pleased.'

The shop bell tinkled again. This time the back-room door burst open and there stood Susan, her small oval face brighter and happier than he'd seen it all day, his mother forgotten.

'I bought some toffees,' she announced. 'Do you want one, Mr Ward?'

As his father shook his head congenially, Matthew

came over and put an arm around her, his mind on her
alone, the poor bereaved woman still living in the past put
aside. Her empty life wasn't his problem. Everyone had
problems these days.

'So you're really going to get married?'

Louise had come home on a weekend leave, declaring
it fortunate to have fallen the same time as her brother's.
She, as yet still in her WRNS uniform, sat opposite him
and Susan in the front lounge regarding him with the
steady critical gaze of a nineteen-year-old who felt she
knew the world. Two weeks ago she had just seen one of
her comrades break down after hearing the news that her
fiancé's ship had been torpedoed; he had gone down with
it. Her gaze was now fraught with concern as well.

'Not much joy being in love in wartime, that's my
opinion. But I wish you both all the luck in the world. I
don't suppose it'll be a white wedding, but the result's just
the same I reckon.'

Susan simpered and sat close to Matthew, looking up at
him for guidance. He gave his sister a rueful grin. 'I hope
to get a twenty-four-hour pass for it if I'm lucky. We'll
have to make do with that. It'll have to be in a registry
office, I expect.'

'Well, perhaps I might wangle some leave. When's it
to be?'

Matthew's smile hovered. 'We're not quite certain
yet. Whenever we can. Probably at short notice. You
should know what the forces are like. It'll have to be in
Birmingham, near where I'm stationed. And with Mum

and Dad down here, and Susan's people up there, I don't suppose there'll be many of our side there at all. It's going to be a rush in the end.'

Louise looked distinctly put out. 'You don't want me there, that it?'

'No, that's not it, Sis.' He was looking dark. 'I want you there. I want all our people there. I'd have liked to have a big white wedding, for Susan's sake. I wish we could.'

At which Susan clung closer to him, his arm tightening reassuringly about her. Louise, Susan thought, for all she was only a year older than herself, had a lot of her mother in her. And as Mr and Mrs Ward came in from the dining room where they had been lingering over a leisurely cup of tea Louise, it seemed, wasn't ready to pull her punches.

'Did you know they plan to get married in a registry office? It's going to have to be done on the quick, so he says. No time for me to arrange leave to be there to see him married. Him, my one and only brother.'

'That's unkind, Louise,' Matthew shot at her, but it was evident she was disappointed. 'Of course you're invited if you can make it. You'd be the first one to be invited. My one and only sister.'

That last sounded dangerously like sarcasm and probably was, and Leonard Ward looked at his son while Lilian stood aside, her face tight. But his was benign. 'Where do you plan to live afterwards, Matthew?'

It was a practical question, but one that betokened acceptance of his intentions, and Susan, feeling Matthew's body relax, realised it had become taut as Louise had railed on.

'We'll get ourselves a furnished flat for the time being, where I can get backwards and forwards from with a special pass.'

Leonard frowned. 'Not much of a start, a furnished flat. You'd need something unfurnished. Something to call your own. Your own furniture, not someone else's rubbish. Your mother and I aren't broke . . .'

'No thanks, Dad.' Matthew stopped him sharply. 'We can manage.'

'I want to say something else, son. It's that if you're posted away at any time or, God forbid, sent overseas, Susan will always be welcome to come here and stay with us.'

Susan's face went blank and Matthew hurried to her rescue. 'That's nice of you, Dad, but we'll get by. Lots of married women have to manage on their own these days when their men go away. And I expect her own family will be there to help.'

'Just a suggestion.' Leonard went to sit in one of the armchairs but Lilian remained standing, her hands clasped firmly in front of her.

'This is all very well. No one has any *idea* when this is to happen. All we know is that it is going to happen. We have merely been *told*. It would be nice if you discussed it more fully with us, your parents, Matthew?'

He matched her hard stare. 'I thought that was precisely what we were doing – discussing Susan and me getting married.'

'Would you be discussing it now if Louise hadn't blurted it out a few moments ago?'

'Probably,' he returned succinctly, at bay.

Susan cut in, amazed at her own boldness. 'We want to get married ever so much, Mr Ward.' It was far easier to appeal to him than his wife. 'I know we've not been together very long, but me and Matthew do love each other a lot. It don't have to take years just to know that. It can happen very quickly sometimes.' She paused for breath, anxious now at having said so much, uninvited.

He smiled at her. 'I know. So how soon would you *like* it to be?'

'Could be next month,' Matthew replied for her, his tone easier now. 'It'll have to be in Birmingham. I've exhausted all my leave so I'll only get a special day off, I suppose. I'll have to beg for that, I expect.'

'We'll try to make it up there if we can,' added his father. He gave a small apologetic chuckle. 'That sounds terrible, I know – try. But nothing's easy these days. Send us a telegram the second you know, and we'll be straight on a train. If I can get some extra petrol coupons . . .' again he gave a chuckle, a somewhat knowing one this time, 'we'll get the car out and use that. It's kept in good working order, you know, but we don't use it, at least very seldom these days. It's yours still, Matthew, sitting there, your twenty-first present. It's in a garage near the shop, waiting for the time you can use it again, Matthew. And talking of presents. Wedding presents of any good quality being hard to come by, would money be okay?'

'That'll be fine,' Matthew said a little tersely, making Susan look at him in surprise. 'But I still have that trust Grandfather left me. We won't go short.'

'Just a token wedding present.'

Susan felt sorry for Mr Ward, hearing the lame ring in his voice. She even felt faintly annoyed at Matthew. Why should he react so unthankfully to his father's generosity?

As Matthew travelled on the train back to Birmingham the following day to be in camp by Monday morning, Susan taxed him on it.

'You shouldn't have gone off at your dad like that, darling. He was only being kind. You acted as if you were bent on having a row with him.'

Matthew was staring out at the passing scenery beyond the carriage window. 'Did you see my mother's face?' he queried without turning. 'In my family we don't need to row. Never a raised voice, but the result's the same – no winners or losers. In a way, worse than any full blown row – no chance for anyone to release their pent up anger.'

He sounded so dark that Susan quickly changed to a lighter subject. 'Your dad said about some money left to you.'

He remained thoughtful for a moment. 'For when I was twenty-one. About five thousand, but I haven't touched it. Wanted to wait until the war was over and I came out of the Army. I expect many of us will come out without a bean, so it'll come in handy.'

'And it'll have made interest,' she added. At the mention of such an amount her eyes had widened. Five thousand pounds. A fortune. To think, being married to someone really well-off. She could hardly wait.

'Let's get married as soon as we can,' she entreated and

had him turn to her to put his arm about her shoulder and cuddle her close, prompting quiet smiles from the others in the carriage with them.

Chapter 11

Jenny gazed through one of the pub windows near which she sat, many of them still damaged by the Blitz and patched up as best as could be until shortages allowed for new windows to be put in. God knows when that would be.

Outside, Whitechapel Road was buzzing with stalls and people this Tuesday lunchtime. Whitechapel Road was exceptionally wide for London. It had apparently been made that way in the days of footpads so that they had no cover from which to spring out on passing horsedrawn mail and passenger coaches. Part of that wide road had, she'd been told, for this last hundred years been railed off for a market which still thrived and the noise of buying and selling came loud through every hole and crack in those of the pub's windows not yet completely repaired.

Despite the war, the market was in full swing; maybe now it evoked the days before the motor car. These days hardly any private cars were being used with petrol rationing the order of the day. Some lorries, though, still tried to make deliveries when they could. But there were a lot more handcarts than in peacetime, and the horsedrawn wagon could be seen in great numbers.

Across the still wide road beyond the hubbub and movement sat the London Hospital, a serene potentate, quieter now that the nightly air raids had passed. The injured were being seen to and sent home with no more being brought in to replace them; the hospital had started getting back now to the normal traffic of poorly children and the ailing elderly, those injured by accident instead of design, pregnant women needing treatment, and the ordinary sick; the outpatients department too had reverted to its normal routine rather than the unending stream of bloodied, bomb-torn bodies. Everyone now had time at last to let out a sigh of relief, Jenny included. She had gone back to work after her first weekend off in ages to find that even in the short time away things at the hospital had quietened still more.

'Penny for them.' Ronald's warm hand closed over her fingers and she quickly withdrew hers.

'Not worth a penny.'

'Ah, well, a ha'penny then.' His light brown eyes were searching her green ones as she looked briefly at him. They were full of adoration. 'No, on second thoughts, Jenny, the smallest thought of yours has to be worth more than a million to me.'

'Don't be silly.' She hated him behaving like this, specially when her inability to return his feelings made her seem hardhearted and his obvious love for her so pitiful. But one couldn't make love happen. 'I was thinking about the people out there, and the hospital. That's not worth a light.'

'Talking shop isn't. Let's talk about us instead.'

'Not just now, Ronald.' She didn't mean to sound so sharp.

Her thoughts as his hand closed over hers had been dwelling on the news she had received about Matthew while home, and then on the surprise glimpse she'd had of him from her bedroom window on the Sunday, his arm around the dainty dark-haired girl he was intending to marry. From her vantage point, Jenny had seen her lift a pretty face ardently to his as they passed underneath her window, and he had paused and kissed her lips. Jenny had felt the passion of that kiss writhe in her bones. It still did.

Gazing through the pub window she savoured a masochistic urge to retain the memory in a moment of self-torture, utterly futile for all it made her feel nearer to the man she knew she could never have. Matthew would marry his Birmingham girl and Jenny would never see him again.

Then Ronald laid his hand over hers, and instead of her private moment being gently suffered as it needed to be, those precious thoughts had raced through her head like a damned whirlwind, to be swept away.

They departed the Birmingham registry office in a thin shower of home-made confetti and a host of good wishes. The reception had been short, a modest gathering filling the little room with perfume, cigar smoke and perspiration.

'I just hope he knows what he is doing,' Lilian Ward said, watching the happy pair go off.

'Of course he knows what he's doing.' Leonard's

own gaze followed the taxi taking Matthew and his new wife off into the unknown; it softened reflectively at the recollection of his son's departing words to him. 'If anything happens to me, Dad, you two will look after Susan, won't you?'

'Nothing's going to happen to you, son,' he had told him sternly, but who could be that certain?

'But it's wartime,' Lilian's voice cut in. 'They don't know what lies ahead of them.'

'It was wartime when we married,' he reminded her gruffly.

Nothing had happened to him, had it, apart from a dose of mustard gas. Left his chest weak, but he'd survived. And so would Matthew.

The taxi going out of sight, he turned back to the registry office with the others to gather up the few belongings they had left behind when they'd gone to wave the happy pair on their way.

Lilian's lips had tightened. She had no wish to be reminded of that utterly mad escapade of hers when she had been young, leaving service to get married to a man going off to join up. She, who had always kept her emotions in check, doing such a headstrong thing! She hated being reminded of it. 'That was entirely different,' was all she could find to say.

'Absolutely.' Leonard gave a playful laugh. 'But we might not have married had I not swept you off your feet.'

'Fiddlesticks!' she shot at him, leaving him to smile after her as she marched ahead of him up the steps of the

registry office to retrieve her hat that went with the smart
suit she had bought with almost a year's worth of clothing
coupons to see her silly, lovesick son married.

In the taxi, Matthew bent towards his wife and tenderly
kissed her. He did it, not just because he was in love with
her, but to reassure himself of their future together. He
badly needed that reassurance.

In the registry office he had stood beside her, smiling,
feeling hot and sticky in his khaki uniform as with one
eye on the large round clock on the wall he received the
felicitations of those gathered there.

Susan had been dewy-eyed the whole time, overcome
by the joy of her new estate, the centre of attraction. Her
sisters had wept obligingly, her mother copiously, as
though her dear daughter were being whisked away to
Devil's Island rather than wedded bliss. Friends and family
on both sides had kissed Susan and shaken Matthew's hand
before wandering off to try the tiny, practically fruitless
wedding cake Susan's mother had made, rations not
stretching to anything more. Its much larger, thinly iced
cardboard cover was impressively decorated to emulate
the fine wedding cakes of pre-war years.

Susan's mother had looked overdressed in fluffy pink
beside his own mother in a tasteful beige suit, yet it was
for his mother rather than Susan's that he felt somehow
more embarrassed; the way she stayed aloof from Susan's
mother as though she were a lesser being.

His father had been different again. He stood talking
to Mr Hopkins, oblivious of the man's rusty best suit, his

tobacco-stained teeth when he smiled, the rolled cigarette hanging wetly from his lips.

There had only been Matthew's parents on his side, and Bob Howlett as his best man, the rest Susan's, relatives, friends, workmates, all laughing and gabbling away in incomprehensible Birmingham accents, filling the tiny room with noise and tobacco smoke. It had been a relief to get away, to be alone with Susan at last, his kiss in the taxi a promise of that to come in the small one-bedroomed flat he had found for them, their own little love nest.

Susan returned his kiss, then broke away, pouting a little. 'I wish we weren't going to have to live in those two tiddly little rooms.'

'Why?' He grinned down at her. Pouting, she looked so pretty, her sweet red lips that he wanted to kiss again pushed out invitingly.

'I was just thinking, Matthew, you coming into that trust your dad was talking about, I mean, surely, couldn't we have got something better?'

'You liked them when we found them,' he told her, frowning. 'You called them adorable, cosy, our own little love nest.'

'Yes, but that was before . . .'

His frown deepened as she paused. 'Before what, darling?'

'Well, before . . .' She tutted, shrugging. 'Oh, nothing. But we will get something better in time, won't we?'

'Yes, of course.' Matthew's brow cleared. He was being stupid about the money coming to him, having for so long conditioned himself against the help his mother,

almost selfishly, tried to give him. Even this trust seemed
somehow tainted with her influence although he knew that
too was stupid. And why should Susan be the loser because
of his ridiculous obsession? Whatever he had was hers as
well, and he shouldn't be selfish in his feelings about it.

'As soon as we get sorted out, I'll look for somewhere
you really like,' he promised and was rewarded by her
instantly snuggling against him, her surge of joy rippling
through him as well.

The taxi began to slow to his directions at a row of
small terraced houses behind spiked railings, with narrow
patches of barren gardens in front. Worn steps led up to
the sepia glass-panelled doors with names above each one:
Rose Villa, Acacia Villa, Magnolia Villa, the taxi finally
drawing up outside the one called Laburnum Villa.

The driver leapt out, opened the taxi door for them and,
accepting Matthew's generous tip, called good luck before
getting back into his vehicle and rattling away to his next
fare.

In the bright sunshine they gazed at their new abode.
The owner of the house, a Mrs Robertson, had recently
lost her husband. It was the first time, she'd said when
Matthew had gone there, that she had ever let rooms, and
from her nervousness and the modest rent she'd quoted, he
had almost been tempted to offer her more, but a corporal's
pay didn't stretch to such gallantry. At the time he had
been labouring under his ridiculous aversion to using any
of the trust his grandfather had left him. He had kept his
mouth shut and guiltily counted his good luck at the poor
woman's expense.

Susan's hand tightened convulsively on his arm. He understood. It might be a modest start but she was still excited at the prospect of entering their first-ever home, closing their door on the world and being alone together.

He patted her hand encouragingly. 'We'll find something much better later. But today's our wedding day. Tomorrow I have to be back in camp, so let's make the best of today.'

This wasn't how it should have been. There should be a honeymoon, somewhere on the coast, somewhere really nice, Bournemouth or Torquay, a lovely hotel. There should have been a church wedding that had taken at least six months to prepare, and a good reception, with lots of money spent on it. There should have been a nice house awaiting them, the furniture bought and sitting inside to welcome them. Bloody war. Bloody Army. Bloody way of having to live . . .

Mrs Robertson was waiting for them. She had given him a key when he paid the deposit money, but motherly soul that she was, she had been waiting for them and now opened the door as they mounted the five shallow steps.

'Come in, dears. Do come in.' Her voice was high, a little weak, a little weepy; that of a woman in her late sixties still not yet adjusted to the loss of a husband after a long married life.

'Now you must treat this place like your own,' she continued, following them to the narrow flight of stairs, eager for conversation. Her main aim in letting her two upstairs rooms had been to secure a little company. 'Don't ever think you have to stand on ceremony now. Come and go whenever you want. It's nice to know there's someone

else in the house besides me. There's a little gas ring and
a portable stove upstairs, as you know, and there's a basin
in the bedroom. My dear George had it put in when we
had the bedroom. But of course, I sleep downstairs now.
If you'd like a cup of tea now, my kettle is on the boil . . .'

'It's very nice of you, but no thank you,' Matthew cut
in, trying not to sound rude. All he wanted was Susan
to himself. They'd have so little time together as it was
without sitting in their landlady's kitchen drinking tea and
possibly listening to her life with her George, dear as he
must have been to her.

He could feel the woman's gaze following them wist-
fully up the stairs, her thoughts no doubt on when she'd
been their age with all her life before her. He felt a surge of
bitterness shoot through him. All her life before her – did
he and Susan have all theirs before them, say forty years of
marriage as she'd had, or would theirs be cut short by war?
A quick, easy calculation, done automatically, told him
that the woman had been married before the last war, but
her husband had been lucky and survived it. Would he be
as lucky surviving this one? A shudder passed through him
and was gone as, reaching the little landing, he shrugged it
away and opened the door to the larger room that had once
been a bedroom, now their living room.

Susan paused on the threshold looking in, not attempting
to enter. 'It's smaller than I thought it'd be.'

'But it's ours. At least for a while.'

He made his voice sound light and jaunty, needing to
brighten up. Flipping open the door next to it, he lifted her
and bore her inside, kicking the door closed behind him,

with her clinging to him, any dejection she might have had dispersing. In one easy movement he tossed her on to the double bed that almost filled this even tinier room. The bedsprings bounced madly under the impact of their light burden.

'That's your place, Mrs Ward,' he announced firmly, and while she lay breathless and laughing, he sat on the foot of the bed, yanking off boots, then socks, battle blouse, shirt, trousers, leaving the clothes draped untidily over the brass bedrail, one or two items already falling on to the floor in his haste as he flung himself down beside her. 'And this is mine. Now – we'll start on you.'

'Matthew!' she squealed as he made to get her out of her suit jacket. 'You'll rip the buttons off. It's a new suit.'

'Well, you do it.'

'No, I want you to do it. But mind the buttons.'

With her he romped and laughed. With her help he rid her of one garment after another, she making a play at struggling, he at Victorian mastery, until finally she lay naked beneath him, his wife, ready for his demands, but still laughing, the pair of them trying hard to keep the sound down away from the woman below.

'I've one night with you, woman,' Matthew hissed. 'And I intend to make the most of it. So behave yourself and do your duty. Now, lie back.'

After love stolen previously in secret, purported to be all the sweeter for that, this love was the most wonderful thing he had ever known. It must have been for her too, for she complied without any of the earlier tension he had always felt in her, the desperation of her acceptance of him. Together, man and wife, it would be the first of a glorious uniting, quite beautiful and satisfying. What more could either of them, or anyone, want than this?

He opened his eyes. He must have dozed. Sunlight was touching one wall of the bedroom; the sun had moved round just a little, so it was still afternoon. He couldn't have slept long.

Turning his head leisurely to look at Susan, he studied her. She lay with eyes closed, vulnerable to his scrutiny so that he felt vaguely guilty in taking advantage of it. Deep in sleep, her breathing sounded gentle; her dark lashes lay against the pale cheeks, lips just slightly thinned as though in a smile of contentment. Matthew watched the quiet rise and fall of her breasts, small and firm with pale nipples, her flesh stretched taut as she lay full length, legs outstretched, the soft darkness rising between her thighs such that he wanted to bury his face there.

He felt his breath come shuddering with a longing to make love to her again. It wasn't purely a physical need, but it still seemed he hadn't been near enough to her even then – could never be near enough. No man is an island? Bloody hell! Of course he was. Trapped and isolated by thoughts impossible to explain, not even to this girl who had become his very life, whom he had this day married. He might try for a lifetime to describe to her how he felt, but she would never really know what it was he was trying to say. In turn could he ever really know her mind? He could bury himself inside her in a brief moment of love, tell himself they were one, yet he would still not know.

They were two people, each with their separate sensations. It was that, he guessed, which really disturbed him, that they couldn't truly ever be one in the sense he wanted – in a sense even he couldn't understand. Suddenly angry at what he could not define, he swore softly and closed his eyes, perhaps the easier to unravel this unsettling need.

Her hand brushing lightly against his thigh brought him suddenly awake. The sun had moved round, now playing on their naked bodies. He glanced at his watch. He had slept away another hour – another precious hour lost in this one day together, and again he felt angered by the thoughts that had plagued him, by fate, by the powers that would soon tear him away from Susan. If only this moment could last forever, the sun hang in its present position, its light remaining warm and luxurious on their bodies.

Susan's hand moved, caressing, not sensuously but possessively, claiming him as her own, reassuring herself of his nearness. The touch brought him back to reality. In the morning he must leave her, go back to the army that had first claim on him.

He stared up at the ceiling, an intense hatred seething inside him of those who could push him this way and that, a puppet manipulated by the strings pulled by some faceless power that had for this one day allowed the strings to dangle and leave him thinking himself free, only to pluck him up in the midst of his happiness to bend him again to obedience. One small jerk on a thread could tug him from this girl he had made his wife; another thread jerked would send him headlong into battle to fight not for his own life but for a continuance of a way of life. And if he should fall, the strings would be severed and he, like the toy he was, would be cast aside, the war going on without him, the peace when it came not for him to see.

Today he had been shown something so sweet, so wonderful; to have it all snatched away now came like a bitter taste in his mouth.

He sat up abruptly, went over and fumbled in the breast pocket of his battle blouse for a cigarette to calm his thoughts. At least moving about had dulled that sensation of panic he had felt. Susan had gone back to sleep. That was if she had woken at all: her hand on his thigh had likely been a purely instinctive gesture. He sat on the edge of the bed and watched her contented slumber. Susan lived for the day. She bent with the breeze, like a slender sapling and harboured no thoughts she couldn't understand. He envied her contentment.

Lethargically, he stubbed out the butt of his cigarette in the ashtray on the round cane table by the bed. The small stab of heat scorched his finger and thumb, making him draw in a hiss of breath. Susan stirred, rolled over on to her side and laid a loving hand on his arm.

'Happy, darling?'

'Uh-huh.'

His reply was purely automatic. He wasn't happy. Their marriage, hardly off the ground, could be cut short within hours.

Her hand began to travel, conveying its own message. Arresting its journey with his own, he held it in a firm grip for a moment, then casting away the dismal thoughts, fell back on the bed and turned until he lay over her.

'You're a little pig,' he told her, masking that earlier anger with a deep-throated chuckle. 'You're a greedy little pig.'

It made her giggle. She fought him as he took command, but only for a moment or two, and it was really she with her gentle resistance who commanded.

Loving her took away the last of his anger and yet this time he took her as a starving man might devour a morsel of bread lest it be snatched from him. And it was a terrified love that burned in his breast.

Chapter 12

'You're going through with it this time then.'

'I owe it to her.' Matthew stared blankly at the dartboard at which they were playing in one corner of the little hut where the NAAFI served refreshments to the ranks.

Bob Howlett grunted and launched his three darts at the board in quick succession, adding up his score as the last one embedded itself in the cork surface. 'Fifty-six. Leaves me double seven.' Retrieving his darts, he stood back, allowing Matthew to take his turn.

Matthew fixed his sight along the line of flight. 'How can I let her exist on a corporal's pay when I could see her more comfortable on an officer's?'

He sent the first dart on its way as though at an enemy. Twenty. All he needed now was a double six to finish, winning him the game and a free cup of coffee from Bob. But he was keyed up. This morning he'd had an interview with the CO, who promised to put his name forward. He'd hear in a couple of weeks, and depending on the selection board he would be sent off to OCTU for that pip on the shoulder that meant better pay and a lot more allowances for Susan. It meant leaving his best mate behind, but Susan's well-being took precedence over all else.

Ever since their marriage last month she had been worrying about that bloody trust that had come his way. Yes, he could have dipped into it, and yes, they could be living well, but there was after the war to think of. After the war he'd have to get himself a job, and if tales of the last war were anything to go on, getting a job with thousands piling out of the forces could take months, maybe years. That trust would be needed to stand them in good stead while he hunted. Oggle-eyed at the idea of five thousand pounds, Susan naturally hadn't been able to see beyond the end of her nose. It was up to him to think ahead for both of them, and a pip on his shoulder, perhaps two in time, would keep her better contented until the war was over.

Bringing his thoughts back to the game, he licked his lips and took aim for the double six, the narrow area between the twin wire rings looking narrow indeed on the right-hand side of the circular board. With a dull thud the dart landed squarely in the single six. Matthew swore while Bob grinned.

'Double three you want,' he blared in triumph. If the last dart landed in the single three section, one-double-one was the only place left to go, the most awkward of scores well named as being up in the madhouse. Bob would surely make his double seven first and the buying of the coffee would be down to Matthew instead, though it was the winning that mattered most.

Balancing his weight on the ball of his right foot, he took aim, let fly. The steel point landed neatly between the parallel wires of the double six as though put there by hand.

'Yes!' he exploded. Susan, his interview with his CO, his ambitions for a commission for the moment forgotten. 'A cuppa you owe me, Howlett.'

Gathering up their darts they made their way to the tea bar. Sipping hot camp coffee in a haze of cigarette smoke, Bob asked casually, 'Did your Susan ask you to put in for an interview then?'

'No, it was my idea.' To avoid Bob's eyes, he gazed around the white painted walls of the NAAFI hut, the corner with the dartboard now taken over by others. At a battered old piano, a group of RAOCs were trying hopelessly to harmonise. *I'll be with you in apple blossom time, I'll be with you to change your name to mine . . .* Mouths hung open, cigarettes burned away in tin ashtrays. *Some day in May, I'll come and say, happy the bride the sun shines on today . . .*

'I'll miss you, y'know, Matt.'

Matthew wrenched his attention back to Bob. 'No you won't.'

'Balls!'

'Well, I suppose I'll miss you too, but I don't think I'll miss any of the others.'

Bob was contemplating the sticky black sludge at the bottom of the thick, straight-sided cup he held as though expecting to see a gold nugget lying there. 'Them too, I expect.'

'Certainly not muck like Farrell.' The man with his coarse turn of phrase had always made a point of taunting Matthew and Bob as snot-nosed college boys, a jumped-up pair of pricks, fairies, a couple of queers, and had more than once referred to Susan, whom he had never seen, as an easy bit of skirt until Matthew once almost punched him. Bob had leapt in and pacified him with the assurance that Farrell wasn't worth wasting the skin of his knuckles for.

Bob gave a small, sagacious smile. 'You'll meet muck wherever you go, in all walks of life. Muck isn't reserved entirely for the ranks, old son.'

They fell silent while across the groups of square tables the singing floated. *Church bells will chime, you will be mine . . .*

'Anyway,' he said as they left the hut, 'Susan will be pleased if I get a commission.'

Monday morning, six thirty, October rain coming down in buckets marking the tag-end of summer. Matthew trudged from the bus stop to the main gate of the camp. 'Ye gods – what a morning.'

The collar of his greatcoat wet against his neck, he thought of the cosy flat he'd left behind as he displayed his pass for inspection. Last night he and Susan had snuggled up together, the curtains drawn while rain spattered unseen on the window panes. She would be getting up now, getting ready for work. Every morning until next Sunday when he, hopefully, would be back with her, granted a sleeping-out pass. He supposed he could count himself lucky. Most could only dream of their wives far away.

She'd been over the moon when he had told her about his name being put forward for a commission. She'd squealed in delight and clasped him to her and they had made ecstatic love. But the weeks had dragged on with nothing more heard. He'd seen his CO, Major Deeks, again, who had said that the wheels of Army protocol turned rather slowly sometimes but he would hear eventually and not to worry. Matthew had nodded and come away, visualising his name lying on some desk at the bottom of a pile of others.

Men were moving about the parade ground. The rain brought up the smell of wet tarmac. Matthew straightened and threw up a salute to a couple of officers as he passed them. They barely glanced at him, swagger sticks in gloved hands half lifted to their caps as they walked on in deep conversation. Elegant, relaxed, the rain seemed hardly to touch them whereas it pelted with malicious glee on other ranks. How long before he would saunter past some poor bloody corporal, hardly noticing him as he returned the stiff salute with a casual lift of a swagger stick? If he was accepted, that was. Depressed by the weather, he couldn't see it ever happening.

Bob was waiting for him inside the mess hall as Matthew pushed his way in. The place echoed to the bass babble of men's conversation, the rattle of crockery and scrape of cutlery across plates. His nostrils were assailed by the clogging odour of cooking grease and the sharp tang of burned bacon over which hung the faint reek of the fish from yesterday's dinner.

Soaked from his own dash to the hall, Bob looked like a very thin Great Dane that had been doused by a bucket of water, his long face drooping. Matthew immediately felt for him. He could only have received some bad news, perhaps from home. Had something evil happened to Bob's wife, his children, his parents? Matthew hurried up to him.

'Something wrong?'

Bob's expression didn't alter. 'Can you stand a shock this time of the morning?'

So it wasn't bad news – not that bad anyway. Matthew grinned with relief for his mate. 'Fire away.'

'We're moving out. The whole unit.'

Matthew gazed up at the pale grey eyes. Dismay had already begun to creep through his stomach. Uprooted after just three short, settled months of marriage. 'You sure? Where to? When?'

'No idea. But soon. Bet your boots on it. Peggy let it out last night.'

They had joined the queue being doled out breakfast. Matthew never had breakfast with Susan, needing to be back at camp on time. He looked with distaste at the congealed mounds of dried egg substitute in the trays, the frizzled bits of bacon, the sticky mass of baked beans, the half-burned slices of toast. A couple were being dumped on his plate with a sound like wooden discs, a dollop of dried egg and a portion of beans unceremoniously plopped on top of each blackened slice, a piece of bacon rattling beside them.

Bob surveyed his breakfast with equal distaste. 'Happy as a bloody sandboy, is our Sergeant Pegg. Said that's just what college queers like us need – a bit of action.'

'Action? What action?'

'It's only rumour so far,' Bob soothed. 'Even though

Peggy delighted in telling us it could be overseas. Silly
arse! He should know about careless talk. Trouble is, old
sweats like him seldom get things wrong. They develop
a sixth sense about rumours after twenty-odd years'
service.'

They found a table and put down their mugs of strong
tea. Matthew sat staring at the cooling mess on his plate,
his appetite gone, his earlier dismay at Bob's news already
turned to premonitory fear. As Bob said, old sweats were
seldom wrong about rumours.

Eddie Nutt, Taffy and Farrell joined them with their
own food, Farrell's narrow face buried in his mug as
soon as he sat down, his slurps carrying across the table.
Matthew regarded him. How the man's wife put up with
him beggared the imagination, unless she was similar.
Birds of a feather.

'Heard our sergeant's bit of news, have you then?'
Taffy asked, seeing Matthew's tight expression. 'Abroad,
it looks like.'

'Fink we'll get embarkation leave?' Farrell spat bits of
half-chewed bacon in every direction as he spoke.

Bob put down his hard-as-rock toast and sipped his tea.
'Peggy could still have it wrong, you know. Though he
shouldn't be babbling on about it.'

Taffy grinned. 'Indeed no. That's all Adolf is waiting
for, isn't it, to hear what's going on in B Troop. Turn the
tide of the war, that will, knowing B Troop might be going
overseas.'

Farrell belched loudly. 'They oughter give us leave.
If they do, I'm gonna do my missus every night till I get

back, give 'er somfink ter bleedin' fink about – anuvver kid. She's always goin' on abart bein' bleedin' bored.' He guffawed at his own joke.

Ronnie Clark, who had come to sit with them, leaned his heavy young chin on his fist. 'If anyone's bored, I am. A bit of action would be welcome.'

'Speak for yourself,' Bob said. 'All right for single chaps like you.'

Matthew pushed his plate away, untouched. 'I think I'll go and get into something dry.'

'I'll come with you,' said Bob, getting up and trailing after him.

The passing days saw rumours gaining momentum. Someone had seen tropical kit being sorted in the QM stores. Two words from a snippet of conversation had been overheard between two officers from their unit – North Africa.

Suddenly it was official: no destination divulged, for obvious reasons, but an issue of tropical kit; half a dozen painful jabs against those nastier diseases prevalent in hot climates that left every victim stiff and aching, and embarkation leave.

Matthew looked in vain for a summons from the selection board. There could be every chance if he were selected of getting out of being sent overseas, at least for the time being, but word from that direction remained stubbornly silent. He'd left things just that bit too late, had been far too bloody complacent, thinking his luck would last forever.

*

Susan stood in the passage, suitcases packed. She had tried to be brave, to keep her voice even and not break down in tears; had tried not to give way to that terrible panic that all but overwhelmed her when he had appeared on the doorstep explaining the reason for being laden down with full kit.

She still felt dazed; had spent much of her time weeping in secret in the bathroom they shared with their landlady, hoping Matthew would not hear her or notice her red and swollen eyes when she emerged; had kept her head averted from him as much as possible in case he did notice. If he did, he said nothing, but cuddled her a lot, assuring her it would be all right.

'Have you got everything you need?'

Susan nodded dismally as they stood in the passage saying goodbye to Mrs Robertson who also looked unnecessarily upset, probably because she must now look for new tenants, these having been with her for such a short while.

Receiving a peck on the cheek from Mrs Robertson Susan picked up the two suitcases and followed Matthew out to the waiting taxi. The rest of their bits and pieces, ornaments, the clock, the little square wireless set, wedding gifts, would be stored in her parents' attic. Susan would have liked to go to live there but her mother had looked askance.

'We got no room here now, love, not with your gran having to stay with us an' all. Her place was condemned after that bomb fell nearby. Matthew's people have got lots of room. You can stay with them, love, can't you?'

She loathed the thought of living for God knows

how long with the formidable Mrs Ward. The woman frightened her. But there was nothing for it except to go there. Matthew was so sure she'd be well looked after that she felt compelled to keep her thoughts to herself.

But in the taxi she couldn't help herself. Clinging to him, she buried her head in his shoulder. 'What am I going to do, Matthew, when you're gone? I'll be left all alone.'

'No you won't.' His voice shook. 'Mum will look after you as though you were her own daughter. And I'll come back. I'll come back.'

He heard the desperation in his words. Susan clinging to him made him ever more afraid of what lay ahead. Would he end up fighting in North Africa? The papers were full of Britain's new offensive against Rommel out there, but British soldiers were still being killed and who could say Rommel wouldn't turn and push them back again with even more men slaughtered, himself, Matthew Ward, perhaps one of them? Never to see Susan again. She would become a widow when she had scarcely become a wife.

The thought stayed with him throughout the interminable journey to London. Their train stopped and started, which seemed the normal thing these days; the delays got worse still as it hit fog just after Watford.

The thought persisted even as he smiled greeting at his parents, his mother taking Susan up to his old room which would now be hers until his return – if he returned. What would happen to Susan if he didn't? Where would she go? She'd marry again, in time . . . God, he had to stop thinking about it, think positive. Of course he'd come back. Yet a premonition that he might not haunted his troubled sleep that night, even though lovemaking helped him wipe it away for the while.

It wasn't that bad coming home, Jenny told herself firmly as, in scarves and warm coats, she and Mumsy walked down to the shops, her mother hanging on her arm in the jaundiced mist of this October Saturday morning. So long as she didn't have to do it every time she had a couple of hours off.

Mumsy, on the other hand, would have relished every second of her free time. But Jenny needed some time with her friends, and there was Ronald too, their off-duty hours coinciding so seldom. What chance they did have to go out together they usually spent going somewhere to eat. Hospital canteen food tasted disgusting and there was not much of it.

A forty-eight-hour week and sometimes eight weeks of night duty when all she wanted to do was go home to sleep, exhausted, until it was time to catch a bus back, took away any desire to go rushing off to see Ronald if he too was off duty. Time off came seldom enough and if he wasn't available it was fun spending it with friends now and again. While she made her way home, which was only a bus ride away, now getting back after lights out, evaded the porter at the gate by climbing the railings; whispers and stifled giggles erupted as they clambered back into the nurses' residence through purposely unlocked windows before the night super began her rounds. She missed all that coming home.

If only her mother would make some attempt to join some women's group or other. There were plenty of them: wives whose husbands had been called up, elderly widows, spinsters, all knitting socks and scarves for 'the boys', or planning charity events, all an opportunity for socialising and filling in their lonely lives, but her mother had never been outgoing and that first approach towards a group of virtual strangers was always the hardest step for anyone to take.

'I couldn't go alone. I wouldn't mind if I had a friend to take me.'

'Then find a friend. Mrs Crompton next door. She lives alone. Or your other neighbour. I know she's younger than you, but she's on her own with her husband away.'

It was easy to say, but she wasn't the one having to do it. Her mother had gripped her arm hopefully. 'Perhaps you could come with me.'

'I'm a nurse, Mumsy. I can't have afternoons off whenever I please.'

She had hated the reluctance that made itself felt, wished she didn't feel so glad at having an excuse not to have to sit with those women with little else to do but discuss children, home life and the ever-tightening restrictions on food rationing as they knitted or planned their events.

Her mother would never understand. Hospital was another world, a little kingdom behind whose walls existed a strictly graded society of doctors and nurses, over which, next to the Matron's, the sister's authority was law. The outside world never penetrated that kingdom; even patients became changed creatures once they came in, lying in their beds in stiff rows, obedient to the ward sister. But Jenny loved it.

Soon to be a second-year nurse, at the moment on the men's medical ward, she was slowly climbing the ladder to the day when those magic letters SRN could be put after her name. Her feet had long ago stopped swelling like balloons and her back aching from long hours on her feet. She could take twelve hours on them almost, if not quite as lively as when she'd begun. She could fold counterpane corners to perfect angles; her mistakes were far fewer than they had once been, her intricate cap folded just right, the leg o' mutton sleeves of her uniform perfect. She'd be sitting for her second state examination early next year and after that her Preliminary. Still a long way to go, but she would get there in the end in spite of Mumsy looking towards the day when she'd leave nursing and go back to doing a nine to five job.

They were coming back home, turning into Victoria Park Road, when two young people came towards them out of the mist through which the sun was at last beginning to struggle. Jenny immediately recognised the figure of Matthew Ward and they halted simultaneously, she pulling her mother to a stop just as he did the girl on his arm. His face lit up.

'Ye gods, Jenny! Didn't expect to see you!'

'Home on leave then?' she asked, trying to control the joy that leapt inside her at seeing him, angering her in remaining as acute as ever, for all the girl with him.

There was a noticeable tightening of his features but he grinned, she was certain, with forced cheerfulness.

When he spoke it was in a similar vein, an effort at banter. 'You're not going to ask me when I'm due back, are you? Everyone asks that, as though they'll be only too glad to see me gone again. But, no, I've been given fourteen days' leave – out of the blue.'

Adding that last on a more intense note, it needed no lecture to know what it meant. The obvious effort he was making to be cheerful helped bear out the message. Her next question, 'Where are they sending you?' sounded stupidly superfluous. How could he know that? He obliged with a shrug, then collected himself and turned to the small, neat girl beside him.

'By the way, this is Susan – my wife. Susan, this is Jen . . . This is Jenny Ross, an old friend from the crowd I used to go around with before the war. Jenny lives nearly opposite my parents.'

His use of her full given name, the first time she could ever recall, now spoken so formally, so neatly severed her from him that she actually felt pain. They'd gone their separate ways, yet even now her heart cried out to be the one on his arm instead of the girl to whom she now cordially smiled, saying it was nice to meet her and politely introducing her mother.

'Me and Matthew's staying at his parents,' the girl supplied in a broad Birmingham accent, her small oval face quite beautiful and full of adoration as she glanced up at him; Jenny could clearly see why he had married her. 'I'm going to live with them while he's away. You living so near then, I might probably see something of you.'

'I expect so,' Jenny obliged, her eyes travelling to

Matthew. All she wanted now was to be away from here to suppress the sick thumping in her breast. It wasn't fair. 'Well, I won't keep you. This damp weather is chilly.' On an impulse she took off a glove and held out her hand to him. 'Well, wherever it is they send you, Matthew, keep safe, and . . .'

Words echoed inside her head, a sharp recollection of what he had once said to her: 'And whatever happens, you'll always be one of my nicer, memories.' She had once had the audacity to think they might have been words of affection, a prelude to something more. But they had not presaged anything.

She had nearly begun to repeat them word for word. Would he have recalled himself saying them? And if so, would he have thought she was being just a little bitter? No, he'd probably forgotten, had never really meant them in the first place, flippant as he'd been those days. And yet, her mind conjured up the look in his dark eyes at the time. He had meant them when he said them, she was certain, but much water had flowed under the bridge since then, and now he was married and in love with his wife, his Susan – that could be seen with half an eye.

'And come back soon,' she finished instead, hardly realising that her voice had dropped to a whisper, almost a prayer, a secret shared between herself and him. But he hadn't noticed as he too removed his leather glove and took her hand, his warmth on her chill flesh making her senses leap. Was it her imagination or did his hand hold hers just that bit longer than was necessary? Was there a spark remaining of that which she thought she had seen in his eyes that day? Silly fool, it had to be her foolish imagination, nothing more.

After they parted she repeated those last words to herself: 'Come back soon.' Now they had become truly a fervent prayer for his safekeeping as she fought the heavy lump in her heart.

Chapter 13

He had meant to make his last night with Susan memorable. Instead, beset by anxiety, he'd failed her, the first time ever. She had been wonderful about it, told him it didn't matter, but he knew she was tearful when she finally turned over to go to sleep, he with his arms about her, cuddling her close.

Mortified by his inability to fulfil her, and himself, Matthew lay awake listening to her occasional sighs as though she was grieving the loss of something precious, yet he knew she was asleep because when he asked if she felt all right there was no reply. Loath to disturb her he left unsaid the words he needed to say.

Awakening to grey light filtering through the curtains and immediately conscious of a deep anger at sleep itself having robbed him of those last few hours with her, he turned to gaze at her sweet face on the pillow beside him, the full lips in gentle repose. He was about to waken her and would have made perfect love to her but for the knock on the door and his father entering in response to his reluctant bidding with a cup of tea for them.

From then on things took on a sense of urgency, washing, dressing, packing his kit, forcing down the boiled egg and toast his mother insisted would 'keep him going', everyone's conversation stilted, shallow, tense.

It had been agreed they'd say their goodbyes here in the privacy of their own home, the severing made clean, but at the last moment Susan pleaded to be allowed to accompany him the whole way to Charing Cross where he was to board the train for Southampton. The prospect of seeing her standing there, a small isolated figure among the seething crowds in that vast station as his train took him from her, was more than he could bear to contemplate; shattering him as well as her. He took her in his arms.

'No, darling, I want you to stay here. It'll only be dragging things out if you come, and the end will be just the same. On top of that you'll have to come all the way home without me.'

She would not see it. In fact his final goodbyes turned into something like pandemonium. Having said farewell to his parents, his father gripping him firmly in a bear hug, telling him to watch himself, his mother kissing his cheek, assuring him she would look after Susan, charging him to look after himself in that cold, stiff manner which he knew hid emotions she had long ago taught herself never to show, Susan standing away from him with her back pressed against the wall of the hall, her naturally pale face now chalk-white, her small slender body as rigid as the wall that alone seemed to be holding her up, she flew at him as though unseen hands had suddenly propelled her forward.

'Matthew, don't leave me! Oh, don't . . . please don't leave me.'

He had to struggle to extricate himself, physically handing her to his mother who held her in a firm grip, her older face like granite. He'd wanted to crush Susan to him, but her demonstration threatened to undermine his own resolve not to give way to too much emotion, so while her tears flowed shamelessly unchecked, his had to remain unshed as he'd put her from him with futile words. 'It'll be all right, love. I have to go. You've got to be brave.' Though what order he said them in he did not know.

He could still hear her calling his name, her voice echoing down the street after him as he stood now on Southampton docks amid long, snaking, khaki queues waiting to board the ship that would take them to God knows where – no one knew as yet, except that they all carried tropical kit.

A fine drizzle sifted down upon the shoulders of the slowly moving queues, upon the loose piles of kitbags ready to be loaded on board, and on trucks and other equipment to be transported the several thousand miles to, where? North Africa? India? It might be India, Matthew prayed. Far away from any war zone. It could be that those in charge thought there was some need of men in that region or perhaps South or West Africa? There they could expect a life of relative luxury, and in time to come back safely. Matthew crossed his fingers as he took his turn to move up the gangway leading to the ship's dark innards.

As soon as permitted, he would write to reassure Susan how well he was and that there had been no need for her to worry about his safety – fair enough, only that he wished he was back with her instead of here. But one must not think of that. Every man here must have loved ones on his mind but knew better than to give too great a thought to it. Pushing that last sight of Susan's tear-ravaged face from his mind, he looked down at the oily green swell rising and sinking between the troopship and the quayside. It was like some slow-breathing animal waiting to engulf them all. From it rose a reek of decayed seaweed, engine oil and bilge water which he could see gushing in small spurts from an outlet below him amid a wreath of steam.

Gaining a position against the deck rail as he and his platoon made it into the ship, he leaned over to watch the water still heaving and sinking, heaving and sinking below the slow climbing of soldiers up the three sets of gangways.

'Get yer arse away from there,' Sergeant Pegg interrupted his reverie. 'All of yer – this way.'

Following him, Matthew found himself in the place where he and the others were to live out the next few weeks; a place with all its port holes well screwed down so no light could escape across a pitch-dark sea to lurking U-boats, their quarters thus promising to become hot and unbearable as they approached the tropics; a place where narrow wooden bunks had been built almost side by side, forcing men by lack of space to share with their fellows most of their personal functions, including seasickness. The all too few, once-elegant toilet facilities for paying passengers, now to be called latrines, had had all but their basic amenities torn out, even their doors, and were painted overall-grey. They needed to accommodate four times as many troops. A line of convenient buckets fixed nearby to make up for the lack of facilities would soon waft their stink to the quarters as they filled before being emptied by fatigue squads. It was a place where snoring, coughing, farting, scratching, conversation and talking in one's sleep would be no secret from anyone.

In this impending claustrophobic atmosphere, Bob dropped his kit down on to a so-far unclaimed area, once beautifully carpeted, now mere metal deck where he and the rest of them would be expected to share their lives in close harmony with all walks of life.

'Like a bloody cargo of meat,' he observed drily and everyone agreed, finding the quip unfunny.

Settled on a top bunk, Matthew wrote his first letters home, the first a brief one to his parents, the second to Susan pouring out all that he had been unable to say to her face. He'd have given the world to see her read it, see her smile with all the confidence he was instilling in her of his safe return.

He could hardly wait for the letter to be collected along with everyone else's and taken ashore for posting prior to moving off, yet it would go with his mixed feelings. In a couple of days it would reach Susan. By then he'd be nearly a thousand miles away. So he concentrated on visualising her beautiful oval face, her tremulous smile as she read, her expression glowing with love, with the certainty of his coming back to her. He worked on retaining that vision. It was one he must carry with him to whatever ends of the earth he was bound for as with the clanging of bells and the deep rumbling of engines vibrating through his whole body, diminishing, then building up again, the great ship began to slide away from the dockside.

His letters sent on their way, Matthew went up on deck – better than meditating below – to watch the huge one-time P&O liner do its majestic about-turn in the incredibly narrow channel, the deep heavy pulsating of engines finally dying away to a regular thumping that in a while would be hardly noticeable, a rhythm to which its cargo of troops would work, rest and think for weeks to come before again setting foot on terra firma.

Jenny sat on the cold park bench staring down at the ring, a band of three diamonds, sitting snugly in the box he had brought from his pocket. What on earth was she to say to him?

'You gave me no warning or what you intended, Ronald.'

It was almost an accusation. What was she supposed to say – this is so sudden – like in those Hollywood films they turned out, those love-scene dialogues so unreal? Don't ask for the moon, darling, when we have the stars . . . Was that it? It would seem laughable if this wasn't so serious.

She turned her eyes from the surprise engagement ring to the man who now held it up for her inspection, ready to be slipped on to her finger. But she had her gloves on. Was she supposed to take them off, or would he? It all threatened to become a clumsy business, stripping it of any romance there might have been. Romance? Really, she wasn't sure she loved him enough to accept his ring. The thing was, she'd let him make love to her. Well, not actually make love, although he'd seen more of her than she'd intended him to see, for every time they got into a clinch, something stopped her, almost as if she were saving herself for someone else. But what someone else? Well, she knew who that was. But it was silly. He was beyond any hope of hers. Married, overseas, his wife waiting for his return. And yet, to accept this ring, this contract for marriage, would be to finally accept the absurdity of that dream to which she had clung for so long.

'You must have known, Jenny,' he was saying, his eyes full of query, his good-looking face a picture.

She looked back at him. Yes, he was handsome. Any girl would have taken him immediately. He could have his pick, but he had chosen her. What did he see in her? What did he see that Matthew had never seen? Yet handsome as he was, there was something missing. What it was she couldn't say. Whatever it was, it wasn't right to hurt him. Ronald, I don't love you.

'I suppose I should have expected it,' she answered instead.

'Then put it on, my love.'

Grasping the fingertips of the woollen glove with her right hand, she pulled it off carefully, finger by finger, making a meal of it, the damp cold December air touching her exposed hand, and held out the hand for him. She watched him slip the ring over the knuckle of her engagement finger with a sort of ritual reverence. It went on so easily, she wondered how and when he had discovered her fit, pondering over it when she ought to have been gasping with pleasure at his wordless proposal.

Hardly giving her time, sitting there in Green Park, to admire what glitter the stars afforded the diamonds with no other lighting, not even a moon visible, he gathered her into his arms.

'Darling Jenny, you've made me the happiest man. The first moment I get, I'll take you to meet my parents. They'll be so surprised.'

Silently Jenny allowed herself to be held, leaning against him at an awkward angle. Seeing her ring glittering but faintly in the darkness over his shoulder she thought of what lay ahead. His parents lived in Bristol. All she could think of was having to go all that way to meet them, of being introduced into his life, quite expected to leave her own behind her. There was her mother to think of. She had no one else but her. Left behind and lonely. There were all the things she had known. Left behind. And there was Matthew, part of her past. Left behind. Panic seemed to take a great bite out of her heart.

'No!' She pushed him away, so hard and suddenly that he all but fell off the seat, regaining his balance with an effort. 'No, Ronald, I can't.'

He looked so taken aback, she could have cried. But there was no altering what she had said. 'I really can't, Ronald.'

'Why not?' For a moment he looked stupid, then he relaxed a little, even grinned. 'Come on, darling. It is a bit frightening I expect, saying yes. But it'll be all right. Let's just sit here quietly for a while. Let you get used to the idea. I shouldn't have sprung it on you like that. But we don't have to get married immediately. A few weeks, a couple of months perhaps.'

'But there's my mother. She doesn't know.'

'Neither do my parents. We'll tell them as soon as possible. I'll write to mine and you write to your mother, warn them . . . no, not warn them, tell them. Oh, Jenny, I've dreamed of this day – me giving you a ring and you accepting. We'll be . . .'

'I haven't accepted yet, Ronald.'

'What?'

'I haven't accepted. You put the ring on my finger, then you grabbed me and cuddled me.'

'You let me put it on. You let me cuddle you.'

'I wasn't thinking. You took me by surprise. It all happened too quickly for me to say anything.'

Comprehension was creeping not so much into his expression, which in the dark she could not properly see, but into his voice, the stiffening of his posture. 'You mean, you don't want me? You don't want to marry me?' His consternation mounted as Jenny remained silent, unable to trust her voice. 'But we get on so well.'

'I know.' She had to say something. 'I just don't . . . I don't know.'

'You don't love me enough to marry me.'

'Oh, Ronald.' What was she trying to appeal to? He got up, took her hand and gently pulled her to her feet.

'We should be getting back to the hospital. I'm on call tonight.'

'What about the ring?' It was as though they were discussing work.

'Keep it for now. See how you feel as time goes on. I suppose I did jump the gun a bit. But I do love you.'

'I know you do.' How could he stay so calm? Another

man would be ranting and raving at her now, for letting him down, making a fool of him.

'Don't you love me at all?' was all he said.

Her heart went out to him. How could she say to him, 'I like you'? How could she insult him like that? In a way she did love him. If only that other face didn't persist in floating before her eyes. Ronald made her feel good when he was around, feel wanted, feel important. His touch did excite. But when he wasn't there, she didn't think about him at all, had never found herself yearning for the time to come for them to meet. So did she love him or not? It seemed she didn't, yet when she saw him her heart leaped with the pleasure of seeing him. They got on well together, never quarrelled. They could chat until the cows came home. She felt easy with him in a way she had never done with Matthew Ward. But Matthew, though claimed, still haunted her.

'You took me by surprise,' she said miserably for an answer as they began making their way out of the darkened park whose gates stood open all night so people could gain access at a moment's notice to the air-raid shelters built there. 'Don't be annoyed.'

'I'm not annoyed.' No, he wasn't annoyed, just deeply hurt.

'I need time to get used to it. I will keep the ring for a while. And I will think about it, Ronald. I promise.'

After all, she must. Theirs would be a stable marriage, she knew that by just knowing him. She would be a fool not to say yes in the end.

'Good girl,' he breathed, his confidence returning, and

gave her a thank-you peck on the cheek as they walked on through the darkened streets.

Bombay had hit the troops newly arrived from the sedate, restrained British Isles, most never having set foot on any foreign soil before, not even France, like a bomb. It was an exotic disturbing place, full of disquiet and unheaval. Fine buildings rubbed shoulders with such squalor as Matthew could never have imagined and made him at first feel sickened. But slowly, confronted by its sights and sounds, its unfamiliar aromas and an atmosphere so indigenous that it seemed there could be no other city in the world like this, his eyes became blinded to all but the worst of sights, and all his prayers were those of gratitude that their final destination had been here and nowhere else.

Amid speculation they had pulled in to Gibraltar, spent a day on the Rock while U-boats reported to be lurking outside the Med were being dealt with by the Royal Navy. They hardly had time to see anything Gib had to offer before the ship sailed onward, not into the Mediterranean as had been expected but south, down the coast of Africa, pausing at Cape Town, then round into the Indian Ocean where they finally disembarked at Bombay.

In the pleasant warmth of an Indian November, Matthew sat on his bed writing letters home to say where he had landed up and thought of the chill sleet of England, and of the commission he'd narrowly missed by being too complacent and seeking it too late. Now he saw it as providential that he had not done so. Had he got a commission, who was to say he might not have ended up on some field of battle instead of here. It *was* providence. He should have known. He had always been pretty lucky in nearly everything.

Leaving her house, Jenny saw Matthew's wife emerge from hers. They caught sight of each other at the same time; she saw the girl hesitate and almost draw back as though about to hurry back indoors. But Jenny wasn't to be avoided. She turned in her direction, her steps rapid. 'Hi, there!'

She had been aching for weeks to have a chat with her, telling herself it was of no consequence to her if she didn't, yet feeling a compulsion to look over to the Wards' house every time she came home. She'd told herself she was only coming home at every opportunity for her mother's sake, yet a tiny voice inside her kept repeating the true reason for her visits. That tiny voice was telling her now of the truth behind the avid eagerness with which she called out, 'Hi, there!'

The girl smiled, nodded briefly, but the ice was broken.

In seconds Jenny was at her side. 'Haven't seen much of you since we were introduced.' She was talking like some schoolgirl, far too fast, far too exuberant.

Susan shook her head rather solemnly. 'I haven't been out a lot.'

'Well, I only get home at odd times. That's a nurse's life for you.' She laughed.

'You're a nurse?'

'Didn't Matthew mention it?'

'No, he didn't.'

They had begun to walk towards the main road, Jenny hiding her disappointment that Matthew hadn't thought of her even enough to mention her job to his wife. But then, he wouldn't, would he?

'Where are you off to, then?' she asked and saw the girl shrug.

'I don't know really. I just had to get out for a walk somewhere. I was going to the park, but it don't matter much where I go.'

She sounded so down. Jenny took a quick guess at what must have driven the girl out. She herself wouldn't relish being closeted with Mrs Ward for days on end. Her own mother with her constant small complaints of loneliness was enough to endure, but Jenny reckoned Mrs Ward could knock spots off Mumsy for driving a person away.

'It's a bit chilly for walking,' she observed as she fell in beside her. A thin fog was threatening to thicken. It clung with cold fingers around cheeks and lips and penetrated the shoulders of the heaviest coat. In mid November, elsewhere on the Continent, flurries of dry snow probably covered everything in glorious pristine white – she still felt a thrill at new fresh snow for all its inconvenience – but here it only got damp and any snow that might fall would soon melt on this seawashed island. Yet she'd rather have all the peasouper fogs unconquered England could dish out than the dazzling whiteness of an occupied Europe. Nineteen forty-two waited just six weeks away – how much longer would this war go on and when would Matthew come home again?

'Have you heard from Matthew?'

Susan appeared to brighten up. 'We had his first letters in the week. Airmail. One for me and one for his parents. From India, Bombay.'

A vast surge of relief poured over Jenny. Far far away from any fighting. Thank God, oh, thank God.

'That's good,' she said evenly. 'I bet you're glad.'

Susan nodded. 'I wish he was here instead. I wanted to tell him my news to his face, not in a letter. It won't be the same written in a letter. Oh, if only he'd been able to stay here a few weeks longer, I could've told him to his face and seen it all light up. I'm going to have a baby.'

'Oh, I'm so glad for you.' It was even more of an effort to keep her voice steady. Marriage, now cemented by a forthcoming baby. 'You must be very thrilled.'

Susan didn't look thrilled. 'I would be if it wasn't for her, his mother. She's really pleased of course. But she's started making plans for it already, telling me what I should do and what I shouldn't do. I really feel like I'm in a prison.'

The same as Matthew had felt; his mother's over-eagerness to guide and help had only been instrumental in sending him away from her. She felt suddenly sad for Mrs Ward, only able to express love by managing the lives of those around her, succeeding only in driving them away with their misguided conception of her actions. Even Louise, with that time she had secretly applied for the Wrens. She had confided in Jenny. 'I never told Mummy at that time until I was quite sure I would be accepted,' she'd said. 'But honestly, Jenny, she can be quite suffocating at times.' Exactly as Matthew had felt, and now Susan.

'I don't know how long I'll be able to stand it,' Susan was saying. She had begun to screw up beneath her winter coat, the damp cold eating into her small frame. 'She watches me all the time. Everything I eat, everything I do. I was sick first thing yesterday morning. That confirmed it but she carted me off to the doctor to be sure. I hate doctors. I hate the smell of their waiting rooms, and ill people all round the room.'

She seemed bent on unburdening herself to someone. 'I was sick again this morning and she said I should stay in bed. She kept coming in every half-hour to see how I was. I don't want to stay in bed. She said I wasn't to go out, I'd catch cold, but I came out just the same. I know it'll annoy her. She'll be all stiff and starched with me when I get back, like I was a kid, or something. I wish Matthew was here. He'd stick up for me.'

She was beginning to shiver. She seemed so small; a waif. 'Perhaps some evenings when I'm home,' Jenny offered readily, 'if you want to come over to us for a chat, you're welcome. It'll get you out of that house.'

She felt she had never seen anyone look so grateful. 'Could I?'

'Of course.' Also Susan would keep her abreast of news of Matthew, though Jenny didn't admit to it even to herself, for all the tiny voice inside did.

The following ten days saw Jenny on nights, taking over from a girl who had gone down sick. Sleeping most of the day, she was unable to honour the invitation to Susan. But she had managed to get Christmas off. Ronald, still waiting for her answer, had asked to take her home to see his parents, but it seemed only right to think of her mother first on this, the one special family holiday of the year. On top of that it was a time when Mumsy would be thinking of Daddy, who had died just one month before the festive season, for all the years were stretching on.

She hadn't told her mother about Ronald yet. The first thing she'd do would be to start fretting about the impending loss of her daughter, as if Jenny would forsake her entirely. Maybe all mothers felt that way but most wouldn't make a meal of it. Not that Mumsy meant to drag on her, but Jenny found herself dreading the day when she must tell her.

That she would marry Ronald was in no doubt. He was kind and considerate and steady, and she did love him – not in the silly way she'd felt for Matthew – still did, she was ashamed to realise, constantly telling herself off about this idiotic wishing for something that couldn't be – but in a comfortable way which common sense told her would last and last.

It did seem a shame to keep fobbing him off so. Perhaps she would tell him her decision when the spring came and the spirits rose with the climbing of the sun. These days she had no deep feeling for love or anything approaching it. The weather stayed too cold for strolling in parks, so they went to the Natural History Museum, had tea in its restaurant, talking of this and that. He held her hand and gazed at the ring she'd begun to wear when with him, capitulating at last. He spoke of marriage, their future

together, again broached the subject of her coming home
with him to see his parents, if not Christmas Day, then
Boxing Day.

'I know it sounds churlish,' she told him. 'But my
mother's all alone. I couldn't dream of leaving her as soon
as Christmas is over. She's made a Christmas pudding too.
Saved up her dried fruit coupons all year for the thing.
She'd be left to eat the rest all by herself on Boxing Day.
They don't keep, you know, not like they used to before
the war.'

For some reason he thought that funny. His laughter
annoyed her for yet some other unaccountable reason.

'I just couldn't leave her,' she stated huffily. The pudding
had been just an excuse. It wasn't funny, at least not all that
much. Even less, again for some unknown reason, when she
remembered that there would come a time when he would
insist on naming the wedding day. Why did her insides
crawl with reluctance at that thought? Later as she melted
into his arms, she wondered why she had felt so reluctant.
This was what she wanted, or what common sense told
her she must want. Security, friendship, someone to be
with, all of those things. And of course love. She did love
Ronald, she told herself severely.

Monday came again, one more week nearer to
Christmas. Jenny was working, swotting for her second
state examination as she had been doing these past months
while Ronald worked and studied towards becoming a GP.
She had been nearly two years doing practical work on
the wards. A couple of years had to pass yet before she
could add SRN after her name, though perhaps in wartime

it might come quicker. But would she ever get it, now that she appeared to be Ronald's fiancée?

She was just going on the ward when a nurse came hurrying towards her. 'Telephone call for you, love. Better cut short whoever it is or you'll make yourself late.'

'Did they say who it is?' Jenny called as she made her way to the old-fashioned phone fastened to the wall down the passage. Her heart had begun to beat. It could only be bad news. Her mother? She had been all right when she'd left home an hour ago.

'Didn't say,' came back the answer, but Jenny was already there, her ear to the earpiece.

'Hello? Hello.'

A girl's frantic voice assailed her ears. 'Jenny – oh, thank God it's you. I tried to get you before you left. But you'd already gone. I had to talk to *someone*.'

'Who is it?' Jenny interrupted the tirade, not recognising the voice.

'Susan, across the road. I must speak to you. There's no one else.'

'Susan, what's the matter?' She felt just a little peeved being made late by Susan's trivial need to phone her. Nothing at all to do with her mother.

'Haven't you heard the news on the wireless?' The girl's voice still held a note of panic. 'Japan's just declared war on America, and us. They've bombed a base belonging to America, called Pearl Harbor, in the Pacific. Matthew's out there in India. I'm so worried.'

Jenny's mind flitted over past world atlases of her childhood, the Indian continent marked in pink, Siam and similar countries further east in yellow, then pink again for Malaya, Borneo, Australia. The Pacific, light blue, dwarfed all else. Where Pearl Harbor was she had no idea but it belonged to the USA and was probably somewhere in the Hawaiian islands. Far away from India. Matthew was safe.

'Susan, if war breaks out there, do you know how far away from it Matthew will be? A good couple of thousand miles at least. If he was still stationed here in England he'd be nearer to a war zone. So there's nothing to worry about. Nothing at all.'

The voice at the other end had calmed a little. 'I've sent off an airmail letter to him to tell him about the baby. He'll get it in a day or two. I know he'll be thrilled. You are sure about him being safe in India?'

'I couldn't be surer,' Jenny said, smiling into the mouthpiece. She was going to be late. 'I must go, Susan. I'm at work. See you soon.'

She replaced the receiver and hurried off. She wouldn't be able to listen to the wireless until she came off duty. Perhaps by then there might be a bit more about this new war so far away. But one thing was certain. Matthew, soon to be a father, was indeed safe and it was best not to let her mind keep dwelling on him.

Chapter 14

Among other things, some of the garrison were staging a panto for Christmas and requests had gone out for anyone with talent wanting to join the chorus to come forward. All the acting roles had of course long since gone to those who'd been stationed there some time.

'Go on, Matt,' Bob urged, hearing about it. 'You've not got a bad voice. How about giving your tonsils an airing?'

Matthew had his pencil poised over a blank air letter. Seventh of December already and he needed to write to Susan again. He was waiting for one from her. It should come any moment but in the meantime . . .

He looked up, gave a small explosive chuckle of self-derision. 'One sound from me and I'd be given the about-turn.'

'Don't be daft. It's not half bad, your voice. Now, me, I'd turn lemons sour. Go on, have a go.'

Again Matthew chuckled, but the idea was tempting. He was bored. Life here was one round of ticking over, being given jobs just to kill time and keep men occupied: in the soporific air of old colonial India they painted flagstaffs, whitewashed stones around brigade HQ, cleaned windows, swept paths, spit-and-polished equipment, attended parades and spent the hotter parts of the day in cool schoolrooms, the strong sunlight thwarted by fretted shutters, the still air stirred by squeaking, slowly revolving fans. With time to laze in the shade, seek somewhere to booze away an evening, what at first seemed delightful had quickly palled.

He was about to say he might think about having a crack at it when Ronnie Clark burst into the barrack room like a tornado. Unable to take in quite what he was blabbering about, those absorbed in reading tatty paperbacks, writing letters, darning socks, looked up.

'Who's bombed what?'

'The Japanese. They've gone and bombed Pearl Harbor.'

'Where the bloody 'ell's Pearl 'Arbor?'

'It's an American naval base in Hawaii,' Matthew supplied, which had Farrell sneering across at him.

''Ark at bleedin' know-all.' But Matthew ignored him. His heart was already filling with a kind of animal fear, nameless and undefined, having nothing yet to draw on, just an instinct of some threat looming from a totally unexpected direction.

'Where did you hear this?' Bob was demanding.

'Over the radio.' Ronnie Clark had been on duty all morning in the communications room. 'A few minutes ago. They've bombed Singapore too.' He looked significantly towards Jeff Downey whose thick lips had dropped open in awe. 'Bet you're glad we didn't go there as you wanted to.'

'The Yanks'll come inter the war now, won't they?' Eddie Nutt said.

'Bugger the Yanks!' someone snapped. 'What about us? Us fighting bloody Jerries, bloody Ities, and now bloody Nips. It ain't fair! Just as we're getting the best of the Jerries in North Africa an' the battle of the Atlantic's goin' our way and everyone's goin' on about us openin' up a second front, now we're inter another bloody war. Ain't it just fair!'

It was Sergeant Pegg who put it all into perspective for them. 'What you lot worrying about them short-arse little monkeys for? Most of 'em wear glasses. Planes tied up with string, like them bloody toys they export to us. I'd sooner fight an 'undred of them than a dozen of Rommel's lot. The Yanks comin' in, all we'll see of them boss-eyed, bow-legged little yeller bleeders'll be their backsides. The Yanks comin' in'll shorten the war in Germany too.'

It all seemed logical and heartening even when days later they were moved on to the transit camp at Deolali; from Deolali station a horrendous three-day train journey across the Indian continent began, to Calcutta, Assam, and on to Rangoon in Burma to join Burmese and Indian brigades there.

Matthew's letters home had been written in fits and starts. Susan's had been delayed because those to her were always precious and needed thinking about, dreaming over. Now there was no time for dreaming. What he had written would have to be sent off as it was. He hadn't heard from her yet, but with all this sudden moving out, hers must still be catching him up. He would get it sooner or later, but it was hell not hearing.

'Knowing the Army,' Bob said as they strolled through

the paved courts of the ancient Shwe Dagon pagoda on their first off-duty sightseeing trip, the hot spicy smells of India now replaced by the milder flowery ones of Burma, 'our mail will all come in one batch.'

'And wait another couple of months for the next lot,' Matthew agreed. Pensively he gazed up at the scores of lesser pagodas that surrounded the great *stupa,* of the Shwe Dagon, its graceful curves clad in pure beaten gold.

His ears filled by the soft slap of bare feet on warm tiles, the low murmur of devotees at prayer, the droning intonation of Buddhist monks, the twitter of birds and the gentle tinkle of tiny bells, he watched a group of Burmese women at their labour of devotion, sweeping the smooth paving with flat, fan-shaped brooms. In crisp, straight blouses over colourful skirts, *longyis*, that wrapped tightly around their legs, their shining black hair pulled into a bun at the back of the head and secured by a gaudy flower, they looked sleek and clean, a far cry from the ragged denizens of Bombay.

'I wish my Susan could see all this,' he murmured.

'Yes, a regular Cook's tour, and not costing us a penny,' said Bob appreciatively. 'Just look where we've been at the expense of the Army. We've stopped off at Gib, West Africa, Cape Town, Bombay, Deolali and now Rangoon. Wonder where we'll end up next?'

'This is as far east as I ever want to go,' Matthew said, his mind on their newest enemy. Short, bow-legged, short-sighted they might be, but they still had guns and shells and mortars, and could kill. He didn't fancy Susan becoming a widow just yet.

Taffy had joined them, coming from a side street with a wide grin of self-satisfaction. Matthew gave him a disparaging look. 'Not in the middle of a Sunday afternoon.'

Taffy's grin widened even more. 'Best time for it, isn't it? Make you pretty thirsty, mind.' He eyed one of the many water-sellers squatting on a corner beneath the shade of a tree, clinking a metal cup against a container with a loud urgent rhythmical clatter.

'Wouldn't risk it,' Matthew warned. 'Wait till you get a beer from the mess instead.'

He paused by an ancient crone squatting under a large spreading tree near some open-fronted shops. Surrounded by several of her family and a few onlookers, she leered up at Matthew, her few remaining teeth stained red by betel-nut juice.

'Tell fortune, soldiya?' she croaked in English. There had been a British garrison here long enough for those like her to have a passing knowledge of their language. Dusty feet splayed from beneath a rusty longyi, the old fortune-teller beckoned with clawed hands. 'You want know of long life, soldiya, love, ha?'

'Go on, give it a go,' Bob urged.

'What about you, Taff?' Matthew asked. 'Might find out you're going to turn over a new leaf and find yourself a decent wife. Put a stop to all that whoring of yours.'

Taffy's handsome face was full of injured pride. 'There's nice! You just leave me be to find me own wife when I'm good and ready.'

Matthew laughed and glanced again at the crone with

her vermilion grimace. On impulse he squatted in front of her, extending his hand, but the woman waved it away. 'You pay. You pay.'

A couple of coins dropped in her palm quickly appeased her and the old witch grabbed his hand to scrutinise it. Tracing the lines of his palm with a piece of indelible pencil until most of them were linked in mystical triangles and trapeziums, she studied the results, her voice a cracked sing-song.

'See baby. See lady. Lady has your heart, soldiya.'

'I bet she says that to everyone,' Taffy interrupted with a chortle.

Matthew was about to ask, what baby? But the woman went on: 'One more lady has heart for you.'

'Two?' Taffy gave another chortle. 'And you talk about me, boyo?'

'Lady with bright hair,' went on the crone.

'No, dark,'Matthew corrected.

The black eyes like polished jet glittered angrily. She glanced round and pointed at the distant Shwe Dagon pagoda glinting like a gold nugget in the sunshine behind the low buildings.

'Bright.' She waggled her old head lest her prediction be contradicted again. 'Like Shwe Dagon.'

He let her have her way. After all it was only a bit of fun. But the old woman's eyes had gone dark. She regarded him narrowly. 'See bad thing here. Binding rope. Bad thing.'

'The ball and chain, that is,' laughed Taffy. 'Don't need your hand read to know that, do you?'

Matthew resolutely kept his palm upwards. 'What do

you mean, bad thing?' Was she referring to Susan? Was everything all right with her? The questions came even as he derided this odd belief in the woman's words.

But the crone had dismissed him, already casting about for other clients. Nor, strangely enough, would she take his offer of any more money.

'A baby! Ye gods, she was right.' Matthew stared at the letter that had at last caught him up. He waved it in Bob's face. 'That old bird who told me my fortune said she saw a baby and Susan says here that she's pregnant.'

For hours last night he had lain beneath his mosquito net studying his palm in the glow of a pale shaft of moonlight through the high barrack-room window, trying to make sense of the marks of the indelible pencil. Now had come Susan's letter. It was uncanny. 'I'm going to be a father.'

Bob, a father of three, regarded him as an old dog might a boisterous puppy. 'Well, if she's pregnant, obviously you will be. You're not unique.'

'I feel unique. God, I feel . . .' There was no way to describe how he felt. Susan, his sweet timid Susan, to be a mother. He thought again of that old crone. Binding ropes she had said. Of course, a baby was binding, tying him and Susan together. Of course. Last night that prediction had worried him, he had been unable to pinpoint any of it. Now it all came plain. 'I'll never doubt a fortune-teller again,' he announced. Bob grinned.

'A shot in the dark. Their stock in trade – make it enigmatic enough and you can read anything you want into what they tell you.'

'Two shots in the dark? No, there is something in it, Bob.'

While Bob chortled, Matthew returned to reading the rest of his letter. It said she was two months pregnant. The letter was nearly three weeks old, so it had happened on his embarkation leave. She would be having the baby around June or July time.

'We might all be home by then,' he said to Bob, roughly calculating the date. 'With the Yanks in the war now it could shorten it considerably.'

Bob's unprepossessing features were wreathed in smiles of joy for him. 'Could be. One never knows. I tell you what, we'll have a drink tonight to celebrate you being a prospective father, wet the baby's head. Drinks on you of course.'

'Thanks very much!' Matthew chuckled, but Bob corroborating his own certainty of being home by next summer heartened him even more.

In this frame of mind he began on his reply to Susan. But it wasn't easy to put into it all he felt. He was in danger of writing a load of drivel and finally had to put it away until the next morning when he might be able to collect his thoughts better. It was the twenty-second of December, with Christmas and its panto, in which he'd got himself into the chorus, not sure if he even wanted to bother, three days away. The next morning the bombers came.

Throughout Christmas and into the early days of 1942, Rangoon continued to be bombed. Detailed to help supervise hordes of terrified refugees pouring out of the city, helping to fill in at the docks now forsaken by hundreds of Indian dock workers who'd also taken to the road, hoping to get back home to India, Matthew's letter to Susan lay unfinished.

His main concern in that letter now was to allay her fears for his safety as news was relayed to England about the fall of Hong Kong and the air attacks on Rangoon. That city would surely be next to fall. Any time Matthew had he scribbled words of reassurance. Above all else, Susan, pregnant, must not be alarmed. He assured her that the bombing had been minimal no matter what the wireless said, but whether some censor would allow that piece of information in his letter to get through was out of Matthew's hands, though he felt better having put it in.

By the middle of January the Japanese were reported to be already concentrated on the Siam-Burma border, the speed of their movements stunning everyone. Matthew's troop found themselves suddenly attached to an Indian brigade very much in need of a signals unit and ordered forward to establish a line of defence just east of the Sittang River which ran into the Gulf of Martaban some eighty miles away.

Gathering up their kit, boarding trucks, they had no time to send last letters home even if they had been allowed to. By the time Matthew was able to scribble a page to Susan, Moulmein to the south was in enemy hands, so fast had the Japanese moved through what had been thought impenetrable jungle.

Two weeks later the letter still lay in his shirt pocket,

darkened by sweat, as he crouched by the side of a dirt road passing on crackling coded messages over his field radio, his nerves jumping, his eyes alert to any movement from the dim jungle on either side of the road.

As yet they had seen no action, the enemy being busy around the Bilin River fifteen miles away. But everyone knew by now just how swiftly that enemy could move through this tangle of rainforest, how adept it was at easing around a battalion, small lightly equipped figures appearing out of the greenery in front of their prey like spectres, cutting off whole battalions without warning. It had happened more than once these last few weeks and no one wanted to be caught napping. Orders had come to withdraw to the railway bridge over the Sittang, to guard it until all transport and equipment was safely across. Then the rest were to cross prior to its demolition to prevent any enemy advance upon Rangoon itself.

As Matthew moved back along the road with his platoon, a staff car passed him, empty but for the Indian corporal driving it. Remembering his letter, Matthew frantically hailed the man and as the car slowed he pulled out the letter and waved urgently at the driver.

A slow gleaming smile split the dark aquiline features. There was no need for any exchange of words; the beseeching look on the taut face of the English corporal brandishing his stained envelope spoke volumes in any language. Stretching out a hand, the driver took it, nodded understanding, and tucking it into his uniform sped off westward in a cloud of dust.

*

Three months she had been here. Three months and still
a guest, not one bit a part of Matthew's family, and she
wondered if in fact she wanted to be.

Yes, of course Mrs Ward looked after her, saw she
wanted for nothing and was apparently very happy with
the knowledge of her son's wife bearing his child. It was
the way she went about it, the way she always conducted
herself, that made Susan feel like an outsider.

She yearned for home, for the noise and laughter, for
her father's uncouth manner and her mother's brassy
warmth, the sharp quarrelling of her sisters and the
tormenting of her younger brothers, neighbours coming
in and out as free as they liked. Their own doors too were
open to anyone who wanted to come in for a chinwag and
a cuppa. Three months here and she knew none of the
neighbours, except Jenny Ross. But she looked for her in
vain to unburden her troubles on. It seemed Jenny Ross
was too taken up with her work nursing, her own friends
and no doubt some young man, to come home at all the
right times. Susan had seen her only once since that time
they had spoken together, but it had been cold with a
threat of more snow when she had glimpsed her entering
her house, head down, glad to be out of the bitter wind
and Susan had felt it too much an imposition to go across
and make herself free as she might have done at home,
especially as it was obvious Jenny Ross was eager to get
indoors and relax.

Life, with winter closing in, the sounds of the world
deadened by the first snows, was turning into a gaol, her
gaoler a well-meaning but dictatorial Mrs Ward whom she

couldn't bring herself to call Mum. Susan merely cleared her throat should she need to gain her attention, which was as seldom as she could get away with. Mr Ward, whom she did feel she could happily have called Dad except that she couldn't address one in-law that familiarly without the other, was so different. He had the same way of looking at her as Matthew had, as though concealing some joke. He said little, but possessed a sort of warmth his wife did not have, and for Susan any tiny port in a storm was a haven. When the weather had been more clement she'd been able to take a walk down to his shop and spend her time there helping a bit, making tea or serving customers with small items or talking to him in the back room when things were quiet. Now that the weather had turned foul, she was stuck here with her mother-in-law, yearning desperately for her own mother. But her mother was far away and in no way could Susan find courage enough to make an excuse to leave and go off to live up there.

In her own way Mrs Ward was kind enough, but Susan could not master her awe of her. And when she'd found herself pregnant, she also found herself practically in close confinement, watched over night and day by a woman with the eyes of a hawk watching its prey, or so it seemed.

'You must stay in bed longer in the mornings. Don't go out of the house without first telling me where you are going. Don't try lifting that on your own, it could be too heavy and cause the baby an injury, I'll do it for you. Don't upset yourself so about Matthew – it's not good for you in your condition. Try to content youself more, my dear – there's plenty of books to read. If you need to go to the library, tell me and I will accompany you. Is it not time you started knitting for the baby? That would help you. We could get some wool and you can make a start.'

And this when she'd only been two months gone. No better, in fact worse, now she was four months. What would it be like by the time she was seven or eight months? Life threatened to become unbearable.

Early Sunday morning, the fifteenth of February, came, with little to do but sit indoors all day as with most Sundays, and probably get on with her enforced knitting. Mrs Ward inspected it every now and again, helping her with dropped stitches, advising her on how to keep the knitting even: 'You knit far too tightly, my dear. That's because you're too tense. Then when you relax, you knit looser. The result is an uneven garment. Try to remain relaxed all the time.'

But how could she? She hated Sundays. She wished Matthew was here. But he was thousands of miles away, in a sunny climate, enjoying himself. Jenny Ross had told her, when she'd got into a panic over the news of war opening up in the Far East, that Pearl Harbor and Singapore which had been bombed at the same time were far far away from him. Mr Ward had confirmed that, adding – she suspected to make her feel better – that Matthew was probably living it up in India. Not that she didn't want him to enjoy himself, wasn't glad he was in no danger from this distant war; she just wanted him back here, a buffer between his mother and herself.

This Sunday she was feeling particularly desperate. It was the baby, beginning to twitch ever so slightly, already seeming to be pushing out the walls of her stomach. She needed to get out of the house without Mrs Ward there to hold her firmly by the arm, like some sergeant major.

That woman, why did she behave as if she had to be responsible for everyone else's well-being? Was it because she herself lacked something, was nursing a sense of inferiority, deep inside, needing to combat it by bossing everyone about? Perhaps it was a way of proving something to herself. But could anyone visualise Lilian Ward as ever having lacked self-confidence? Susan could imagine her at four years old, bossing all the kids about, even then managing everything for them; could imagine her in her crib consciously manipulating her mother with a cry, a squeal, a smile. Lilian Ward had been born managing. But she wasn't going to manage her!

Susan made up her mind. The weather looking passable, Mrs Ward was upstairs clearing out a cupboard in one of the back rooms, which she loved doing on Sunday mornings, Mr Ward looked ready to settle back with his Sunday paper, which he was never allowed to read over breakfast. Susan hastily donned coat, scarf, boots, and gloves and quietly opened the front door to let herself out. Just a short walk. She'd be back before they knew she'd gone. Mrs Ward might even assume she'd gone to lie down in her room for an hour though there was a chance she might look in to see if she was all right. There was never any need. Susan felt her health was magnificent. Gone was all that dreadful morning sickness when Mrs Ward would hurry into the bathroom after her, embarrassing when she was being sick, to wipe her brow and advise on how to prevent morning sickness: drink cold water, eat an apple.

'Is that you, Susan?' Her mother-in-law's bat-hearing had detected the door opening. Now she must answer.

'I just thought I'd wander down the road a bit. I need some fresh air.'

'Oh, no.' Already Mrs Ward was coming downstairs. 'The pavement is still a little icy. You'll slip and fall. You must not harm that baby.'

It was all she cared about, Susan thought uncharitably, the baby, the mother just an incubator for her son's child, someone else for her to fuss over, think for, do for, the way Matthew had described on one occasion.

'I just want to go out,' Susan blurted. 'I need to go out.'

'I'll come with you. I think I need a little fresh air myself.'

There was only one thing Mrs Ward really needed, to keep an eye on her. Slumping a little, Susan waited as the spotless flowered apron was taken off and outdoor clothes put on, the lightly greying short hair given a brief tidying pat and a hat put on over it. Mrs Ward had a wonderful clear skin, virtually unlined, and Susan thought as she waited for her that when young she must have been a very handsome woman. She still was, but so forceful. Meekly, Susan allowed herself to be conducted a short way across the icy road, in through the park gates, as far as its nearest bench and then back – a distance of no more than five hundred yards, not really a walk at all, and all the time with the woman's arm stayed tucked through hers, practically holding her up as though she were crippled or something. Susan was glad to get back indoors if only to escape to her room on the pretence of a lie-down after the walk, Mrs Ward approving wholeheartedly.

She had hardly closed her door and gone to her bed than she heard voices slightly raised downstairs. While Mrs Ward's voice had a penetrating quality to it, her husband's was always soft and thoughtful. Now, however, his could be heard above hers. Susan got up and opened the door again, the better to eavesdrop on this mystifying rise of voices.

'I think we should let her sleep on, rest, before we say anything,' he was saying.

'I think she should be told immediately,' came the reply.

'I don't think so, Lilian. You know how quickly she gets herself into a state.'

They had to be talking about her. What had she done to cause an argument? They had a damned cheek discussing her when she wasn't there. Becoming angry, she crept out on to the landing.

'Even so, he is her husband. She has a right to be told and as soon as possible.'

Susan made for the stairs. What had Matthew done that she must be told immediately of it? He hadn't found someone else, all those thousands of miles away? She felt sick as she ran into the living room. The two people were standing, their backs to her.

'What mustn't I be told?'

They had turned, were looking at her with a sort of dumb fear in their eyes. It was Mrs Ward who moved towards her first. Susan noticed that Mr Ward was holding the Sunday paper, half folded, half crumpled.

'My dear . . .' Mrs Ward began.

Her voice broke. She reached out and took Susan's arm in a vice-like grip but which Susan felt had been meant to be comforting. 'My dear, you must be strong. You mustn't allow yourself to become panicky.'

'What is it?' Susan asked, her heart already pumping like a little frightened animal behind her ribs although she had no idea why except the two people before her looked frightened and anxious, lending their anxiety to her.

'It's Matthew . . .' Mr Ward began, then checked himself. 'Well, not exactly Matthew, but it concerns him.' With that, he unfolded the newspaper and held it out for Susan to read. She had read with dismay of the fighting that had broken out in Singapore, how the Japanese had come down from the north through hundreds of miles of tangled jungle hitherto thought impassable for any human being, taking that city by surprise, and she had been mildly worried, but Singapore was still a long way from India.

Taking the paper from him while Mrs Ward turned away to gaze out of the window at the bare trees of the park opposite, Susan stared at the large black headlines:

SINGAPORE FALLS. GENERAL PERCIVAL SURRENDERS ON
ORDERS OF MR CHURCHILL TO PREVENT LOSS OF LIFE.

and then a smaller heading:

CHURCHILL TO ADDRESS NATION TONIGHT ON RADIO.

Susan looked up, imploring the couple as though they might

be able to do something to make it all better. 'But they said Singapore could never fall. How could it happen?'

With the Japanese capturing Singapore, would Matthew be with those sent to recapture it? He would have to fight, and she had thought him safe. He could be wounded, killed. She'd never see him again. The thought filled her whole being as though glue was being poured into her body. Susan felt herself beginning to sway. The baby seemed to be jumping about inside her.

'I don't know,' Mr Ward was saying. 'All their defences point out to sea, they were so sure no enemy could ever come from the north. But they did. That's all I can say.'

But she hardly heard anything he said for the buzzing in her head. The room had begun to spin. The floor was coming up to meet her and she felt her body grow limp and lifeless. She vaguely felt someone catch her, felt herself being picked up and carried upwards in a jerky manner, guessed in her faint that this was the stairs. But her faint had become complete before Mr Ward ever laid her on her bed.

Chapter 15

It was a day of stifling heat. Vehicles lurching from one bomb crater to the next sent clouds of dust over the sweating shoulders of those trying to clear the road of stricken transport on this twenty-second day of February.

The railway bridge over the Sittang River, hastily converted to allow single-file traffic, was making progress slow and hazardous, on top of which a truck had run off the temporary decking, hopelessly blocking the bridge, the tailback now grinding to a standstill.

They were at the mercy not only of enemy aircraft, but of Allied planes who had been ordered to attack the advancing Japanese but not informed that any troops west of Kyaikto would be British, and thus were strafing the waiting columns out of hand. With more transport being knocked out and more men being killed and wounded, the state of the road became steadily worse.

Beneath a smoking carrier a dozen men lay huddled, heads down, as dive bombers screamed over the muddle of men and machinery. Bullets whining like angry hornets ricocheted off the metal sides of the vehicle, and in the ensuing din Bob Howlett's voice had as much power as the squeak of a mouse, begging that they make a run for it to the safety of the jungle.

Some had already sprinted for the trees looking for an easier way to the river, but orders were to hold the bridge for as long as was needed to get the transport across before they were all cut off.

Matthew held on to Bob's shirt to prevent him from making for the deceptive shelter of tangled greenery each side of the open road. 'Stay put! The Japs could already be there. A whole platoon of 'em would be on top of you before you could see them.'

Scarcely any of his mob was left. Taffy – poor libidinous Taffy – dead. Hadn't known what had hit him. Ronnie Clark with his hankering for the excitement of battle, dead. Eddie Nutt, Lieutenant Grice, dead. Sergeant Pegg, somewhere back there along the road, both legs gone, had grabbed Matthew by the shirt front and pulled him close, his bullet-head unbowed, his eyes still glaring through his pain. 'Yer in charge now, Ward. Yer wanted t'be an officer. Now see if yer c'n make somefing of yerself, prove yer can . . . Now git to it!' Letting go Matthew's shirt he sank back to stare at the bloody earth where his legs should have been and waited for the stretcher bearers, if there were any and if he was still alive by the time any did come for him.

Others of his platoon had been separated; of the survivors lying here beneath the shielding carrier, none of them was worth a light: Jeff Downey with chubby cheeks flabby and pallid with terror and fatigue, one side of his shirt stiff with blackening blood, his or someone else's, Matthew hadn't felt inclined to find out; Farrell nursing

Matthew stared blankly at him, as yet incapable of a response. 'We've hurt men here.'

'Then get 'em on board and get this damned thing moving.'

The order brought Matthew back to his senses. No longer needing to be a leader, he could take relief in letting someone else do the leading. He and Bob, Bob now coming back to himself with an apologetic grin for his previous show of weakness, helped get their own wounded aboard. Farrell was the first to climb in.

Men's weight was pitted against machine. 'One – two – three, heave!' the officer shrieked. The vehicle lifted, its back wheels back on firm ground; the driver touched the accelerator. The wheels spun, briefly spraying dust over the men, then slipped back.

'Hold it! HOLD IT!' The officer's voice was full of panic. 'Again. One – two – three, heave! For Chrissake, HEAVE!'

From the direction of the crossing came the sudden rapid hammering of Bren-gun fire followed by the staccato crack of rifle fire. Caught by the knowledge that those at the river were having to turn and fight an enemy that had crept up on them, the men struggling with the truck paused.

The unsuspecting driver braked frantically but ineffectually and the vehicle slipped violently backwards. Cries of pain came from the wounded unceremoniously thrown about. Eyes rolling, the Indian soldiers exchanged cries of alarm in their own tongue, but it was Farrell leaning out over the tailboard of the stricken truck who said it explicitly.

'Oh, my bleeding Gawd, we're cut orf. We've 'ad it.' Very agile for one who a moment ago had been counted among the helpless injured, he was over of the tailboard and off, bolting towards the jungle.

'Stop that man!' To the officer's yell, Matthew added the power of his own lungs.

'Farrell – stay where you are!'

Farrell paused, Army training prevailing for all his panic, but his face as he turned twisted in an animal snarl of fear. 'Yer can't stop me. I've got a right ter git back ter me own lines. I'm pissin' orf.'

In one quick movement, Matthew unslung the rifle he still had on his back, levelling it at the man's groin. 'You do and I'll cripple you.'

In that moment he knew himself capable of carrying out the threat. It was as though he were another person, not because of his dislike of Farrell, but cold, clinical, the indurate soldier, Army-crafted, a machine, hating what he had become. But he'd halted Farrell who for a moment stood uncertain, though whether he would have defied his corporal's threat or not was not to be discovered as twin dark shapes roared over the rim of the trees, their shadows passing between the sun and the men below. A clatter of machine-gun fire scattered men in all directions, as though a stone had dropped on a cluster of marbles.

Matthew did a nightmare scramble for the carrier again, it seemingly a mile away as he felt rather than saw a line of dust spurts heading his way. In his own panic, he never even heard the explosion of the direct hit on the truck he had been helping to shove.

The attacks continued into the afternoon. In the centre of the road the truck was ablaze, now interlocked with a ten-tonner that had come from nowhere it seemed. From the smoking cab the officer's body hung amid shreds of burned clothing gently wafting away in the upcurrent of heat from the vehicle. Of Farrell there was no sign. He had legged it to the trees and was gone.

The sun going down saw the waves of planes depart. The bridge was at least still being defended, with the heavy hammering of a Bren-gun which sounded almost dignified against the excited clatter of an enemy machine-gun. Occasionally there came the dull flat detonation of a mortar bomb. At one time he fancied he could hear the hollow cough of a bomb as it left the mortar's barrel, the enemy too close for comfort if he was right. After a while it ceased, the operators perhaps moving closer to their goal, ignoring the broken vehicles nearby, but his uneasiness lingered. Those passing him in the sudden darkness that descends in the tropics trod warily, bent double, weapon held tense as they tried to probe the shadows either side of the road.

It made the flesh creep, this sensation of being watched, imagination magnifying fear tenfold. But fear had no place here. There was work to do, a way to be made for vehicles laden with wounded and supplies to get through to the bridge. In the darkness lit by lurid flashes, Matthew heaved and sweated helping to clear blockages While all around came the incessant chirruping of insects impervious to the racket of men locked in battle. At least while the sound of fighting continued there was hope of getting through.

Should it cease, it would mean the enemy had taken control.

It was with relief that he saw a staff car approaching out of the darkness, followed by a lorry full of Indian troops. The staff car held two obvious junior officers, even though they had ripped off their lapels and thrown away their caps, and a burly senior officer also minus his insignia.

With the road narrowed by the shattered ten-tonner, the car stopped. The burly officer got out. 'Where's your officer, corporal?'

Matthew indicated the body hanging from the burned-out truck. The man sighed, surveying the tangled wreckage. 'Not having much luck here.'

As Matthew explained his lack of men and tools, the lips beneath the dusty moustache gave a small, tight, tired, smile. 'My men will take over, corporal. Corporal . . .?'

'Ward, sir,' Matthew supplied.

'I'm Captain Weatherill. You and your men get some rest. You may need it.' He nodded towards the flashes around the bridge up ahead. 'By the way, the Japs have cut the road at Mokpalin,' he added as calmly as if announcing a cricket score.

Mokpalin, only three miles back, meant they were virtually caught in a neat pincer movement. For a moment, a feeling of doom spread through Matthew together with an irrational impulse to run towards the bridge, to race across and keep going until he got home to Susan and safety. It came to him that he might very well never see her again.

'Dear God,' prayed the panic within him, 'please, get me out of this. Let it all be a dream.'

Beside him Bob's voice came hollow. 'You mean we're trapped?'

The sound of that voice returned Matthew's sanity to him in a rush.

'We're going to get out okay,' he said, more to still his own fears than to reassure Bob. His mouth sour, he lifted a hand to his eyes and with finger and thumb grubbed out the caked dust that had collected at the inner corners. To ease the ache between his shoulder-blades he straightened his back. It was a gesture Weatherill immediately took as determination.

'Good man,' he grunted and left them to find a hole by the road to creep into and rest for a while.

Beside him Bob was fast asleep. Other men also were sleeping, but his own rest was fitful. For something to keep his imagination at bay he took a sip of the warm metallic water from his canteen, rinsed it around his mouth and spat it out, thick and evil, then took another sip and swallowed it. In the canteen the water slapped hollowly. How grand to have been able to wash, if only his face. To think of millions of gallons of fresh water flowing by just half a mile away. He listened to the spasmodic firing and wondered how much longer the two sides would continue taking pot shots at each other. He thought of Susan, the child she bore. He thought drowsily that if he were to get up now before it got light and go towards the firing, the river, there might be a chance . . .

A hand on his shoulder brought him awake, grabbing for his rifle. The grip tightened.

'Easy, lad.' Weatherill stood over him. 'Be light in a few minutes. Get your men together.'

Firing could still be heard from the bridge, a little more energetic in the fast-brightening tropical morning. The driver of the staff car, a cheeky Cockney, was handing out cubes of corned beef, the tin opened with his bayonet. 'We're orf, mate,' he said to Matthew. ''Ad a dekko darn the road. It ain't so bad furver along. A few obstructions but we can all git fru. Once we're over that bleedin' bridge we'll all 'ave a nice cuppa tea at HQ.'

Matthew grinned at his Cockney optimism and was on the point of helping himself to a greasy cube of the corned beef when a terrific triple explosion rocked the already pink dawn.

For a second or two the firing from both sides stopped as though paralysed by the tremendous paroxysm, and in the lull its echoes rumbled away into the distance with slowly diminishing reverberations.

'Mother of Jesus! What the hell was that?' one of the junior officers called out, running over.

Weatherill's answer was one of incredulity. 'They've blown the bridge.' A pall of smoke was spiralling slowly above the tree-tops.

The other man's voice shook. 'Bloody HQ. Couldn't wait for us. Left us in the lurch, thousands of us. They panicked.'

Weatherill didn't dispute him. Headquarters had probably had no alternative if the Japanese had been threatening to swarm across. It had been the plan, to delay the enemy's advance on Rangoon enough to allow Allied reinforcements to arrive.

After the first shock of the explosion, hostilities resumed with even greater ferocity, each man now desperately fighting for his own life, gone all thoughts of saving transport and artillery.

Weatherill lost no time. 'We'll try the river further upstream. Thank God this isn't the monsoon. The river should be low.'

'What about the wounded?' Matthew asked. The enemy, it was rumoured, had its own methods with casualties. Weatherill didn't even look at him.

'If they can walk and if they can be quiet, they come too.'

His words were met by silence, the men around him knowing there was no other suggestion to be made. He waited a moment or two for any there might be, then turned and without a word moved towards the trees. The others followed mutely, the green world closing in barely thirty feet into the trees, hiding the abandoned wounded quickly from guilt-ridden sight.

Here even any continuing rifle fire was muffled, the canopy a hundred feet or more above them cutting out all sunlight in a tangle of vines and parasitic growth, echoing only to the whirring of insects and the bell-like early-morning calls of forest birds. Grey wreathing mists of morning lay in motionless flat layers, but as the sun rose they turned delicate pink and lifted steadily through the ceiling of miniature jungle above to disappear. Within minutes that ceiling was pressing the heat down on the men, saturating them with sweat, the soft and spongy earth under their feet smelling dank.

Progress remained snail-like. In some areas the great mottled tree-trunks stood like dead-straight pillars of some vast cathedral, lianas draped from one to the other with curtains of green moss hanging from them. Sometimes the forest thinned enough to allow shafts of sunlight through and vegetation to become rampant, scrambling for light with vivid colouring, thick clumps of bamboo around which the men must time after time make diversions. In half an hour they had covered just half a mile, bearing northeast as much as those diversions allowed.

Breathing heavily from the now steamy heat which by midday would reach ninety degrees or more, arms aching from pushing aside the tough, woody creepers, legs aching from negotiating a surprisingly undulating terrain, from somewhere to their left came the gurgle of water.

'Should see some open space soon,' Weatherill predicted in a whisper. 'Paddy fields probably. We could be easily spotted. Keep your heads down.'

After ten more minutes pushing through undergrowth, they came upon a proper path, the forest beginning to thin.

In the sudden brilliant sunlight, Weatherill crouched just off the path, beckoning to his men to follow suit. 'I think there's a village ahead. Could be sitting ducks if we blunder in there. We'd best skirt it, find the river and somewhere to swim across. Come on, but quietly.'

He stood up, the rest taking their cue from him. A sudden movement of foliage, the metallic sound of hands

on rifles, froze the group. In a strange language, a guttural
voice grated out a command.

From nowhere there appeared small men in drab tunics
with double belts, short legs bound in puttees to the knee,
and split canvas boots that divided the big toes from the
rest. Black shoe-button eyes trained on the group from
behind levelled rifles with incredibly long bayonets; for all
their size each man looked strong, immensely capable and
very much a fighting man, utterly at home in this hostile
environment.

One by one the surprised men let their rifles fall and
lifted their arms in the time-honoured abject signal of
surrender as their captors moved closer. There were some
twenty-five of them plus their officer – that many moving
so silently no one had heard them at all.

With a sickness pounding in his chest, Matthew lifted
his arms with the rest, submitted himself to be searched
by a soldier reaching only to his shoulder in height. His
pockets and ration pack were emptied of all he possessed:
silver cigarette case, lighter, a little Burmese money, a
photo of Susan. It was the photo that hurt most, seeing
it scrutinised then torn into four pieces and flung away.
The silver cigarette case and lighter were handed to the
Japanese officer who immediately pocketed them with a
satisfied smile.

Chapter 16

'We'll get another letter from him very soon. You really must stop fretting, Susan. It isn't good for the baby.'

Susan eyed her mother-in-law, just managing to hold back the tears that threatened and which always annoyed the woman. But every time she thought of Matthew's last letter she couldn't help them rising to the surface.

The one prior to that had said he had been over the moon about her news of the baby, and she'd been so happy that he was happy. It had said they were leaving Bombay though where for, as usual, hush-hush.

His last letter had come two days ago, a single page written in pencil in such an obvious hurry she could hardly read it, the soiled notepaper in an even more soiled envelope telling her not to worry, he was all right, that in itself worrying her more although she wasn't sure why. It bore a military Rangoon postmark. Rangoon was in Burma, Mr Ward had told her, and she had heard fear echoing in his tone.

Her geography never good, she'd quickly consulted an atlas, alarmed how near the fighting Matthew had been sent. News from that part of the world had all been of disaster: the sinking of two large Royal Navy ships, the

Prince of Wales, and the *Repulse*, the fall of Hong Kong on Christmas Day, then Singapore on the fifteenth of February four weeks ago. Now it was March. There was fighting in Burma and Matthew's last letter, grubby and stained, made her shiver with imaginings she daren't voice; none of them dared, though the look on their faces said they were thinking the same as she was.

Why was it, Jenny thought, that when she was with Ronald she could talk without a pause about all sorts of things, completely at ease in his company, yet the very anticipation of going to meet him never failed to fill her with strange reluctance, wishing she didn't have to?

'Have a quick drink in the pub tonight?' he'd whisper as they passed in a corridor, if their off-duty hours coincided. 'Wait for you outside.'

She would nod, smile, aware of a sinking feeling, a wish to be doing anything other than meeting him, even preferring to go home to spend a dull evening with Mumsy. There was none of that excited palpitation a girl in love was supposed to experience – the way she used to feel all those years ago when Matthew Ward came into sight or inadvertently touched her. The touch of Ronald's hand on hers did nothing, though if he kissed her, her body would stir, responding of its own accord. Then her head would start to send messages that this wasn't love, but a natural response to the touch of any man halfway handsome. Yet it made no sense to shy away from the knowledge that marriage to Ronald could be the best thing to happen to her; she would become the wife of a general practitioner.

'It's still early days,' she'd hedged. 'Too many people are rushing into marriage because it seems the right thing to do.'

'Don't you want to marry me?' he had asked only last week, towards the end of February. What could she say?

'Of course I do.'

But was she lying, to him and herself? They had had their very first row, as far as it was possible to row with Ronald, who was always even-tempered.

'Then for God's sake why delay it? It's not as if I've nothing to offer you. My family's pretty well off. My father's a GP. Soon I'll be one as well.'

She knew that. He was taking his finals in a couple of weeks and was more than certain that he'd pass. He had talked often of the day when he too would be a GP expected to go in with his father as a junior partner. Perhaps it was that which made her so reluctant about marriage and the assumption that she would accompany him to Bristol. It meant leaving her mother, who still deemed herself lonely after all this time with Jenny not getting home regularly each night. Her mother was destined to become even more isolated if Jenny went off to live on the other side of the country – the other side of the world as far as she was concerned.

'If you go into your father's practice I shall end up in Bristol,' she argued obstinately and saw his lips tighten a fraction. 'There's my mother to think of. I can't leave her all on her own.'

She could have suggested he find some other practice around here, but some quiet little voice said it would be tempting fate – he might agree and she would then have no option but to say yes to his expectations of their marrying.

He had fallen quiet, had sat away from her, his brow furrowed. She too had sat silent over her mild ale and the evening during which they would normally have chattered away like a couple of monkeys had become long and tense until it was she who said she ought to be going to catch the last bus home. He had nodded, got up, got her coat for her and helped her on with it and had said, 'See you tomorrow then. I'll see you to the bus stop.'

This week, during another quick drink in the pub opposite the hospital, the row that had been simmering, exploded. Quietly, but it exploded just the same.

'I've had enough of this, Jenny.' Ronald's voice was harsher than she had ever heard it. 'What the hell do I have to do to show you how much I love you?'

She had to say it now. 'I don't want to go to live in Bristol all that way away.'

'I can't go without you.'

And now she must add: 'Then can't you try for a practice somewhere local, around here?' There, she had said it, had burned her last bridge.

Ronald looked at her, his brows meeting in anger at her selfishness. 'You want me to scratch around here looking for some half-baked practice that'll take me years to get anywhere with when I've an already made place with my father? You must be mad, Jenny. Don't you want to see me get on?'

'Of course I do.' She felt lame.

'Don't you love me?'

'Yes, Ronald.' She wished he wouldn't keep pushing that question.

'Well, it doesn't sound like it to me.'

A group of American servicemen with smooth smart uniforms and girls on their arms, bustling past, filling the pub with their loud easy twang and high spirits, put paid to the couple's quiet argument. Ronald threw them a frown, and repeated his statement a little more audibly. 'It doesn't sound like it to me.'

'Because I don't want to go traipsing all the way to Bristol, leaving my mother? What is this, Ronald – a demand for self-sacrifice?'

'In a way, yes.'

'But you're not prepared to sacrifice yourself when it comes to you.'

'Look, I shall be the breadwinner. I've got to consider what's best for our future. Can't you see that? If you really loved me, Jenny, it wouldn't seem to you like self-sacrifice – as you call it.'

There came screams of laughter from the GIs' girls. Jenny felt tears come into her eyes. 'If that's what you think of me, Ronald, the little lamb ready to follow its shepherd up hill and down dale, I've got a career too. I've studied hard, and I've still got a lot of studying to do, and I want to get somewhere, not just be a GP's wife, sitting at home, joining nice little ladies' clubs and doing your book work. Eventually I'd have liked to go into the QAs.'

This was the Queen Alexandra's Imperial Military Nursing Service Reserve. She hadn't really thought about going into the QAs before, but she thought of it now, more out of anger than ambition.

Ronald was staring at her. The ruckus from the GIs and their girls was getting worse, but they had good money to spend and the landlord would suffer them. The look on Ronald's face tore at Jenny's whole being.

'I had no idea that was all you cared for me, Jenny. You'd sooner join up than marry me.'

'No, darling, that's not what I meant. I want to marry you.' Now, suddenly, she did, seeing herself throwing away the chance of a lifetime. Did she really think she wanted to go on nursing for the rest of her life, to go off and be a Queen Alexandra's nurse, to take orders when she could live in comfort with a man who loved her? 'Ronald, I really do love you.'

He sat looking at her for a long while, as she watched him, visualising what was going on in his mind, her protestations fallen short. Then he stood up, and got her coat, as always helping her on with it, for he was a caring man even when hurt and angry. Wordlessly, she let him guide her from the now noisy pub. Outside, he took her in his arms and kissed her.

'Perhaps I have been rushing things,' he said in the quiet night, the sounds from inside muffled by the closure of the pub door. 'What I wanted to tell you, darling, is that I got my results today. I've passed.'

She leaned back from his embrace. 'Why didn't you tell me?'

'I don't know. I was going to, but somehow we ended up discussing something else instead.' He wouldn't say row. Easier to call it discussing. But he wasn't finished yet.

'Jenny, darling, I know now that you're not yet ready to commit yourself – not to me or to anyone. But I love you. And I think, deep down, you love me, but there's something in the way. Maybe it's your mother. But you must break away from the hole you're stuck in. So I think it best I let you consider things before you make up your mind what you want to do. In a week or two I'll be leaving to go home to start up in my father's practice. I'll write to you and if you do change your mind about coming to Bristol, I'll be waiting. I'll keep on loving you, Jenny. I won't give up hope. I just want you to think about everything and what we are throwing away.'

Tears were streaming down Jenny's cheeks. Now was the time to burst out that she did love him, that she wanted to go with him. But she didn't. For the most futile of reasons. And the moment vanished.

A bleak spring had followed a bleak new year, that first elation at the United States coming into the war dissipating; everywhere Jenny saw set faces that spoke of grim determination to believe things must only get better.

In the Middle East, Rommel, seemingly invincible, had struck back and recaptured Benghazi. At sea the German battleships *Scharnhorst* and *Gneisenau* slipped their hide-out at Brest under the very noses of the British Navy and in attempting to sink them the RAF lost forty planes. Ceylon was raided by the Japanese, the British Eastern Fleet withdrew to Kenya; Britain had abandoned the Far East.

The London Hospital's outpatient department seemed to

be full of women showing the strain of trying not to dwell on loved ones away. Women with drawn faces, complaining of backache, neuralgia, stomach pains, stiff necks, strange agitation, trembling hands, 'I c'n 'ardly keep meself still in the mornin', doctor'; 'I'm fair sick of this bloody back of mine'; 'I've got these legs, doctor, wot keeps on swellin''; and usually as he examined whatever complaint presented itself, came the inevitable self-diagnosis: 'Wiv'art me ole man at 'ome I feel lorst.'

Jenny, helping in outpatients, knew how they felt thinking of those absent faces. Too often she thought of one absent face in particular. Since the fall of Rangoon in Burma, Susan Ward said she'd not had any letters from her husband and the Wards were growing anxious. Lots of wives and mothers were going through that strain, added to which was the constant worry of eking out the rations for those still at home. Shoppers needed to be ever more watchful for opportunities to present themselves in the food line.

It wasn't unusual to see whole streets come to life with hurrying women. Coats, aprons, scarves billowing like schooners in full sail as they converged on some butcher's shop from which whispers had emanated: ''E's got offal!' Jenny's mother and even the proud Mrs Ward joined in the hasty advance. Jenny would pass a growing queue of women now waiting patiently and not leaving until every last scap of off-ration meat had gone. Nothing stopped the unending search for something nutritious to fill a plate: horse meat, goat, stringy fishy-tasting whale meat being tried out.

'I got a little bit of goat meat,' Jenny's mum told her on one occasion – succulent, tender meat it was too, except, unused to such rich fare, they were both sick. Jenny stayed off duty all next day much to the displeasure of the ward sister. Otherwise, things went on as normal, the tip-and-run daylight raids on country towns like York and Bath and Exeter (Jenny thought of Jean Summerfield whose family had left London to escape all that) virtually ignored by Londoners, who had suffered the Blitz.

The evening she came home from the hospital, still a little queasy from the enjoyable meal of goat meat, she met Susan wandering along by herself, her coat tight about her stomach. The early March evening was still light, summer time's extra hour still prevailing. Susan looked wan, and hardly smiled as she saw Jenny coming towards her from the bus stop.

'Have you heard from Matthew yet?' was the first question out of her mouth. Susan shook her head.

'Nothing yet. I hope he's all right.'

'He's bound to be. Otherwise they'd have said. You'd have heard.'

'It's been nearly three weeks. I've not been out of the house in ages. I'm so fed up. I'd like to go to the pictures or something, but his parents don't go. I can't go on my own, so I'm stuck.'

Jenny found herself amazed at how easily the girl had slipped from concern at not hearing anything from Matthew to talking at far greater length of her own boredom. She would have thought the former worry would oust everything else from her mind.

'If you like,' she offered, giving Susan the benefit of any doubts, 'we could go to the pictures together. I'm off next weekend. *Casablanca* is on at the Regent in Mare Street. There are bound to be long queues, but we could go early on Saturday afternoon, if you can stand lining up.'

Susan's face was a picture of eagerness. 'Oh, that's ever so nice of you. I'd love to do that, I really would.'

'Then that's what we'll do.'

In her bedroom Susan stared into the mirror at the hardly noticeable lump. It would get larger and larger and she'd never be able to escape. Going to the Regent with Jenny Ross looked like being her last trip out, with Mrs Ward getting ever more attentive.

Just over four months pregnant, and being slightly built, even that tiniest bulge made her look dreadful. There was no one to reassure her that she still looked beautiful, no one to lay a loving hand on her stomach or to gaze on her with pride in her and himself at what they had achieved, no one to tell her she was a clever girl and that he adored her. When this baby was born there'd be no one there to hold it and gaze down on it in wonder. Only God could say when Matthew would return home. As yet she'd not heard a thing from him since that last letter at the end of February. It was March now. Early March, it was true, but waiting made it seem longer. She trembled for him, dared not think of his never coming back. Whatever would she do without him? The thought made her feel sick.

Hastily, she turned from the mirror, trying to push such dreadful thoughts from her, and feverishly got dressed.

They'd get his letter soon. Military mail from that part of the world was a bugger, the time it took.

A ring on the front doorbell swept away all her dismal anxiety. Maybe it was the postman. Hurrying from her room she leaned over the banister in time to see her father-in-law closing the door. Aware of her standing there, he looked up, his eyes wide as though with guilt, but she knew it was fear for she had seen the telegram he held. Even from here the blurred bold black letters OHMS leapt out at her, searing through her brain, sending her rushing headlong down the stairs. 'Matthew! It's about Matthew.'

Leonard caught her as she reached him, took her arm and guided her into the lounge through which the early March sunlight was slanting.

'Lilian,' he called as he sat Susan down in one of the armchairs; she felt struck dumb with growing terror. 'Lilian, come here, dear. It's important.'

As Mrs Ward came hurrying in, Susan found her voice. 'It's Matthew! Oh, God, it's Matthew!'

Neither took any notice of her or seemed to hear her as Leonard tore open the envelope, extracting the buff paper to read. He looked up bleakly.

'It says Matthew's missing.'

'No!' Susan's voice rose to a scream. She leapt up, tore the telegram from his hands, but the words blurred, her brain seemed to be exploding and the scream that came from her lips seemed not to be her own, a hollow screaming that went on and on: 'He's dead . . . Matthew's dead . . .'

The telegram fell from her fingers and she felt herself taken on a blind, headlong rush from the room, though

where she was going she had no idea; she found herself
clinging on to the newel post of the stairs, unable to let go
of it. And still the hollow, terrible screaming continued,
consuming her.

What happened next was a vague blur of being picked
up, of being carried, of being laid down, then shaken until
her head felt it would fall off her shoulders. That irrational
fear was what brought her to her senses and she found
herself looking into the stern face of her mother-in-law.

'Get a hold of yourself, Susan. You must remember the
baby – his baby.'

Damn the baby! Tears squeezed between her eyelids as
she screwed them tight. 'Matthew's dead . . .'

The hands holding hers were like stiff, dry claws giving
no comfort at all. 'He's not dead, Susan. It says he's
missing. They will trace him soon. We must cling to that
hope. You must cling to it. For his sake. For the sake of his
baby.'

'That's all you care about,' she burst out in her grief.
'*His* baby – a baby to take *his* place. You don't care about
me at all, how I feel.'

'We do, Susan.' They didn't, but she had no strength
left to argue.

'The pain's still there in my stomach,' she complained from
her bed. She'd been in bed for two days, ever since the dull
ache had started. Now she saw Mrs Ward's expression of
sympathetic concern change to one of apprehension.

'The doctor said it isn't what we thought it might be,
but that you are upset and probably strained yourself when

you lost control of yourself, and that we must just keep an eye on you. But doctors can be wrong and I really think we ought to get you to a hospital if this doesn't improve.'

'No!' Susan's voice rose in terror. She had a naked fear of hospitals; it dated from when she had been a child and had had her tonsils out. It had been an awful experience. The smell of the place, a mixture of antiseptic and ether, its green and cream tiled walls and age-yellowed ceilings, all pressed in on her, and the hush of the ward as night had come down emphasised the feeling of being alone away from her parents, shut away from the cosy world outside as though it was a different place – as hell might be, or death. She'd cried for her mother and a stern-faced nurse had told her to be quiet. Taken on a hard, rumbling trolley along corridors and into a stark white room with horrid glittering steel instruments hanging from the ceilings, an evil-smelling rubber mask had been put over her face until her mind seemed to swirl away into a roaring blackness. The next day her throat had hurt terribly and she wasn't allowed to eat and when she cried another nurse had told her off. And all the time that peculiar rustling hush and muted voices and that horrible disinfectant smell. She'd never been near a hospital since, unable even to bring herself to visit anyone in there. The mere thought of going into one brought back the memories of its smell. It must have done something to her because to this day her whole body would cringe from anything savouring of it, from those with a hacking cough to someone with a cut finger. Even an unsightly scar could make her body tingle with revulsion. How Jenny Ross or anyone could bring herself to be a nurse was beyond her.

Mrs Ward was looking down at her. How could she be expected to understand? 'If the pain gets any worse, you will *have* to go to hospital.'

This left Susan gritting her teeth against the dull ache for fear of the threat being carried out. Bidden by the doctor to lie as still as possible in bed for the next week, she did all that was asked of her, determined no one would get her anywhere near the gates of any hospital.

Mrs Ward wrote to Susan's parents. They came hurrying down from Birmingham; the content of Mrs Ward's letter had frightened them. They found Susan looking much better than they had thought, with the pain almost gone, but she was still confined to bed – just in case, said the doctor.

As soon as Susan saw them, she burst into tears and, when Mrs Ward prudently retired from the room, she threw her arms around her mother to be cuddled and crooned over in privacy. She hadn't realised until then how much she had missed her mother.

'Mum, oh, Mum – take me home. I hate it here.'

Her mother let go of her slightly to gaze around the pretty pink bedroom. 'Whatever for, love? This is really lovely. Matthew's parents look after you so well, better'n like I ever could in our crowded house.'

'Don't talk of Matthew,' Susan pleaded tearfully. 'The telegram said he's missing, but it's only another way of telling us he's bin killed.'

'Don't say things like that, Sue.' Her mother leaned

back to look up at her husband, seeking help from him, to which he responded in his usual way, merely repeating what had already been said as though that cemented it all perfectly.

'No, don't say things like that, Sue.'

'You've got to 'ave faith, love. He'll come back, right as rain, you'll see. When this war's all over, love, you and him, you'll both pick up like where you left off, and you'll 'ave a little baby then to look after, like. So you got to be strong and look after yourself, for Matthew and for his baby's sake.'

'I could do, at home,' Susan whimpered as her mother gently broke free of her arms, almost as though she were glad to be released of them. 'If I was home, Mum, with you to look after me, everything'd be all right. I hate it here. With Matthew gone, I don't feel I've got any business here.'

'Sue, love, he ain't gone. He's alive somewhere, waiting to be found by the Army. You make it sound as if you think he'll never come back. And look, love, we couldn't have you home with us. You know there's no room. There was hardly no room when you was single, much less when you've got a baby with you. And honestly, our Sue, look what you've got here. No, love, I do think you're better off staying here with Mr and Mrs Ward. They really are nice people and you're being so well looked after.'

So that was that. Abandoned by her own family. Over the next couple of weeks, she rested, slowly recovering, the baby still firmly entrenched inside her. There had been moments when she would have put her hands together if she had lost the baby. Growing more convinced that Matthew must have been killed, lying unfound somewhere in the jungle with creepers and undergrowth hiding his body and (the mere thought made her weep until her eyes appeared permanently red and swollen) the horrid creeping things slowly devouring it, a baby would only be a painful reminder of the love and happiness they'd once shared. She couldn't give her love to a baby when her love for Matthew was of no use to anyone any more. Then, as she recovered, she wasn't so much glad as relieved that she hadn't lost the baby after all. It hadn't grown so much that she was yet attached to it in her mind, but if Matthew had really been killed and was at this moment actually looking down on her, he'd never forgive her for such thoughts about it as she'd had.

If only she'd been asked to go home, it might all be so different. But now she was being pampered all the more by Mrs Ward, who was nothing to her, this in-law business thrust on her, yet was assuming the role of loving mother. She could see no escape. At home she might for the time being go out and enjoy herself, still go off to dances, perhaps dance with some of the young servicemen, Yanks, Canadian, the Free French, the Polish and the British boys, and still be admired for a while. Here, she was trapped, expected to play the wife when there was no one to play wife to.

To escape the sensation of being smothered and continually watched over, she would spend hours in her room reading the limp, buff-coloured magazines that wartime austerity forbade shiny covers. Sometimes she read increasingly tatty books from the library, love books mostly – easy-to-follow love stories with handsome heroes and violet-eyed heroines. They'd bring back a flood of memories, desolate now, of when she and Matthew had made love, had been in love. She'd pretend he was still making love to her, but it brought such wishing that she tried not to imagine it too much. Then she'd throw the book down and weep with loneliness, stifling her sobs in her pillow in case Mrs Ward came hurrying in to see what was the matter. As if the woman couldn't see why she was crying.

Chapter 17

Halfway through April, when her stomach was really beginning to show and not much chance of going out anywhere presented itself, there was no one to talk to. With Matthew's sister serving as a Wren in Southampton even Louise's company was denied her. She'd have felt even more trapped if it hadn't been for Jenny Ross popping in now and again. She'd become a good friend and confidante.

For Jenny, an hour or two with Susan on those evenings when she wasn't with her friends from the London could be a change from sitting with her mother who seemed to want to lean on her more and more. She often wondered how Mumsy would have coped had she married Ronald.

It had been strange not seeing his face about the hospital. She had found herself looking for him, missing him, but as anyone would miss a face no longer there, she told herself. One didn't have to love the person in order to feel keenly that empty place his going had left. She busied herself and put him from her mind.

As promised, he had written to her, a friendly letter, a little formal perhaps, wondering if she had thought any more about the things he'd last spoken of. He phrased the question itself slightly obliquely – no mention at all about the ring, which she still had tucked away in a box. She had replied, sounding just as friendly, just as formal, skirting the question. She had not meant it to be such a short letter, but there wasn't much to say. Time had gone on too long for that. She had wanted so much to say she'd changed her mind but when it came down to it, couldn't.

As time went on the wish had diminished, the dilemma's sharp edges had blunted somewhat. His departure had left a hole, but had she truly loved him, surely it would have left a much larger hole that would have taken a lot more to fill. And that impulsive statement she had made at the time about joining the QAs, then just a silly idea to get out of a spot, began to take more shape. The more she thought about it, the more attractive it was becoming. She'd be given a chance to travel overseas, to see the world, to meet new people, to expand her life. Mumsy wouldn't be too pleased but she had to get out of the rut that Ronald had accused her of being in. The QAs had such smart uniforms too, grey and scarlet with ties and snappy-brimmed hats, unlike the drab dress of ordinary nurses. She'd be tending fighting men instead of, now the Blitz was over, ordinary civilian ills and ailments. But first she had to pass her remaining exams. Prepared to work hard, she'd thrown herself into her work and looked very like passing her exams with flying colours come summer. All that would remain then would be to sit her finals that would turn her into an SRN. Then it would be off into the QAs in earnest.

She sat now talking to Susan in the living room. Mrs

Ward was out at one of her many women's meetings, Mr
Ward in the lounge listening to the evening news on the
wireless and reading his evening paper.

'The Red Cross hasn't come up with anything at
all,' Susan was saying, sitting back in a fireside chair
nursing the growing bulge over her stomach. She looked
particularly down this evening. 'His parents have made
lots of enquiries, but he's never been traced. They can only
guess he might be a prisoner of war but the Japanese aren't
giving out any lists.'

'But they should,' Jenny said, aghast. She had felt the
news of Matthew, or lack of it, as keenly as anyone, and
in private had shed tears. 'The Geneva Convention says all
sides must declare lists of prisoners.'

'The Japanese apparently think they're exempt because
they never signed anything, or whatever. So no one knows
if Matthew's been captured or gone missing or been . . .
you know.' Tears flooded the deep blue eyes.

'You mustn't give up hope,' Jenny said in an effort to
console.

'What's the point?' Susan got up and began pacing the
room, going to fiddle with the heavy curtains that concealed
the blackout material, drawn now with the gathering dusk
outside. Jenny watched her.

'If he's been taken prisoner, that has to be better news
than it might have been.' Meant to give comfort, it only
came out clumsy and tactless. She tried to amend it.
'You've just got to hang on to hope.'

Susan swung round, almost viciously. 'Hope! It's all
right for you to talk. You didn't love him like I did, so how

do you know what it's like not knowing what's happened to him?'

To combat the pain that retort invoked, Jenny got up and came to stand beside her. When she spoke her voice sounded flat even to her. 'Can you be that sure no one knows how you feel?'

Susan gave a sullen shrug. 'All I know is that if he's a prisoner of war, it'll be years before he ever comes home again, not till the war's over, and that could be God knows how long. And in the meantime, there's me stuck here. If I go on living in this mausoleum much longer, I'll go mad. I've got to get away from here before I get any bigger and can't at all.'

Again came the feeling that Susan wasn't thinking so much of Matthew, possibly in danger if indeed he hadn't been killed, as of herself and the loneliness *she* felt. Everyone was lonely who had a loved one away fighting, not knowing if they'd be killed or captured, but they usually kept it to themselves. Susan was too outspoken for her own good. It made her look bad.

'Where would you go if you left here?' she asked.

'Home. And as soon as I can. Trouble is, there's no room at me mum and dad's with our Robert and Les and our John there, and June and our Beryl. I'd rent a room somewhere nearby, but at least I'd be near my family. I'd have me mum near me. If only I wasn't having this baby . . .'

She broke off, not in shame at what she'd said, but swamped by the injustice of it all; Jenny could hear it in her tone. The girl's next words confirmed it.

'Why did all this have to happen to me? It's not fair! Landed with a baby, and Matthew God knows where.'

She began to pace around the room again while Jenny followed her with her eyes, the sympathy she had initially felt for the girl draining away.

'Haven't you stopped to think how dreadfully unfair it must be to Matthew?' She couldn't control the anger in her voice. 'Wherever he is, he can't be having much of a time either.'

She refused to think him dead. It was unthinkable. One day he would come home and take up his life again. That was all she ever wanted, to see him come home and be happy. The wish for that caught her like a pain. But not as great a pain as being compelled to keep her feelings for Matthew to herself when all she wanted was to sing them from the rooftops.

A day didn't go by that she didn't pray for his safe return. The notion of never seeing him again tore her to pieces. It was bad enough to know that if and when he did come home he and Susan could go off into the blue, that she would never see them again. But at least he would be in this world, somewhere. Far worse to know that he was gone from this world entirely. How dare this girl, his wife who professed to love him so dearly, take the news of his being missing as though she alone suffered – *her* loneliness, *her* grief, *her* plight, not his plight, not the worry and grief of his family, but hers.

Beneath the anger that welled up in Jenny was a dull ache for Matthew which she was sure would stay with her the rest of her life if he never came home again.

And here was Susan thinking of him only in terms of herself.

'Wherever he is?' Susan's voice had risen in near hysteria. 'Wherever he is? Don't you understand? He's dead. Matthew's dead! And here I am trying to be a wife, living with people that mean nothing to me.'

'You're carrying Matthew's child. His parents' grand-child. That's what they should mean to you, Susan.'

'Well, they don't. Everyone keeps saying he's been taken prisoner, but I *know* he's dead, lying out there some-where in that terrible jungle where no one can find him, his body being . . .'

'Don't talk like that!' Susan had conjured up visions in her mind too awful to bear. 'There had to be others with him. They'd have reported . . .'

'I don't care! All I know is he's not here and I am, and I can't take much more of this living with his parents. They're not *my* family.'

'They're your baby's family.'

'I don't care,' she said again. 'I don't want this baby anyway, not now Matthew's gone. All I want is to get away from here. I have to get away.'

She broke off in a flood of tears and threw herself back into the fireside chair, head twisted into one of its wings, her small body convulsed with weeping.

The door opened. Mrs Ward in hat and coat came hurrying into the room. 'Susan! What is the matter? I could hear you shouting as I came in.'

Mr Ward had followed her in, also alerted by the cries. 'What in God's name is going on?'

'Susan is upset,' Jenny offered but neither of them looked at her.

Mrs Ward came forward and lifted the still-weeping girl from her huddled position in the chair. 'This happens each time someone tries to offer sympathy,' she said sharply, and Jenny might have taken umbrage had she not seen the girl's reaction for herself and heard the things she had said.

'Come on now, Susan,' Mrs Ward was ordering as Jenny stood aside, unsure whether to stay or go, both of which seemed ill-mannered. 'Pull yourself together now. We're all worried and anxious, but it does no good to give way like this. We all have to be strong. We all have to believe he'll be returned to us. You're doing yourself and the baby no good. Matthew wouldn't want that. I'm taking you up to your room and you can rest there.'

Helping the girl to her feet, she looked at Jenny for the first time.

'Having visitors seems to upset her even more,' she said with a small, cold smile which Jenny could only take personally, this time smarting from the rebuff. But the things Susan had said made Jenny herself prefer not to pop in and see her again. Let the girl do what she wanted. It was none of her business. And yet came the thought that in the depths of her, Matthew *was* her business, would always be her business wherever he might be.

She had intended to wait until at least after the baby was born. But after one miserable evening in early May, still with no news at all of Matthew, and with Mrs Ward telling her for the umpteenth time that they were all worried and anxious for him, Susan made up her mind. Early next morning, she got up before Mr and Mrs Ward were awake and feverishly packed her suitcase with a few essentials. It mustn't be too heavy. She was nearly seven months and she didn't want to harm herself in any way carrying it.

She had enough money, thank God, something under twenty shillings a week serviceman's wife allowance, and her National Savings book. Mrs Ward had never taken anything from her for her keep and she had been able to save quite a bit.

She left a scribbled note to Mrs Ward on the kitchen table, lacking the courage to face her. Retrieving her ration book from the shelf where they were kept, she silently let herself out.

The sun hadn't yet risen. The horizon of Victoria Park with its trees clad in young green glimpsed between the houses opposite was a mere blush, and seemed to emphasise the quietness. It was Tuesday, just gone four thirty, too early even for workers to be up off to work. She couldn't remember the road feeling so quiet or looking so wide. Lined by trees in new leaf, it was filled with the fresh, clean fragrance of the park and the new day, in May not even tainted by chimney smoke. She mightn't have been in London at all. It was a morning that should have been savoured, but it only made her shiver.

Alone in this empty road, all the large bay windows of the bedrooms looking down at her like empty eye sockets witnessing her flight, for a few seconds Susan stood uncertain, fighting the impulse to run back indoors away from those accusing, silent windows that seemed to be asking what she thought she was doing. At least her mother-in-law's home offered protection and comfort. With no idea exactly where she would go, a strong temptation to run back was growing stronger. Then she thought of the woman becoming even more dictatorial once the baby was born. With a final shiver, not at the silence of the morning, but at the well-intentioned if unwanted help of her mother-in-law, Susan turned her face towards Mare Street and Cambridge Heath Road, the bus stop and freedom. Once she got back to Birmingham and her own family she would be all right. It was her only comforting thought on this lonely morning.

Euston was a mad-house of hurrying people by the time Susan got there. Panting engines, the sudden shriek of released steam, the rumble of trolleys full of mail and parcels, deafened her. The last time she was here had been on Matthew's arm, with him to defend her against all this. Now she was on her own, her figure pulled out of all shape by the baby it carried inside it. She felt lost, conspicuous, but no one took a blind bit of notice of her, being more locked up in themselves: people getting to work; couples saying farewell to each other; the men going back off leave. Uniforms of other countries jostled past her, the ever-attentive Americans alone giving her pretty face a quick appreciative glance until seeing her condition and looking away.

By now her mother-in-law would have been bringing her up a cup of tea, telling her she could get up when she felt like it or could have breakfast in bed if she didn't, coddling her, concerned and managing. Suddenly that managing seemed preferable to standing here not knowing where to find the platform she was supposed to be on. Panic came and went in waves as she tried to gather her thoughts together, attempting desperately to hold back the tears her plight was prompting.

Once she found the right platform, the man at the ticket barrier told her the train would be leaving in five minutes. Hauling her suitcase, five minutes seemed hardly long enough to find a carriage and she worried that the train would pull out to leave her standing helplessly on the platform. So few trains ran these days, she could be stranded for hours. She struggled on, the suitcase banging against her legs, almost ready to turn round and head back to Hackney.

The first four carriages were full of people standing in the corridors. The fifth carriage seemed less full and with a struggle she got herself in. There'd be no seats, not here with the corridor partially occupied by servicemen. How could she face standing all the way to Birmingham? If an empty seat couldn't be found, she would go back home. Home. It seemed odd that she should think of it as that now she was away from it. Her heart seemed to sink down at the realisation. She had no home. Common sense told her there was no room for her with her family, and she had shunned the one she'd left behind. Mr and Mrs Ward would be up by now, would have read her note, devastated, not knowing how to find her and bring her back. And she so desperately wanted to be brought back at this moment.

Just as she was on the verge of turning round and forcing her way off again, a voice with a faint northern accent spoke in her ear.

'Pardon me, my luv.'

She turned to see an elderly man in a cap rising from a seat in the near corner of the apartment beside which she was standing.

'Have my seat, luv,' he said, and taking hold of the suitcase, added, 'Allow me,' and hoisted it up on to the string rack above.

'When you want, I'll get it down for you, like.'

Indecision had been taken neatly out of her hands, and she accepted gratefully. The sailor next to her looked a little crestfallen that he'd not offered his seat as the train gave a jerk, then with several more slowly began to move.

'Ooh, love, what you doing here?'

Her mother, her blonde hair in curlers, stared at her from the back door on which Susan had prudently tapped rather than surprise her mother by walking in on her after all this time away. 'How'd you get here? Is anyone with you? You're not on your own?'

'I've come home, Mum,' was all Susan could gulp.

'Good Lord. You'd best come in, love. How'd you get here?'

'I came on the train.'

It had been a long, drawn-out journey, the train stopping and starting as all trains seemed to do in wartime, sometimes to let a troop train through or one carrying munitions, sometimes for no known reason at all. She'd eaten a Spam sandwich she'd bought at Euston, somewhat stale, its grey corners turned up, but there'd been nothing to drink; that train had not carried refreshments. People going on journeys usually brought their own, just in case.

At New Street station she'd had some baked beans on toast and a much-needed cup of tea, then had come straight here on a bus. She felt tired and a little sick from the rather strong-tasting baked beans that were already repeating on her.

She was glad to follow her mother into the single living room. Nothing had changed, the room still looked worn, shabby, comfortable.

Susan had expected to find no one at home other than her mother, with everyone this afternoon still at work or school. So she was surprised to see her grandparents sitting there, having looked up expectantly at her entrance. Now her grandad was rising on his rickets-curved legs to greet her.

'Now then, there's a surprise, gel. Didn't expect to see you, like. What you doing 'ere?'

'That's what I asked her,' her mother put in as Susan leaned forward to give his lips beneath their bristling grey moustache a kiss.

She went over and kissed her grandmother too, feeling the bristles on her chin dig sharply into her like tiny needles. Her grandmother cut them with scissors.

'Nice to see you, luv. Y'look a bit peaky, love. 'Spect it's the baby. Y'r mam told us, but you ain't never come a-visiting. Is y'r husband with you, love?'

'He's away,' her mother explained quickly as Susan's

eyes began to mist. 'An' she will look a bit peaky, like, not getting any news about him. I told you, Mum, they reported him missing, like, and nothing more's been heard. Come on, now, our Sue. Sit down and tell us why you're here and I'll get you a nice cup of tea. And I expect you're hungry an' all. So why're you here then, luv?'

'I couldn't stay with Matthew's people any longer – not now he's not here.'

'They ain't turned you out, have they? I wouldn't think . . .'

'No, Mum, I left there.'

'Whatever for? A nice cosy place there to live, everything you want there.'

'I can't stand it there, Mum. I can't stand being told what to do and when to do it and what I should eat and when I should rest, and when I should go to bed, and I mustn't do this and I must do that. I can't stand it.' The words flowed out of her, all the pent-up things she'd been unable to say to anyone.

'But . . .' Her mother was looking at her, bewildered, a little concerned and, with the truth of her visit dawning on her, a little wary. 'But where d'you think you can go? Look, love, I don't want to appear hard and unkind or not caring or anything. I do care. But there's no room here at all, if you're thinking of coming here. I'd love to look after you, you and the baby, when it comes. I'd love to. My first-ever grandchild. Y'r grandma here'll be a great-grandma. Y'r looking forward to that, ain't you, Mum? But staying here, that's another thing, love. Y'see, last week they was bombed out in one of those daylight tip-and-run raids. House was condemned. Cracked walls and the roof's had it. Until it's repaired they've had to come here to live. That's why they're sleeping down here, don't y'see?'

For the first time Susan noticed the sagging double bed in the corner where the old scratched oak sideboard used to be. The sideboard was probably down in the cellar with all the other junk. Too damp for anyone to sleep down there even though during the night-time raids before she'd met Matthew, all the family had endured its damp conditions for safety's sake.

'I didn't know,' she mumbled. 'What am I going to do now?'

'Well, I think you ought to go back to Mr and Mrs Ward. They won't be cross with you, I'm sure. Just say you wanted so much to come and see us all up here.'

'Like this?' Susan looked down at her small bulging stomach.

'Well, you've got to say something. They'll understand. But you do see you can't stay here.'

But she could find somewhere to live nearby, some cheap room for the time being, until her grandparents could return to their repaired home. Her mother must have read her thoughts.

'The council people said your gran and grandad's place might not be repaired until the war's over. There's so many homes needing repair. Some people've had to be evacuated all over the place for the duration. At least your gran and grandad won't have to do that at their age when we can at least give them a roof over their heads, awkward as it'll be for them. You do see, love, don't you? I don't know what you can do except go back to London and I don't think you'd want to bunk in with any of your aunts and uncles, would you?'

No, she wouldn't. Go begging cap in hand to any of them, asking to foist herself on them, saying her own mother couldn't put her up, and them all knowing she already had a posh roof over her head down south.

Her mother appeared to think the problem solved. 'You can't go back tonight. You look all in. We can make a bit of room for you in with June and Beryl. It'll be a bit awkward for them but it'll only be for one night. But you can see, it couldn't be permanent, not with a baby to look after when it comes – nowhere to put a cot or anything. You do see, our Sue, don't you? Well . . .' She brightened as though everything was solved. 'I better get you this cup of tea and a quick sandwich of something. And when the boys come home and your dad and the girls, we'll all have a nice tea. I've got a nice big stew for us all.' Susan had smelled it as she came in and her mouth had watered and her stomach rumbled at the lovely aroma.

'I can get a better bit of meat with your gran and grandad's ration books added to ours,' her mother went on.

Susan fished into her handbag. 'I've got mine.'

Her mother looked horrified. 'Good Lord, love. I don't want yours, not for one meal. We've got plenty of stew. We won't even know it's been stretched. But, Sue love, you must go back home in the morning. Dad'll see you to the station all right. It won't matter if he's a bit late going into work.'

'I shall be all right, Mum.' It sounded pathetic, her mother using the word 'home'.

'No,' her mother argued as though bequeathing some bountiful gift. 'I won't have you going back to New Street on your own with the workmen. Y'r dad'll take you. He'll see you all right.'

Chapter 18

She hadn't felt so tired in all her life. The suitcase seemed to weigh a ton. Outside Euston station Susan checked the money she had left. There wasn't a lot, not enough to waste on a taxi back to Victoria Park Road and she just couldn't face the bus ride, nor see herself creeping back mollified to face Mrs Ward's wrath or relief, whichever it turned out to be. But where else was there to go? No one here to help her, no one to care for her, she felt as lonely as it was possible to be. She just wanted to sit here on her suitcase and burst into tears.

Nearby a news vendor's raucous voice was calling out: *'Standard, Ev'n Standard*! Get *y'r Standard.'*

It was getting late though daylight was still being drawn out. It had taken more than half the day travelling from New Street to Euston. And now she had either to go home to Mrs Ward before it got dark or find somewhere to stay at least for the night, she was so weary. But her remaining money for this week wouldn't stretch to any hotel. Misery rose again in her throat, which she fought to hold back with large gulps. She had been such a fool, it had been such a daft escapade. And now even her brain couldn't think properly. She saw herself sleeping here where she sagged, a policeman moving her on in the night like he might a tramp. She wasn't a tramp. She was a fool and she was seven months pregnant. If only she could stand here and cry her eyes out.

'Get y'r *Standard*! Fifty farsand at Second Front demonstrashern.'

Of course, buy a paper, look in the rooms-to-let columns, the logical thing to do. Feeling uplifted, Susan bought a paper. She wasn't going back to Mrs Ward, she would stand on her own two feet. At least for a while.

Half an hour later found her on the doorstep of one of the somewhat shabby-looking houses off Mile End Road whose address was the one she'd selected from the to-let column: 'Two furnished rooms, large family home, shared bath/wc, seven and six pw.' She had to knock twice before anyone answered.

She felt and looked sick, and the woman who finally came to the door took one look at her condition, her suitcase, and said: 'Gawd 'elp us – you orlright, dear?' the Cockney accent closing around Susan like a warm blanket.

'I . . . I saw your ad,' she began, unable to say any more for the sick giddiness that was overwhelming her.

'Better come inside, dear,' the woman was saying. 'You don't look too good, and that's a fact. I'll take yer case for yer. Come on in.'

Taken into a cavern of a room, Susan gratefully allowed herself to be eased down on to a sagging brown leatherette sofa that puffed explosively under her small weight. The suitcase was plonked at her feet. 'You stay there, dear. I'm gonna make yer a cuppa tea. Look as if yer could do wiv one. I won't be a tick.'

Left alone to recover, Susan stared about her. The room had a high ceiling and a huge, stained marble Victorian fireplace but was bare of all ornaments and embellishments, almost as though the family were on the point of moving out and had packed away everything easily movable. All it held was two large armchairs that matched the sofa, half a dozen straight-backed chairs and a scratched oak sideboard with a radio on it. There was only lino on the floor and set in the centre was a circle of linked-up toy railway lines with a couple of Hornby trains, their carriages lying on their sides, and nearby some very battered toy cars.

As she sat looking at it, a boy of about thirteen came in. Staring at her from under a thatch of unkempt tawny hair, he said, "Ello.' Susan smiled through her tiredness.

'Mum's gorn ter make yer some tea,' he announced gravely. When Susan nodded, he went on, 'I'm Malcolm. I've got two bruvvers. They're Percy an' 'Enry. They're younger'n me.'

Again she nodded, too weary to make conversation with small boys. A silence fell and finally Malcolm wandered off leaving her to continue gazing at the square-patterned lino and the indifferent beige wallpaper. The once-heavy green brocade curtains at the long Victorian bay window were faded at the edges by sunlight. Against the wall were propped makeshift blackout shutters of thick black paper in flimsy wood batten frames. The woman returned with a steaming basin-like cup on a wide saucer which she put into Susan's hands.

'Yer'll feel a lot better after this,' she said and sat on one of the chairs while Susan sipped what was the best cup of tea she'd had in what seemed like ages.

'About the advert,' she said at last.

'Oh, yes,' said the woman as though only just recalling that was why Susan was here. Now Susan felt better enough to take note of her, she saw a smallish woman of about thirty-five with uncurling fair hair roughly cut straight about her ears and forehead. Her hands were rough and she wore a washed-out flowered wrapover pinafore over a green dress.

'Well,' she said now. 'I'm Emma Crawley. Me 'usband's often away fer days on end – works fer the Gas Board, reserved occupation, but 'is job takes 'im all over the place and I get a bit lonely. I need a bit of company. That's why I'm lettin' out the rooms.' She eyed Susan. 'An' your 'usband?'

'In the Army,' Susan obliged quickly. 'Abroad. At least he . . .' She faltered to a stop, then added hastily, 'I've got my marriage certificate.'

Mrs Crawley burst out laughing. 'Lord luv us, I don't disberlieve yer, dear. Where is 'e, or is that 'ush-'ush?'

'He's . . . he's been posted missing.'

'Oh, yer poor duck!' Her earlier hilarity swept away, the woman's face creased with pity. 'An' you wiv a baby on the way. But ain't you got no 'ome or anythink? 'Ave yer bin bombed out, then? Not in London though, dear?' She had taken note of Susan's accent. 'D'yer come from Manchester way?'

'No, Birmingham.' Susan was surprised that tears

hadn't flooded her eyes at the mention of Matthew, but guessed she was too tired for that.

'Birmingham. They've 'ad it nasty up there too. 'Ad some of them daylight raids. They've left London alone this time, thank Gawd. We 'ad enough of our share in the Blitz. Shockin' it was rarnd 'ere, flames . . .'

She pulled herself up sharply. 'Look, come upstairs and take a look at the rooms, see if yer like 'em. Yer can cook up there. I've put in a gas ring but there ain't no place fer an oven. But yer can eat wiv us if yer like. Might save yer a few bob in the meter. Don't s'pose yer get much allowance from the Army. Come on, dear, I'll show yer. Leave yer suitcase there fer the time bein'. What's yer name?'

'Susan. Susan Ward.' She got up, put the cup and saucer on the floor because there was nowhere else to put it and followed Mrs Crawley out and back along the passage, its thin runner rucking up under her tired feet, and up the narrow lino'd stairs.

Opening the door to the large bedroom which had been divided into two at some time to form a sitting room as well, Mrs Crawley stood back for Susan to enter.

'Everythink's nice an' clean,' she said. To someone who had been travelling for much of the day, it looked like heaven, despite the well-worn furnishings and, if one had been finicky, really only being one divided room. 'I 'ope it's suitable for yer.'

Suitable! Susan could have cried at the sight of the large brass bed on which she could have flopped this very second, it looked so inviting and comfortable. She turned to the woman. 'I'd like to take it. But do you mind me being . . . like this?' She nodded towards her midriff.

'Bless yer, no. I like kids. Got free of me own – all boys. Wot I'd like is a gel. Well, yer never know. Ain't too old yet. An' Geoff, that's me 'usband, it's Geoffrey really, but 'e's called Geoff by everyone – when 'e comes 'ome, yer never know, it could 'appen and I could spark again. But it'd be nice 'aving a bit of female comp'ny in this family of boys. Me 'usband too – as much boy as any of the kids, I can tell yer.'

'Well, if it suits you to have me here, Mrs Crawley . . .'

'Call me Emma. An' I'll call yer Sue.'

Susan smiled. The woman was motherly, and she needed someone motherly right now, someone like her own mother. Her mother spoke real Brummy, Emma Crawley spoke Cockney; it was all the same when someone saw no point to putting on airs and graces.

'Emma,' she repeated, already feeling at home.

The first thing she intended to do once she was settled in was to write to her mother telling her of her good luck. As to writing to Mr and Mrs Ward, she would think about that one, but she supposed, as their son's wife, she really should let them know where she was. This she did and bravely prepared herself for their onslaught. It wasn't long in coming.

'What did you think you were doing, Susan? You had us worried out of our wits. You seem to have no conception of what you have put us through. No consideration. Didn't you ever stop to think how worried we'd be?'

In her room, which she had already made even more cosy, Susan withstood the tirade by keeping her head bowed and saying nothing.

'After all we tried to do for you. I don't think we've been unkind or made you do anything you didn't want to do. We've treated you as though you were our own daughter and done all we can to make you feel at home. Not only for Matthew's sake but your own, a girl away from her parents, her husband . . .' Mrs Ward gulped back a wave of emotion, thankful the landlady Mrs Crawley wasn't present to see it, having decently left this family to its argument. 'Her husband, our son, not with her,' she finished.

Collecting herself, she paused again, this time for some sort of reply. When none came, she pushed on. 'How could you have been so thankless, so unkind, so thoughtless as to cause us all this worry?'

'Don't you think you were being just a bit unfair?' Mr Ward added with a little more calm, saving Susan the awkwardness of answering his wife's angry question. 'God knows, we've done you no harm to have been treated in such a way. What *have* we done to you, Susan, to deserve it?'

This was said in such a heartfelt manner, tears began to surge up in Susan's eyes. She hadn't meant to cry, had even steeled herself against crying. So finding herself on the verge of doing so made anger rise up instead.

'You've never let me lead my own life,' she blurted. 'Watching every move I made, you made me feel like I was a prisoner. I want to lead my own life. I'm not a kid. I can look after myself.'

'It looks like it,' Mrs Ward remarked, gazing about her, exactly as she had done on entering the house. 'This place is disgusting.'

'But it feels more like home to me than your fine house ever did.' It didn't matter that she sounded rude. She felt angry. 'Mrs Crawley's like a mother to me, which you never was.'

'Well, that is the absolute limit . . .'

'Now look here, Susan,' Leonard Ward cut in again. 'There's no call to talk to us like that. We have, truly, tried to do our best for you. If the way we did it wasn't what suited you, I'm sorry, it's the only way we know. You must admit, you wanted for nothing. Did you?' he ended firmly.

'No,' she said in a small voice.

'Then where have we failed?'

She was crying now. 'You haven't failed. I didn't mean to upset anyone. I suppose I should have told you how I felt. But it's done now.'

'It isn't. You can come back with us.'

'It is. I want to live on my own. I'm sorry, but I feel smothered. I just want to live on my own.'

There was a long silence, both of them looking at her, she not daring to look at them.

'But the baby . . .'

'I'm all right,' Susan cut across her mother-in-law's lame words. 'Mrs Crawley's got children. She's made me feel wanted and comfortable here.'

'Meaning we haven't?'

'It's like I said. I don't feel comfortable in your home.

I want to be on my own. I need to be on my own. I don't want to be smothered.'

'Well, all credit to you, Susan,' Leonard Ward muttered then turned to his wife. 'I can't see anything we can say altering her mind. I think we'd best go, Lilian.'

'I'm not . . .' she began, but again he interrupted her, firmly raising his hand towards her.

'There's no point us trying to argue any more. I give you credit for wanting to stand on your own two feet, Susan. I didn't think you had it in you, but obviously you have. Well, we're not far away if you need us. If we hear anything from Matthew, we'll let you know immediately. Obviously we have no way of writing to him except through the Red Cross, which we will do, and I expect you will too. You're as anxious as us to hear something, no matter what. I expect it's the strain of all this that's made you do what you did. We're going now. But, Susan, keep in touch. Don't alienate yourself against us, whatever it was we did to displease you. Of course, we want to know when the baby is born and if you're all right. You will do that, won't you?'

Dismally she nodded. He came forward, laid a kiss on her downcast cheek and took hold of her shoulders to give them a small encouraging shake. It was like having Matthew touch her and it was all she could do not to fall into his father's arms to receive his hug. Instead, she stepped back, lifting her tear-streaked face, shaking her dark hair from her eyes, a small defiant gesture, and he too stepped away, defeated. It showed in his eyes, again so like Matthew's though a few shades lighter.

Mrs Ward just stood there, not quite looking at her, her face set like granite.

'Take care, child,' Leonard Ward said and his wife, still without looking at her, gave a stiff nod of concurrence and turned, leading the way out of the room.

Susan stood listening to their footsteps echoing down the uncarpeted stairs. She heard Mrs Crawley saying to them before they left, 'I'll see she keeps in touch. She's in good 'ands 'ere.' Then the door closed and Emma Crawley's footsteps came quickly back up the stairs.

'I'm gonna do yer a nice cup of tea, Sue. Make yer feel better.' It was Emma's way of solving all crises. More often than not it worked a treat, just as it did now as Susan smiled at her through her tears.

A fierce stab somewhere in her stomach awoke Susan with a start and for a moment she lay rigid, frightened by a pain that could bring her out of what had been a deep sleep. There was only a dull ache now that wasn't really an ache at all – she wasn't sure what it was – just a feeling. The clinic had told her she had only a week or two to go now, though no one could say quite when. So was this her time? No, it couldn't be. Probably just wind. The fear began to subside but it had left her wide awake.

Turning over she closed her eyes again and tried to sleep. But sleep had gone and all that were left were thoughts, the sort of reflections that come at night, persistent, refusing to be ignored.

All this time, there had been no news whatsoever of Matthew. But she wouldn't think about that. Once on that track it would persist, plaguing her with memories of those wonderful days with him, thoughts of the days that now stretched ahead of her without him, forever and ever. She would end up crying into her pillow. She mustn't think of him. She would try to think of something else. Something positive. Something happy.

It had been the best move she had ever made getting away from his parents. Emma was such a wonderful, motherly person, she couldn't have wished for a better landlady, more a friend than anything, so free and easy. It was a rough-and-ready-come-and-go-as-you-please sort of home. Meals were never the ritual they'd been at the Wards' home. The only time anyone sat around a table – the big bare table in the back room – was when Geoffrey Crawley was home, and even then everyone came one after the other as each plate was filled, leaving the same way, as soon as the plate was empty – no waiting for anyone else.

Helping around the house, going shopping with Emma who held her arm as she got bigger around the middle, was enjoyable. So were these long July evenings. As the sun went down on kids playing in the street, the drawn-out twilight of double British Summertime fading, the Crawleys' flimsy blackout shutters would go up amid a dozen bits of advice how to make them fit so no light finally showed. With the sounds in the street finally muted by the closing of the thin curtains, they'd all settle down to an evening around the wireless, laughing at ITMA, Arthur Askey and Stinker Merdock, Vic Oliver, Ben Lyon and Bebe Daniels; listening intently to the news read by Alvar Lidell or Bruce Belfrage, hoping to glean a little joyful tidings from the war front. Sometimes she and Emma would have a go at one of the dozens of old jigsaw puzzles that lay around the house, the wireless still blaring to itself, while young Malc sat at the other end painting from a tin paint box on bits of old paper, his brothers playing noisily with some toy or other, Geoffrey in his creaking old fireside chair reading the evening paper or studying his work sheets for the following week. All nice and cosy.

With all this going on around her there was little time for fretting any more, although now and again she did, picturing herself and Matthew together in a little home of their own. But this was the nearest to it, and Emma and Geoffrey were so nice, she should think herself lucky. Geoff was an easygoing man. It wasn't at all difficult to talk to him. Mr Ward had been nice too, but it had not been so easy to talk about things that she liked – films, popular songs, singers, the big bands, her life in Birmingham. Geoff would talk about his life too, telling outrageous tales of the people he met in his work, making them all laugh. He told her how he had met Emma, how she'd caught him on the rebound from a girl who'd given him up for a prizefighter. The girl had been a real wow and Emma hadn't measured up to her, he said, but Emma fell for a baby and they'd hastily married. 'Had to,' he said, 'for her sake.' Susan felt a little sad for him that he'd had to take, as it seemed, second best, though Emma had, he admitted, been a bloody good wife to him, more than the other girl might have been.

If Matthew were to come home now, Susan mused as

she lay wide awake, she would make sure no one else could match her . . .

A second stab of pain broke into her thoughts, making her gasp. It was not as bad as that first stab had been, but she was consumed by a sense of urgency, an ancient instinct that lies dormant within each woman so that she knows instantly what it is without being told.

Swinging her feet out of bed, she hoisted herself up and, holding her stomach in which there was now only a dull grinding feeling, she got to the door and out on to the landing.

'Emma.' Her raised voice sounded small and terrified even to herself. 'Emma, quick. Something's happening.'

Geoff was away. Emma came running out from her room and guided her downstairs to sit her in one of the old armchairs in the cavernous front room, the most comfortable place she could find. 'Stay 'ere,' she ordered. 'I'll go up an' get yer clothes an' fings for yer.'

She was back within seconds with a shopping bag holding a towel, flannel and soap, hairbrush, a change of nightie, and over her arm, Susan's coat and a scarf, and a pair of shoes dangling from her fingers.

'Can yer put yer coat and shoes on yerself?' she queried anxiously. 'I've got ter get meself dressed. D'yer think yer can walk? We've got ter get yer to the 'orspital. It's only half a mile darn the Mile End. Yer've only just started. Yer'll be able to make it if we walk slow.' To which Susan let out another gasp at a fresh small onslaught of pain.

Lights were on all over the house; the boys wandered out of their bedroom asking, 'What the 'eck's up?' before

being told by Emma to go back to bed – it wasn't none of
their business.

There came a loud hammering and knocking on the
street door, a harsh voice shouted: 'What th'ell are you
lot up ter? Yer showin' a bloody great light – like a bloody
searchlight art 'ere.'

'Oh, Gawd, the blackout!' Emma rushed in panic to the
window to find one corner of the blackout frame leaning
inward towards the room, not having been put up properly.
Only then did she run to the door, flicking off lights as she
went, leaving Susan in pitch-darkness.

Her voice was breathless at the street door. 'Gawd, I'm
sorry. We've got an emergency 'ere. Me lodger, she's only
young, 'er 'usband's overseas, an' she's just started 'er
labour pains. I've got ter get 'er to the 'orspital.'

'Can't yer get an ambulance?'

'It's only 'alf a mile ter the London.'

'Yer can't ask 'er ter walk 'alf a mile, not in labour.'

In pitch-dark, Susan felt the pain returning. In panic she
cried out. From the door, the voices grew more animated.
'Can't she 'ave it 'ere, in the 'ouse, save walking all that
way in 'er condition at one in the mornin'?'

'It's 'er first. She ought ter be in 'orspital. I told 'er
'usband's people I'd look after 'er. I can't be responsible
for anyfink goin' wrong.'

'Well, she can't walk. Tell yer what. I've got a bike. We
could put 'er on that and wheel 'er. Save 'er walkin'. It's
got a wide saddle. And paddin' as well. I got piles an' I
'ave ter 'ave a wide saddle wiv a lot of paddin' on it.'

Sitting in the dark listening, Susan wasn't sure whether

to laugh or cry as the present bout of pain began to fade a little.

The baby, a girl, arrived the next day around three in the afternoon. 'Quick for the first,' a nurse told her, but it had seemed like eternity to her as she writhed in terror and pain, a young mother not knowing what was expected of her, what to expect. Throughout she had been alternately encouraged and scolded, assured that it wouldn't be long now, that she was doing wonderfully, then in the next breath upbraided for making a fuss, getting into a needless panic, yelling when there was no need, not co-operating. And when during easier moments she wept for Matthew, she was told she must be brave for him, that he, a stalwart fighting for his country, wouldn't want to see her less brave, breaking down like this.

She couldn't bring herself to tell them he'd been reported missing. Though his family hung on to the hope of his having been captured, she knew deep inside her that he was dead, that she'd never see him again and would have to bring up his child alone.

Chapter 19

Jenny stood by Susan's bedside. Susan's in-laws had just left and her parents, who had further to come, had yet to see her.

Jenny herself had heard of the birth of Susan's baby by chance, being told at teatime by one of the nurses, creased up with laughter, of a woman in labour having arrived at maternity around one thirty in the morning on a bike. 'What people don't do in wartime,' the nurse had giggled over her bread and jam sandwich.

'You mean she rode herself here on a bike?' Jenny had joined in the general laughter. Odd things happened in hospitals, but that one had taken the biscuit.

'Well, not exactly rode herself. An air-raid warden was pushing her. And her landlady apparently kept helping her off every time she got one of her pains. They had the saddle all padded.' This last brought a fresh gale of laughter.

'I'm not surprised,' Jenny had said over the laughter. 'Where were her parents then?'

'She said they lived in Birmingham. She'd walked out on her in-laws or something and lives about half a mile from here. Seems it was easier to get here on a bike than having to walk. I ask you! Can you just see it – some old air-raid warden wheeling a pregnant woman on a bike all the way to the hospital, her hopping on and off every so often? It must've looked a sight. Lucky for her it wasn't midday. Honestly, some people!'

But Jenny had no longer been laughing. Now she stood looking down at the girl's face, pale from the hard work of bringing a baby into the world, looking wan and down in the mouth when she should have been glowing with pride at her achievement.

'Have you seen the baby, Susan?' she asked for something to say after having enquired how she was, a question which had been met by a tear being squeezed from between the closed eyelids.

'What did you think of her?' she pressed as Susan merely nodded without speaking.

'I'm too worn out to think anything. Except that Matthew's not here and I'm all on my own. I'll never see him again, and no one cares.'

'Of course they care. His parents care. And your family – they care.'

And Matthew, he'd be over the moon with joy and pride if he was here to know about his baby daughter. But there was no way he could know, no way he could be told, could be contacted. Her mother had relayed what little news she happened to glean from his parents, which was hardly anything. And having for a while lost the run of Susan, all she knew of Matthew was of the ongoing but vain efforts of the Red Cross still to trace him, one way or the other. Wonderful people, but as far as she knew they'd hit a complete blank.

Gazing down at the despairing Susan, Jenny bit her lip, refusing to believe Matthew could be dead. Somewhere he had to be alive. She clung to that hope with all her heart, and inside that heart those feelings she had always had for him beat as strongly as ever.

She had tried to put it away from her, had assumed she had at last conquered it when she had written to Ronald Whittaker, finally confronting the stupidity in letting such a chance go of getting Matthew out of her system once and for all by marrying Ronald as he'd once asked. His parents had replied for him, saying they were sending her letter on to him, that against their wishes he hadn't gone into practice with his father but instead had joined the Army Medical Corps. Slightly dismayed, she had got in touch with him at the address they'd given. Ronald's reply had been kind and friendly but said that he had met a girl to whom he'd be getting engaged on his next leave; that he was sorry Jenny hadn't written earlier because they'd got on well together but it wouldn't be right for him to drop the girl he now loved for the one he had thought at the time he loved. He'd always remember her with affection and hoped that it wouldn't be too long before she too found herself someone to settle down with. She had felt hurt, angry with herself and very aware that her only avenue of escape from the love inside her for Matthew had been cut off.

It made her furious that Susan could lie here lamenting her lot and assuming her husband dead when she should at least be fighting to fill herself with optimism that he would eventually come back to her. She didn't even seem interested in her baby as a mother would normally be.

'What are you going to call her?' Jenny asked and received an apathetic shrug.

'I don't really know. I've not really thought about it.'

'Then don't you think you should? What do Matthew's parents say?'

'They suggested a few names.'

'And?'

Another shrug. 'I can't seem to like any of them. I got confused and said I'd think about it. Mrs Ward said don't take too long about it.'

'You'll have to come up with something.' Jenny herself thought about it for a moment, then said, 'How about Mattie?'

'Mattie?'

Yes, it was a lame sort of name and sounded even more so on Susan's amazed lips. 'It's short for Matilda.' Matthew had always loved shortening names. '. . . Hi there, Jenny . . .'

Jenny swallowed back the sentimental restriction of her throat. 'Matilda is the feminine of Matthew. It would remind you of him, and . . . when he comes home.' He would come home. 'When he comes home he'll know you were thinking of him. Make it Mattie, Susan. It sounds better.'

She spoke positively. Susan was by nature a malleable person and she was at her most malleable now. 'Well, I hadn't got any name ready for her. I suppose it's as good as any.'

She couldn't care less, Jenny thought angrily, but she smiled. 'I had better go or I'll get into trouble,' she said brightly. 'I'm supposed to be on duty. Another nurse is covering for me, so I could only have a few minutes. I'm glad you're okay and I'm glad the baby, Mattie, is okay. She'll be something for you to cling to until Matthew comes home.'

Giving Susan no opportunity to argue with that, she turned smartly on her heel and with a quick wave went back to work.

Sitting by the lounge window for a better light by which to see her knitting pattern, Lilian Ward glanced out at the dull November weather, her fingers still busy with the clicking needles. She had no real need to look at them; the pattern itself had become partially imprinted on her brain so often had she used it to knit the exquisite little dresses for Matilda. The weather was getting colder. Wool was hard to come by, so second-hand woollen garments were usually found in jumble sales, unravelled and re-knitted, but the child needed some warm clothing. Left to Susan, she'd have nothing warm to wear. It seemed to Lilian the mother had no interest whatsoever in Matilda. She insisted the child's name be spoken in full. None of this silly Mattie business. But in truth the shortened name reminded her too much of Matthew. Where was he?

Nothing, absolutely nothing. The Red Cross were even mentioning the dread word. But she wouldn't have it that Matthew was dead. He was *somewhere*. He had to be. Why *couldn't* they find him? Not trying, too many other missing servicemen to trace. But her son was as important as they. Meanwhile this war was dragging on. So what if on the fourth of this month came the long-awaited tidings that German forces were at last in full retreat in Egypt, the wireless announcer hardly hiding his excitement? So what if the Allies had landed in Algeria? So what if the church bells had rung across the whole country to mark Montgomery's victory? One or two swallows didn't make a summer. Meanwhile Matthew continued to be missing. His daughter was going to grow up not knowing him. Susan, his wife, was gadding about as though she hadn't a care in the world, leaving Matilda in the dubious if willing care of her landlady, just as if her husband, missing or dead, meant nothing to her. No sighing after him or, Lilian was certain, tears, except, when she and Leonard went to see her – then she'd weep buckets. Lilian's needles clicked angrily in the dull November daylight.

Crumpling the brief letter into a ball, Susan threw it across the kitchen.

'She never gives up, does she? Says she's got another cardigan for Mattie. I don't want her making clothes for my child. Anyone'd think I can't dress her myself. She looks all right, don't she, in what I put her in?'

Carving hunks of bread for when the boys trooped in from school for their midday break in half an hour, Emma looked up from the kitchen table. 'She means well, Sue. She knitted you both lovely Christmas presents.'

'Means well? She always means well. It's the way she goes about meaning well that gets my goat. Treating me as though I've not got a clue on how to bring up a baby. I know she doesn't approve of me going out every once in a while. That's all it is, once in a while. I'm not gadding about with soldiers. I just need a break now and then.'

'Of course you do.' Emma continued spreading the doorsteps with the thinnest scrape of margarine, her family's rations dwindling towards the end of this week's allowance. She put a small smear of plum jam on them and pressed the slices together, the resulting sandwiches almost too wide for any child's mouth.

'The way she talks,' Susan went on, 'you'd think I was on the streets. I like going dancing with Edie. And we know how to behave ourselves.'

In September, for a bit of extra money, she'd started a part-time job in the Whitechapel High Street near Aldgate East station in the stockroom of a wholesalers of men's underwear and hosiery, Fishman & Sob. The owner's son had been called up. Edie Barrows, who worked with her, also had a husband in the forces, and like herself needed to get out now and again and see a bit of life rather than be stuck at home – it was easier for her, having no children. There was no harm in it, the way Mrs Ward intimated.

'Neither of us are going to go off the rails, both married. We just need a break now and again, that's all,' Susan repeated.

''Course yer do,' Emma murmured. 'Do yer want jam or a bit of yer cheese ration in this sandwich?'

'Jam'll do.'

She began mixing Mattie's bottle with dried baby milk and a tiny drop of cod-liver oil. Her own milk had dried up earlier. Susan wasn't sorry. Though making bottles was a chore, she wasn't confined to the house or to rushing back home having to breastfeed at inconvenient hours.

She set the bottle in a saucepan of cold water to cool for when Mattie woke up. 'I think I do all right with Mattie's clothes. That exchange shop's a real godsend.'

In the Mile End Road near the old Empire Music Hall, a small derelict shop had been set up with a system whereby mothers could barter clothing their toddlers had outgrown for larger clothes. It saved on clothing coupons and it was cheap. Mattie looked a treat in some of the baby clothes Susan had managed to find.

'Trouble is, she inspects everything I buy for Mattie, as if I'm putting her into something lice-infested. The way she purses her lips if Mattie looks the least bit messy! You can't keep babies clean all the time. She's bound to sick up a bit of food on her clothes, and she always manages to come in when Mattie's messy, never when she's clean. I'm sure she times it.'

Emma laughed and glanced at the battered alarm clock on one of the kitchen shelves. Twelve thirty. The boys'd be home any minute, all three of them bursting into the house as ravenous as if they hadn't eaten for a week.

'Wait till she starts feeding 'erself, then yer'll know what messy is.'

When the post fell lightly through the letter box, Lilian was neatly folding the finished baby dress, ready to take with her tomorrow morning. It looked pretty; the pink and white wool she'd picked up from the WI skeined and washed, almost new. Susan should be pleased, though

Lilian could bet she wouldn't show it if she could help, merely look askance at it as though she, Lilian, were interfering. How could she be interfering, the child's own grandmother? More than them up in Birmingham ever bothered themselves – she allowed herself that little grammatical lapse in referring to Susan's people who as far as she knew hardly ever came down to see their daughter, much less sent her presents of clothing. Out of sight out of mind. They probably wrote now and again and thought that good enough.

At the sound of the post, she left the dress on the round occasional table in the bay window and hurried into the hall to see what had arrived. Always in the back of her mind was that one day the post would contain a letter from the Red Cross or some other authority to say her son had been traced. At the same time there lingered that fear of being informed of his confirmed death, so that she never approached the envelopes lying in the wire cage attached below the letter box without pausing, to carry on more slowly in trepidation at what might be there.

This procedure she followed now. Pray God there was no bad news, bills excluded of course. But what was bad news and what was good if it concerned Matthew? Was missing good news? But surely better than that dread which invariably throbbed in her mind. Whatever it was, it had to be faced.

There were several letters, most of them bills and invoices concerning Leonard's business, two private letters, both face down. What would they contain? One had an official look to it. It was that one which she swept